SEMI-PSEUDO-SUPERHEROES
Neighborlee Book 2

Michelle L. Levigne

www.YeOldeDragonBooks.com

Previously released as **Dorm Rats**, 2018
Revised

Ye Olde Dragon Books
P.O. Box 30802
Middleburg Hts., OH 44130

www.YeOldeDragonBooks.com

2OldeDragons@gmail.com

Copyright © 2020 by Michelle L. Levigne
ISBN 13: 978-1-952345-02-9

Published in the United States of America
Publication Date: July 1, 2020

Cover Art Copyright by Ye Olde Dragon Books 2020

Welcome to Neighborlee, Ohio.

Where? Somewhere on the North Coast of Ohio, south of Cleveland, right off I-71, north of Medina, in the heart of Cuyahoga County.

What is it? That's a little harder to explain.

Neighborlee is a place you need to experience.

The most important thing you need to understand: Neighborlee is *magic*. Some people say the town is alive. It exists to protect the weird and wonderful (and sometimes a little bit scary) from the cold, practical, material world.

More important, Neighborlee protects the outside world from the weird and wonderful that come to visit … and sometimes come to stay.

First stop: Divine's Emporium, a four-story Victorian house sitting on a hill overlooking the Metroparks. Whatever you really need, you can find at Divine's. Even if you don't know what you're looking for when you walk in the door. The shop is often bigger inside than it is outside. Angela is the proprietor. Please stay on the first floor. You don't want to find out what is hidden and locked safely away upstairs. Like Aslan, Angela is good, but that doesn't mean she's safe. And neither are the secrets and wonders and doorways to other worlds that she protects … and keeps securely locked.

Come in and explore. Meet the people who help Angela guard Neighborlee. Share their adventures of magic and wonder, danger and sacrifice. You never know who or what you'll run into as you walk the streets and listen to the stories of their lives.

Chapter One

My parents have always been and always will be the coolest parents in the world. Consider it: who else, besides the Kents, would adopt a kid who might possibly have dropped down out of the sky? Even for the town of Neighborlee, the Lost Kids, as we call ourselves, are a little "out there."

Either lost or abandoned, what does it matter? We were toddlers, alone when no child our age should be left alone. Never reported missing. No identification. While it might be fun to imagine ourselves the stuff of mythology, or fantasy or science fiction books or TV shows, the pressure of not knowing who we belonged to, how we got to the outskirts of Neighborlee and why some of us ended up semi-pseudo-superheroes ... not quite cool.

Thank God for people like my folks, Charlie and Rainbow Zephyr, investigators and reporters on the weird and wonderful. They came to Neighborlee Children's Home, fell in love with me, and adopted me when I was six. We made a family out of a man with a long, gray ponytail and moccasins, an Asian woman who dyed her hair a different color every week, and a little girl who was learning "the rules" by reading superhero comic books.

Further proof how great my folks always will be? When I revealed I wasn't normal, and flew to put the star on the Christmas tree, they didn't freak out.

At.

All.

They just accepted it and didn't slow down loving me for two seconds. Then when Felicity with her ability to call every dog in the county and let off uncontrollable EM bursts joined me and Kurt in trying to figure out the semi-pseudo-superhero rules, Mum and Pop became our counselors and support staff.

So I need to apologize to my folks for being such a snot the fall of my junior year of high school. They took me, age sixteen, and Harry, age nine (adopted two years ago), to England with them for nearly two months. They could have left us at Neighborlee Children's Home under Mrs. Silvestri's care. Or with Ford and

Charlotte Longfellow. Maybe even Angela, at Divine's Emporium, the fountainhead of the magical, strange, and sometimes frightening in our town.

But no, Mum and Pop took us with them. To England. London, Cornwall, Oxford, and Stonehenge. Did I appreciate it? Well, once we were there, yes, but at the time our folks announced the details of the trip, I sulked. And whined. Basically all the tantrums and hormonal adolescent stupidity my folks had avoided the last few years because I was so busy learning to be me. Who had time to be a so-called normal teenager?

I would miss basketball tryouts. That was my big concern. Missing tryouts meant I would miss out on the entire basketball season. Coach Kalnbach did a lot for my ego by being first stunned, then visibly upset when I told her I couldn't play that year. Not to brag (too much), but I had proven myself a valuable member of the team in tenth grade. I planned to be on the starting team my junior year. And no, I didn't use my telekinesis to be a great basketball player. I'm proud to say my own skill, sweat, and dedication did it. Too bad that maturity didn't carry over to my reaction to the plans for the trip.

So I need to say again, my folks were and are the coolest parents ever. They let my sulking and pouting and whining just slide right off. They never once said, "I told you so," when we got to England and I had a blast.

Being Charlie and Rainbow Zephyr's kids got Harry and me into places that ordinary tourists couldn't go. Armed with cameras and digital recorders, we were official assistants. When that didn't smooth the way, the incredible luck or unbelievable coincidences that usually surrounded our folks came to our rescue. Once people got over a graying Hippie, an Asian woman with emerald or amethyst hair, a brunette teen with hazel eyes, and a husky Latino boy being a *family*, they ignored the background weirdness.

Being the Zephyrs' kids got us some frustrating and slightly embarrassing moments, too. We were nearly trampled five times by fans in search of autographs. You'd think we would have learned the warning signs after the second near-death experience.

Or the time Mum and Pop had a booksigning in this cool little bookstore north of London. This huge woman at the front of the line nearly shattered glass, yelling at us, when Harry and I showed up and tried to get into the bookstore before it officially opened. The bookstore owner, Mr. Cloverdale, was a little man who Harry and I both swore had slightly pointy ears. Like some of Angela's friends who dropped by Divine's Emporium. He was watching for us, since we'd left the inn a good half hour after Mum and Pop that morning. At first, he didn't see us trying to sidle through the crowd to get up to the door because the crowd had grown to about forty people by then. Plus, that huge woman was right in front of the door. While the bookstore had enormous picture windows, we were hard to see because the windows were full of books on display or posters of Mum and Pop and information on the booksigning.

The big woman's voice, raised in a shout that would have stunned a dinosaur, alerted him that we had arrived. The British are supposed to be so reserved and dignified, but this woman...? Maybe she was also a soccer fanatic when she wasn't going into ecstasies about Mum and Pop's latest investigation. As soon as Mr. Cloverdale realized Harry and I were there, jammed between the locked door and the woman, he came running. The old-fashioned roll-up blind covering the door zipped up with a *rattle-clatter-hum-bang* and the keys chimed as he unlocked the door. I could hardly hear all that through the woman's furious lecture on the rudeness of the two of us trying to get to the head of the line and sneak in ahead of people who had done the sensible thing and gotten there two hours ahead of opening time. Seriously? She was waiting there *two hours?*

As soon as Mr. Cloverdale opened the door, the woman's volume dropped and she turned to him, pointing at Harry and me. We weren't afraid, just kind of stunned, and ready to laugh about some of the rabid fans of Mum and Pop's books. Mr. Cloverdale jammed his fists into his hips and glared at the big, angry, noisy woman. She quieted down and seemed to shrink about ten percent in height and width. He ushered us inside and locked the door, then told us not to mind her, Beatrice was a wonderful lady who loved books. She simply hadn't had her first pint of the day yet.

Yeah, that's right. Pint. As in Guinness. First thing in the morning. The sandwich shop/pub next door connected to the bookstore by a door about halfway back in the shared wall. The lock was on the bookstore side of the door. The sandwich shop opened at 10 in the morning, and when the bookstore opened the connecting door, Beatrice got her first pint of the day. That was her routine. Step into the bookstore, get copies of all the morning papers, and cross into the sandwich shop and pub. Get her first morning pint, then cross back to the bookstore and settle into the big easy chair next to the fire to read for the next hour.

Well, that morning, her routine changed slightly, because she wanted to get Mum and Pop's newest book before she got her newspapers and pint. As she told us later, over the most incredible meal of gazpacho, goulash and chocolate soufflé, in her old age the slightest change set her off. Hormone therapy didn't help, lithium didn't help—only set routine, and her morning pint. Yes, we had dinner with her. By the end of the day, she was Auntie Bea, and we laughed a lot over our first encounter.

Bottom line: Harry and I had a blast. The coolest part of the whole adventure was seeing Mum and Pop as other people saw them. Charlie and Rainbow Zephyr were loved by both sides of the whole debate over the weird and wonderful. On one side were the cynics who lived their lives to debunk mysteries and wonders and miracles. They admired our folks for their honesty. On the other side were people who wanted desperately to believe in the weird and wonderful, in miracles and aliens, doorways to other dimensions, reincarnation and ancient astronauts. They also admired and respected Mum and Pop because they didn't mock or set out to shred whatever the extremist radicals held dear. No matter what conclusion our folks arrived at by the end of their investigation, both sides were at least happy with the rational and respectful treatment of the issue or question or mystery or theory.

Back home in Neighborlee, they were just Charlie and Rainbow. In England, they were celebrities, somewhere between priests, philosophers, and explorers. Back home, Harry and I were just the Zephyr kids. In England, we were envied and admired. Despite being Americans.

Bottom line: the trip to England changed our lives in so very many dimensions. The most important being Pete. I'm getting ahead of myself a little bit, since Pete wasn't even born yet. We met his parents, Jake and Emma Crowder, during that England visit.

Our first two weeks in England, we stayed in London and the suburbs. We hit bookstores every day. Two kinds of bookstores. In the first, Mum and Pop dug through musty, dusty, shadowy old bookstores for research books, sending twenty-pound crates home, in care of Angela and Divine's Emporium. In the second type, our folks did booksignings or talked to reader groups. Harry and I had our tasks, to help search or to help set up for the talk and signing, or to run errands. We preferred the last option, because it left us free to explore the village and find something fun to do in the afternoon or evening.

Harry caught on to the whole weird money system on the first day, so he handled purchases and decided if something was worth the price being asked. I learned the bus routes and how to read village maps and route markers, and had a good knack for deciding if we should rent bikes or hike or take a cab or bus to our destination. I was good with maps. Maybe it tied into my ability to kinda-sorta fly, like built-in radar or something. Admittedly, it helped to be able to rise fifty or a hundred feet in the air and get a bird's-eye view of the terrain, orient myself on the roads and fields and spy out landmarks to compare to the map.

Our sixth day in England, Mum and Pop had a booksigning, followed by a hike to the other end of the village for a private luncheon with a historical society. The building where the society met was reputed to be haunted. Harry and I speculated for a short time that our folks were going to be asked to determine if it really was haunted, or if something else explained the odd noises and lights and visions that people experienced. I wondered if it might turn out to be another "weak place" in the fabric of space and time. Kind of like the situation in Neighborlee. I wanted to wander the village and determine if they had their local equivalent of Divine's Emporium and Angela. It made sense to me that other places in the world needed something and someone to reinforce the weak spots and channel all the magic and weirdness for profitable use. The person and the shop would protect the village from the rest of the world, and the rest of the world from the village.

Harry liked my theory, and we had an enjoyable two hours going about on scooters provided by our host at the little guest house/hotel where we were staying. Then we had to get down to the haunted building to meet up with everyone for lunch. We got there about five minutes early. We could look down the street that ran straight through the village to the bookstore at the other end, and see the people coming out the front door.

A couple was sitting on a bench in front of the building. This was our introduction to Jake and Emma Crowder. They were researchers like Mum and Pop. And Harry's parents. I never made the connection until years later. Emma and Jake's work was midway between Mum and Pop and Harry's parents, meaning they did a lot more "unofficial" government-type investigations than our folks did, but they didn't get into trouble and danger to the point of threatening their lives, like Harry's birth parents.

"You have got to be Lanie and Harry." Emma stood up to greet us when Harry and I approached the building.

I honestly to this day have no idea what to call it—house, shop, office, headquarters for interdimensional visitation? After all, it was reputed to be haunted, and people from all different disciplines or theories of haunting had investigated it. My folks had access to historical documents and records of the weird goings-on through the years. How many times the building had burned and even been bombed out during various invasions and revolutions in England's history, and the multiple uses it had been put to. House, store, jail, apothecary, hospital, morgue, schoolhouse, or barn.

Pop remarked, our second night in the village, that the building wasn't haunted so much as it had grown a personality from all the uses and turmoil it had endured through the centuries, and all the Human energy that soaked into it. People's reactions to the building varied depending on their personalities and beliefs. Five people could go into it at the same time, hear the same sound, but hear it differently, giving it a different cause.

I know this is true because Harry and I went exploring the first time we got inside. We found out later that nobody knew the attic was there until we found it. How could people *not* see the door and the steep, really skinny stairs all these years?

We were climbing around in the attic and our folks were downstairs, going through boxes of crumbly historical documents, when a delegation from the village came in to speak with them. They wanted a progress report on what had been found after only one full day of investigating. I heard the door creak-bang open and signaled Harry to be quiet. He was in the middle of leaping from one rafter support beam to the next. Kind of hard to land on the next beam without making noise, but he managed.

He didn't land square, though, and started to fall backwards.

Not a problem if this was an ordinary attic, built by sensible people, with plywood sheets stretching from one rafter to another, to provide a solid platform for storage. Keep in mind, Harry and I had to jump from one rafter to another *because* there was nothing solid between them. A layer of fluffy gray stuff that was more likely to be dust than insulation was all that lay between Harry's backside and the thin sheet of plaster and paint that made up the ceiling of the room below us.

Fortunately for Harry, his big sister had telekinetic power. Unfortunately for said big sister — *moi* — it isn't that easy to catch a husky nine-year-old going through a growth spurt, either with hands or with mental powers. Something gets strained, muscles or brain. Harry yelped. I snagged him so he metaphorically skidded to a halt in mid-air, with his bottom about three inches from breaking through. I let out a muffled *yelp-argh*. Sorry, but that's the only way to describe the involuntary sound that came from the sensation of a spike going through my left temple and out my right eye. Fortunately, only a temporary sensation. We froze in that position until I could regain my breath, while my stomach settled back into place after trying to come out my nose.

Down below, the five people with Mum and Pop all froze and looked upward at the ceiling. Mum knew what had happened, because she had seen us in action about twenty minutes before, when she came upstairs for the last crate of historical records. Don't even get me started on her fury over the deplorable state of those records. Mum froze, and Pop took his cue from her, even though he didn't know what was going on. He didn't notice the delegation at first, immersed in deciphering a document that later turned out to be over three hundred years old.

Mum said everyone just stood there, looking up at the ceiling, waiting for something to come through. She waited a few seconds, then asked them what was wrong. Mrs. Guttersnatch declared that was proof the building was haunted by the spirits of children who had died there when it was a pauper's prison. Mr. Wimbly said it was the spirit of a schoolteacher who had been driven insane by the imbeciles he had to pound learning into, and who had committed suicide. Note: she was an advocate for prison reform and believed in communication from the Great Beyond. He was a teacher who had been forced to retire after a nervous breakdown. Miss Wilson-

Smythe countered that the rats had come back, despite the promises of the rat catcher.

Mum nearly laughed aloud at that, because she knew if I had heard I would have screamed. I'm all right with rats if I have warning they're there. Tell me rats are around when I'm already in a dark, dusty, spooky place, and that's a recipe for trouble. Even my ability to hover doesn't protect me from the oogies. My imagination shows me rats taking running leaps and dropping on me from holes in the ceiling.

If I had heard Miss Wilson-Smythe, I would have screamed, and probably lost my mental grip on Harry, sending him through the fragile pseudo-ceiling, and probably right on top of the visitors.

The fourth member of the party was Mrs. Grendel. I am not lying. Honestly, who would keep the last name of Grendel in the land where Beowulf made his stand? She said the building needed better security measures, to keep children from sneaking in and playing where they were likely to get hurt. The fifth member of the group never did give his name. He left immediately, snarling about the ceiling being ready to fall down on them. They might as well tear the place down and build a parking lot. Who gave a royal fig about historical preservation anyway?

That proved what Pop said: everyone explains the unexplainable based on their own beliefs and experiences.

Where was I with this story? Oh, right. The day before the incident of almost falling through the ceiling. Meeting Emma and Jake Crowder, future parents of Pete.

Emma said, "You have got to be Lanie and Harry."

"Why do we have to be?" Harry said.

Yeah, that was my brother, the literalist. Harry liked playing with words. He also got a kick out of the reactions of everybody when he played word games, especially when he went very strict with the literal meaning of the words.

Emma gaped for about two seconds. Jake tipped his head back and laughed. They both grinned at us and held out their hands and introduced themselves.

"Right, we aren't supposed to meet up with your folks for two weeks," Jake hurried to say. "Our plans changed on us, so we thought we'd pop in before we shuffle off across the channel."

"What's there?" Harry said.

"Besides France?" I said.

He scowled at me for about two seconds, then all four of us were laughing. Then our folks got close enough to see us and for Pop to recognize the Crowders. The handful of people from the bookstore who were hosting the luncheon welcomed the Crowders, even though they didn't recognize their names until after Mum gave the titles of their published investigative books.

The meal was served buffet-style, which made it flexible for people who couldn't show up right away or those who had to eat-and-run. That also made it easier for the organizers to include the Crowders without having to set more places at the table. That was good, and bad. Honestly, who ever thought it was a good idea to have tiny folding chairs with seats only big enough for a Kindergartener's behind? With a visibly antique and valuable plate balanced on one knee, trying to hold a paper cup of punch or lemonade while eating and not overbalance said plate, so it became very expensive shards on the floor? Pop pointed out that at least we weren't struggling with paper plates, as we had three days before. Every item on that menu was wet in some way. Either the food soaked through the paper plates, or the plates folded in half, allowing the collected liquids to run into the lap or down the leg. Mum was the only one who escaped unscathed by embarrassing stains.

Poor Harry proved what a trooper he was. Someone had done enough homework to learn Harry was adopted and Hispanic. Said sucker-uppers invited several exchange students from Latin-American countries to come to the luncheon, just so Harry could have someone to speak to in his native language. Nice in theory, but the exchange students were from Brazil, they spoke Portuguese and Harry spoke Spanish. It wasn't the difference between England's version of English and United States English. More along the lines of Chaucer trying to talk with someone who spoke Ebonics. No Star Trek universal translators handy to help out. Somehow, Harry managed to get through it. Nobody was mortally embarrassed.

"Isn't Harry an English name?" he demanded, when we discussed the weirdness of the day that evening, in the sanctuary of our suite in the guest house.

"Yeah, it should be."

"Then how come nobody treats me like I'm English?"

It took a few seconds to decipher what he was getting at. I was tired, my head hurt, but I was alert enough not to irritate him by pointing out that he wasn't English, he was American. Duh, I knew what he meant.

"It really doesn't make sense. You don't even have an accent anymore," I offered.

"I know."

"So what makes them think you speak Spanish when you don't have an accent?"

"Maybe they think my American accent is Spanish?"

We were tired enough to be punchy, so we laughed. Mum and Pop heard us and came out from their room to join us. Our suite took up the top floor of the guest house, with a bathroom, three bedrooms, a sitting room and a little kitchenette.

We spent our evening relaxing, talking, checking our maps and writing up our journal entries for the trip. We learned more about the Crowders. They were researching a book on folk heroes and legends that had been taken over and adopted/adapted by more modern storytellers, especially Hollywood. For instance, the heroes during the French Revolution who helped French refugees and became the foundation for the tales of the Scarlet Pimpernel. Or the real warriors and rebels behind the tales of King Arthur and Robin Hood. The Crowders' research had headed down a rabbit trail when they dug up journals written by several noblemen who had married the daughters of exiled French nobles. After the demise of Napoleon, they and their sons had gone back to France in search of hidden gold, jewels, and chests of incriminating state documents, buried to keep them out of the hands of the revolutionaries. The book on folk heroes was turning into a treasure hunt that promised to uncover secrets that had lain buried since the revolution.

The next day, we had our little episode where Harry nearly fell through the rafters. That illustrated a theory our parents had espoused for years: whatever someone brought into a hunt for supposed truth usually dictated the result.

Chapter Two

We spent two more days in that village. Harry and I proved very useful. The local children felt safer talking to us and telling us stories they didn't want their parents to know about, which we passed on to Mum and Pop. Nobody was surprised to learn the haunted building had a couple of secret entrances, which weren't really that secret since they had been passed on to succeeding generations for more than two hundred years. The adults conveniently forgot about the escapades they pulled off inside the building, the hiding places, the tricks they played on each other and their parents, the odd noises they created by accident or on purpose, and the near misses.

Harry got a good ghost story, but I preferred to think it was a sighting of some Fae at work. Think about it: if I had passed on to my reward, I would not want to come back. My college theater friends expressed it best. Earth is the "green room," in theater parlance. It's all dress rehearsal, preparation, training for the Great Adventure of eternity. If you can get out on stage, why stay in the Green Room? I choose a Fae sighting instead of ghosts, because I have had a chance or two to talk to real Fae. It cleared up a lot of misconceptions while threatening to turn my brain into a rubber ball for someone to bounce around the room.

So, Harry and I managed to get some good stuff for our folks, just by virtue of being Charlie and Rainbow Zephyr's kids, which gave us free passes between many different social circles and levels, during our time in England.

When we finished up in that village, we took some time off for touristy things. Such as Stonehenge. We had fun, getting impossible aerial shots. Well, impossible for someone without a crane or access to a helicopter. Or the ability to kinda-sorta fly. Harry played lookout.

About two-thirds of the way through our tour of jolly old England, we visited the Tower of London. Mum and Pop got some ideas for a new round of research. The general idea was comparing prisons throughout the world, and throughout history, the legends and fables and ghost stories and famous escapes, famous prisoners, and the basic humane or inhumane conditions. Mum and Pop went into full plotting mode, throwing ideas back and forth in their verbal shorthand, and not paying any attention to the people around them. The smart tactic when that happened was to get them out of traffic, seated somewhere, and wait until they came up for air. So we did, then went off to do some looking around of our own.

Harry and I made one circuit of the courtyard, then I heard an irritating voice. Irritating because it was familiar. Which was impossible. That voice absolutely should not have been there.

Correction: that voice deserved to be there back when the Tower of London was a functioning prison.

I nearly ran over to Mum and asked her to check if I was feverish, because I had to be hallucinating. There was no way in the world that Sylvia Grandstone, the self-proclaimed queen of Neighborlee High, would be there at the Tower of London, thousands of miles and multiple time zones away from home.

Among all those British accents, that whiny voice with a touch of nasal from the Lake Erie effect stood out like a foghorn cutting through gull cries. Not that I'm making any kind of comment about British accents. Some of them are pure music, others are so thick with snobbery they make me gag.

Despite what horror films teach (run, don't look in that room), I had to turn around and look. Self-preservation instincts said to identify the source of trouble and get out before it targeted me.

At first, all I saw was a sea of green plaid and gold-trimmed black. As in uniforms. Pleated skirts and jumpers with white blouses under black blazers or black sweaters with gold trim. Topped with ridiculous little black visor caps somewhere between lawn ornament jockey caps and baseball caps. A few seconds of studying the gaggle of girls, ranging in age from maybe ten years old to the late teens, made it obvious these were the la-de-da of society, daughters of the rich and powerful, who spent more time on their figures and their hair and makeup than they did on homework. Honestly, the obvious field trip to the Tower of London was more likely to show off jewelry, makeup, or a new manicure than to educate. Listening to Sylvia holding forth now on the wives of Henry VIII, maybe the field trip was to get the girls out of the school to give the teachers a little peace and quiet.

"She's got it wrong," Harry said, stepping up next to me.

I lost track of my little brother for those few seconds it took to find Sylvia standing in the middle of a group of girls who looked either stunned, confused, or amused by her lecture. Harry paid enough attention to our surroundings for both of us. Sometimes we would tease each other that he was along to watch out for me, not for me to watch out for him.

"Yeah, she does."

We grinned at each other.

Sylvia lumped Lady Jane Grey in among the eight wives of Henry. There were *six*, and he didn't kill them all. One died from childbirth. Okay, that might count as him "killing" her, but seriously? Lady Jane Grey was a cousin of his children, and ruled for a few days in between Edward and Bloody Mary.

From the expressions of the girls with Sylvia, I guessed who were cowed by her, who admired her, who despised her, and who thought she was amusing and not worth their trouble. Judging by her smug expression, Sylvia believed herself admired, maybe even adored. From the way some of the girls whispered to each other, sneering at Sylvia just like she sneered at our classmates at home, she couldn't have been more wrong.

After all the misery she had put our classmates through since Kindergarten, I wanted so much to witness her being put down by people she probably considered her equals, her natural kind. Grandstones often rewrote reality to suit themselves. Sylvia had probably convinced herself by now that she had demanded her family send her to England, and she was right where she wanted and needed to be.

Okay, I admit it, sometimes I am not a nice person. Stamp "work in progress" or "under construction" or "please be patient, God isn't finished with me yet" on my forehead and my heart. Maybe a big sticker across my mouth, while we're at it.

I realized I was anticipating the impending humiliation with some glee. Right there, in public, in front of tourists from around the world. I shook myself, mentally and physically, and turned to walk to the other side of the courtyard. I was a junior in high school. I was a guardian of Neighborlee. My folks and Angela and Pastor Rocky would all be disappointed by the nasty thoughts going through my head and how much I enjoyed them.

"Uh oh." Harry yanked on my sleeve and stopped me when I had only taken two steps away.

I turned around to see another girl in a uniform saunter up to the group gathered around Sylvia. The other girls separated before her approach like the Red Sea before Moses.

This was visibly the queen of the school. She radiated that power and confidence that didn't need makeup and fancy hairstyles and jewelry. Her hair was straight and cut short and simple. No curls or clips or ribbons or streaks of color. She didn't have any visible earrings or necklaces, no eyeshadow, and from where I was standing about fifteen feet away, she didn't seem to have more than lip gloss, no visible rouge, and the hand she raised to point at Sylvia didn't sparkle with rings and bracelets and had no nail polish. Yet she seemed to glow.

Sylvia's mouth finally stopped flapping. She took a step back, her chin went up, and I was close enough to see her nostrils flare. Some of the girls took a few steps back.

The other girl gestured, counting down, with the forefinger of one hand ticking off the fingers on the other hand. A handful of the older girls ranged behind her with those hungry, smug looks of anticipation. I knew just what was about to happen. A put-down that I wanted too much for it to be good for me to witness it.

The school queen went through the list of the wives of Henry VIII and how they died or earned a divorce. With proper dates and details like their ages and how long they were married. It was like the outline of a PBS special. She knew her stuff. Then she stopped and spread her hands in question.

"Excuse me? I don't seem to see Lady Jane Grey anywhere in that list. Could I possibly be wrong? Or could you?" Then she started in on a biography of Lady Jane Grey, the nine-day-queen, as some had called her.

Sylvia spluttered and looked around for support. None to be found. I finally figured out what a sharkish expression meant. The other girls looked like they were ready, in their patrician way, for a feeding frenzy. Her head tilted back a little more, her mouth flattened, and a red haze spread across her cheeks. I knew what was about to happen next. I did not want to witness a Grandstone explosion of self-righteous martyrdom. Been there, done that, burned the T-shirt. Honestly, I was trying to be a nicer person. I had all that whining and pouting to make up for.

"But Lanie," Harry began, as I turned and walked away. He hurried to catch up with me. "That was her, wasn't it?" he said, when we had put a noisy crowd of Spanish-speaking tourists between us and the private school shark-girls.

I didn't deny it, just gave him my best eyebrow-raised-in-question Spock look.

"That—" He used a string of Spanish words I didn't know. From the impression of garbage in the mental atmosphere, I didn't want to know. Kind of frightening yet impressive, coming from my nine-year-old brother who had lost his accent within six months of coming home with us. "The one who ran away from home and got her folks so mad at her. They sent her here."

"I was hoping for Switzerland. I mean, make Sylvia learn a foreign language, please."

We traded grins and he fluttered those thick, unjustly long lashes at me. When I held out my hand, he gave his and we walked around the corner to the little mobile cart that sold exorbitantly priced soft drinks. Honestly, it was rather unjust that Sylvia got off easy, going to a country where her prison guards spoke English. If there was any justice in the world, she should have been sent to a school where she had to learn French, at the very least, and another language altogether to navigate the town outside the school gates. But no, Sylvia Grandstone got off easy, going to England.

Of course, thinking back to those watching sharks, maybe she didn't get off that easily.

"Any chance she'll come back home a little nicer?" I asked at dinner that night, after we related what we had witnessed.

We had picked up carryout food and brought it back to our hotel suite, to have a relaxed evening and some privacy. While we were pretty much immune to the odd looks that our mixed bag family got, we treasured the freedom to have long conversations over dinner without worrying about people nearby overhearing something the wrong way.

The kind of research my folks did for their books often made for bizarre dinner conversations. Twice, people at other tables asked to be moved elsewhere in the restaurant, four times they complained to the waitress, who came over and asked for an explanation. A dozen times, people looked at us long enough that they recognized our folks from the photos on the backs of their books, which led to requests for autographs. And once, the people were frightened by a discussion about unexploded German ordnance being buried under the streets rebuilt after WWII. They called a police officer to ask Mum and Pop to "mind what you say around folks what got sensitive ears, if you catch my drift?"

"Well, you can pray about it," Pop said, with a sideways glance and a wink for Harry, "but just remember that God doesn't always answer our prayers the way we want."

"Charlie," Mum scolded softly. Her eyes sparkled with laughter.

"You know what?" Harry said after we had folded up the cartons and paper plates and tossed everything in the totally inadequate wastebaskets provided in our suite.

What was with English kitchens that everything was so tiny? Refrigerators that only held a quart of milk at a time, for instance. Very inconvenient, when Harry could drink a half-gallon all by himself for breakfast.

"Enlighten us." Pop tossed a package of cookies across the tiny sitting room to him.

"I think I figured out what's wrong with the Grandstones." Harry snorted as he tore open the package. "I think they stay in Neighborlee because they do have magic. Only they don't want to admit it. So it kind of turned itself inside out a long time ago. It's all twisted and negative, like the evil empire in Star Trek. You know?"

Harry had caught on early that yes, magic was real, and there were rules. Few people had it. Usually, those who had magic had a responsibility to use it the right way. Some people were given magic to protect everybody else from the people who misused their magic. "Magic" being a generic term for anything unusual and outside the bounds and definitions of "Normal." Whatever that was.

Remember, Harry came to Neighborlee when he was seven, settled right in and made a place for himself, and didn't blink or stop breathing the first time he saw his big sister kinda-sorta fly. Harry figured out that if he could see the magic things, that meant he belonged in the magic place. He didn't get jealous and he didn't get whiny and he didn't freak out over the magical ordinary everyday weirdness of Neighborlee.

Maybe Harry's magic was his insight, and ability to figure things out that most nine-year-olds couldn't. Think about it. Most boys his age focused on tormenting the girls in class, making rude noises, and avoiding things like homework, chores, and Sunday school. God put Harry in our family to give us insight into our mortal enemies.

"Makes sense," Pop said after we had all sat and thought about it for a few minutes. He frowned and gestured at the package of cookies, which Harry had decimated.

Another nice thing about Harry was his ability to eat eight cookies without choking or the attendant foundation-shaking noise and a blinding shower of crumbs that most nine-year-old boys produced, all in the space of about half a minute.

"It would certainly explain the Grandstone ability to persuade people to support them," Mum said, with a wink for me. "Mind control. The ability to bypass common sense and civility. They always have a gang of followers, willing to participate in nasty pranks when they're children, and support sometimes criminal activity when they grow up."

"And marry them, to produce more monsters and villains to torment the next generation," I added.

Case in point: Reggie and Freddie Grandstone had managed to get accepted at snooty, expensive universities. As a stringer reporting on school sports for the *Neighborlee Tattler*, I spent a couple hours at the newspaper office every week, and helped with odd jobs, like sorting the mail and maintaining the morgue. Nearly every week, one of those universities sent a press release about the Grandstone boys and their social activities. Either Grandstone magic or hefty bribes persuaded the PR people at their schools that their home town was dying for regular updates on who they were dating, what fraternity they had joined, and social events they had participated in. Honestly, with all the parties and dances and debutantes the Grandstone boys were dating, did they ever step into the classroom? Every picture sent to the *Tattler* was tossed in the garbage or used as dart targets. Need I mention the *Tattler* and the Grandstones were not on friendly terms? The Grandstones alternately tried to buy the *Tattler* or sue the owners for slander.

"Think that's why Sylvia was sent here?" Pop muttered. "Find some impoverished duke or earl and blind him with all the money she'll inherit someday, to trick him into marrying her. That's all we need, a Grandstone with an eventual claim to the throne."

"That's the plot of a lot of really outrageous romance novels," Mum said with a chuckle.

"You forget, sweetheart, it really happened. A lot of American heiresses married into nobility in the last century. A lot of rich fathers traded their fortunes for pedigreed descendants."

"Think it'd do any good if you sent a warning through your friends in the military?" I asked. "Like, give them an idea of what Grandstones have done in the past, and then remind them about the sleeper agents the Nazis and Communists sent to the US?"

Pop pretended to give it serious thought. Mum just laughed.

~~~~~

Four days before we were scheduled to leave England, we made a stop in Cornwall at a "select academy for young women" that shall otherwise remain unidentified. Don't for a moment think that description makes it easy to identify, because in England they grow select academies like the average Midwestern front lawn grows dandelions.

The academy was supposed to be one of our first stops when we arrived in England, to go through the archives. Just before our flight, we learned our visit would have to be either postponed or canceled. The academy's librarian, Mum and Pop's contact, Dr. Butterfield, had to take care of an emergency in New Guinea. Nobody else on the staff was qualified to oversee the search. We learned later, that actually meant no one was willing to work with Yanks. They changed their minds fast enough to make Linda Blair's head spin in the opposite direction, when Dr. Butterfield returned and the staff found out who they had snubbed.

We had planned to spend the last day in England doing the shopping-tourist thing (Harrod's, Selfridges, other landmark and famous stores). Instead, we packed up and zipped down the coast to a truly beautiful and rocky and wild section of Cornwall. From the top of the cliff that bordered the school grounds, we could see the coastline and the crashing waves. If it had been near dusk, I might have taken a chance of floating down to the water's edge, maybe get some water-smoothed rocks for souvenirs.

We spent about eight hours at the academy. Dr. Butterfield had already done the preliminary work, narrowing down the specific
~~~~~

hand-written, ancient books and loose-leaf stacks of records. My folks "only" had five books to look through out of the enormous, nine-hundred-year-old archives.

Once again, the Zephyr reputation worked for and against my folks. The academy administration finally linked Dr. Butterfield's long-distance research friends with the authors who, according to the papers, had been taking England by storm. The humanities and arts teacher begged Dr. Butterfield to bring my folks down to the school immediately, for an extended stay. She claimed she wanted to provide a "delightful educational experience for the girls," but based on her fan-girl reaction to Mum and Pop, the real reason was for her to go nuts. She was just giddy enough to confess, giggling, that she had "mistakenly" considered them "filthy, foreign intruders, unable to appreciate the treasures of the academy's archives." Until Dr. B returned and revealed his friends' identities.

The headmistress was an even bigger fan, but she was reasonable and had some dignity. She and Dr. B teamed up to get some concessions out of the snobs who had thrown up the original barrier. For the sake of the students, of course. Everything came together, including paying for our transportation to Cornwall and the sprawling manor that had been turned into a private school, and get us back to Heathrow on schedule.

An unoccupied faculty apartment was set aside for my folks to do their research in comfort, instead of working in the room Dr. B had set up before he went to New Guinea. In exchange, they were asked to spend a few hours talking with the students about all the aspects of research and writing, journalism, the pros and cons of authorship and the globe-trotting lifestyle. We had to laugh a little about the last part. Mum and Pop had left the globe-trotting part of their job description behind when they settled in Neighborlee. Sure, they still traveled, but no longer ten months out of the year.

As soon as the first green plaid skirt and black sweater trimmed in gold strolled into the meeting room-slash-former chapel for the first question-and-answer session, I got that sick feeling of impending doom. Harry was sitting with me in a small balcony where we could see and hear everything, but we weren't on display like Mum and Pop. He was busy with a pretty cool hand-held video game Dr. B gave him, and he didn't pay any attention to the students filing into the room and jockeying for one of the sixty seats, until I groaned.

"What?" He scooted over on the bench seat and rested his elbows on the balcony ledge, to look down on the growing audience. He frowned at the girls filing in, then at me. "What?"

"Don't you recognize the uniforms?"

He shook his head and shrugged.

"Remember the Tower of London?"

Chapter Three

"I remember that Grandstone... Oh." Harry patted me on the shoulder. "Maybe she's sick today."

"Grandstones are always sick, but it's not the kind that gives *us* any relief." I slid back on the bench, away from the ledge, even though chances of anyone looking up and seeing us were slim.

"Well, you think she's going to come here to listen to Mum and Pop if it's voluntary? I bet the only thing she reads is a supermarket gossip rag or else something about Hollywood. That's why she got sent over here, because she wanted to go into acting. Right?" He waited for me to nod, then bent his head over his video game again.

Honestly, my little brother was a really smart kid.

Too bad his theory was wrong. Sylvia came strolling in among the last of the first group for question-and-answer. She didn't look happy about being there. Maybe because she strolled in entirely alone. No followers, no admirers, no co-conspirators.

I paid attention to the Q&A because these select academy girls asked smart questions. Maybe because the students who came to the first session *wanted* to be there. They were interested in writing and doing research and what else they could do with their study focus on language and writing skills when they got out of school. I listened instead of turning down my mental volume control. There were no multiple repetitions of the same inane questions, proving nobody was listening to anyone. I liked listening to my folks talk about writing, about research, about fun and freaky things that happened to them or that they discovered. Mum made them laugh when she admitted how she tried her hand at writing paranormal romances, and while doing research on druids she learned about the Roman occupation of Britannia.

She then related how researching the Roman occupation led to learning about Boudica, the tribal queen who united the tribes in revolt against the Roman overlords and destroyed ancient Londinium. Yeah, nothing like infuriating a warrior queen by declaring that since her husband was dead and there was no male heir, the Romans were going to disband the tribe. Excuse me? Her husband was king because he married her. That was how some Celtic tribes handed down the leadership: the man who married the previous king's daughter became king. When you think about it, a very sensible way of handling things.

Mum never did write her story set in ancient Britain, but she got the girls interested in doing research and just having fun learning bits and pieces. From some of the comments I heard as they passed under the balcony on their way out, she got them interested in Boudica and their own history, too. That was Mum.

Harry escaped while the girls were still filing out. I waited until everyone was gone before I came downstairs. Pop went back to the archives with Dr. Butterfield, and Mum walked off with a knot of girls with specific questions about resources and searching.

There was nothing to pick up and move after the Q&A, not like other talks where Mum and Pop had books or visual aids. I wandered around the room, looking at the stained glass, the chimneys on the lanterns with all the fancy brasswork and colored glass, the inlay on the ends of the benches. There was a lot of history in this little room of ten rows with two five-seater benches in each row.

"Thought so," a familiar, whiny voice said, punctuated with a snort.

I looked at the door. There was Sylvia Grandstone, arms crossed, head tilted to display her golden curls. I wondered who she was trying to impress. Ninety-five percent of the staff were women, and this was a girls-only school. That was followed by a sense of "whew!" Her entrance stopped me just in time, before I acted on an idea of floating up to look at some writing in the stained glass panel at the front of the chapel. While I didn't really care what Sylvia Grandstone thought of me, I wasn't stupid enough to risk her making a fuss that the wrong people might listen to.

I always had to keep in mind the rules Kurt and Felicity and I had made up to protect our talents or powers or whatever let us do what we did. Hide what we did, hide what we were, hide from trouble. There was no telling when the weirdness factor of Neighborlee would fail us, and those people who spied on the children's home would return, notice us, and make us vanish.

So it was good that Sylvia didn't catch me kinda-sorta flying.

"Am I supposed to ask what you were thinking?" I asked, after we stood there for a few minutes in silence.

Sylvia was the one Grandstone who had learned some patience. Where just staring down her cousins, Reggie and Freddie would get them to mouth off and get themselves in trouble, silence didn't get under Sylvia's skin. She could stand there and smirk, or give indications of the mental gymnastics she was going through, and wait for someone else to talk.

The smart tactic was to take control of the pseudo-conversation when Sylvia was involved. Besides, the more time she had to think, the better the chances she would twist the situation around entirely in her favor. For instance, if I made her stand there long enough, by the time an argument arose and she started screaming, she would have convinced herself that I had tricked her into staying behind after the Q&A. Since I had survived ten years of attending school with her, the odds were good that I could predict what she would say and do, and even how she thought. If the mental gyrations in the gray matter of a Grandstone brain could be called "thinking."

"Just how long did you think you could keep that secret?" She adjusted her stance so the other hip was cocked out and she leaned against the other side of the door.

"Uh, it's a secret to me, I guess."

That got one of her trademark squeal-snorts. "Your parents."

"It's no secret that I have parents."

I fully expected her to harangue me with the fact that I was one of the Lost Kids of Neighborlee. Former resident of Neighborlee Children's Home. A reject. A throwaway. Sloppy seconds.

"They're famous!" Sylvia came out of the doorway, jamming her fists into her hips. "Your parents are big-time, famous writers! How long did you think you could hide it? Some people!" Another squeal, with only a touch of snort.

"Uh, I never tried to hide it."

What I tried to hide was my grin. Until that first booksigning where people were lined up halfway around the block, it never really registered that my parents with twenty books to their names were indeed popular writers. People paid good money and waited eagerly for first editions in hardback.

"I can't believe I never made the connection." Sylvia tipped her head to one side, letting her hair fall in her face. "I mean, yeah, they're the weird, hippie Zephyrs, but they're *famous*. They've got about a gazillion books that people buy. You are rich."

Uh huh. So that was her problem. Nobody in town was allowed to be rich other than the Grandstones.

"How did you con them into adopting you? Like, you're gonna be rich when they kick off. Both of them are so old. You have got to tell me how you did it."

Why? So she could con someone into adopting her?

"I didn't do anything. I was only six when they adopted me." I barely managed to hold back "remember?" because of course, the only time Sylvia paid attention to me back in school was when I stood between her and what she wanted. "Right place, right time, right people, I guess." I couldn't really say my parents were warm, loving people who were looking to share their love. Sylvia would not understand at all.

"Some people get all the luck." She straightened up and shook her head, with that calculated, slow kind of movement that I swear she had to practice in the mirror. How else could she get her curls to respond like that and lay just so on her shoulders? "You're rich. Who would have thought it? I mean, you don't act it."

"What does acting rich mean?"

"Well ... not dressing like that, for one thing." She fluttered her fingers at me.

Then she stopped, frowning. My deceptively casual outfit was brand new. Mum and I spent half a day at Selfridges with a personal shopper, putting together outfits. Mum liked casual, but she also liked quality. She liked stuff that lasted. Yes, sometimes she wore jeans so heavily studded with rhinestones that she almost couldn't lift her legs to walk, but she also liked good quality, casual fashion. For the first time on the trip, I wasn't wearing my usual comfy jeans with an overshirt and T-shirt.

"What's wrong with my clothes?" I had to ask.

"Better get your money back from that shopper chick who was helping you spend all Pop's money," Harry said, leaning into the doorway. He crossed his eyes and stuck his tongue out, then straightened out his expression when Sylvia turned to look at him.

"You have a personal shopper?" she drawled, her disbelief so thick in her voice, the pitch slid up the scale about an octave. "What is your problem? Why are you acting like you're a stupid poor hick all the time?"

"How should I act? Like a spoiled brat arrogant snot who thinks she should run the world, and just makes herself look like a brainless twit?"

"Like you?" Harry added.

Sylvia let out a steam whistle shriek and launched herself at me. How unfair was that? Harry said it. She never would have realized I was talking about her until he said it.

Someone must have been teaching Sylvia boxing. She got in a good right hook between my left temple and eye socket before I realized she was getting physical. Sylvia hadn't tried to inflict capital punishment on those who crossed her since fifth grade.

While I didn't use my telekinetic power to shove her away, pin her to the wall, maybe even shove her through the wall, honesty compels me to admit that Harry saved me. Maybe he had a little ability to fly, or least do the long jump fast, and hard. He body-slammed Sylvia from behind while she was spinning around and coming back in for another strike. I was still catching my breath and seeing stars. Then suddenly the male five percent of the faculty and staff stormed into the room and got hold of Sylvia.

Dr. Butterfield had heard everything, and proved he had a future writing political speeches with the great spin he put on the whole encounter. Without repeating a single word that either of us said, he put everything on Sylvia. She was a resident at the school and I was a guest. She had come back to the chapel when she should have been heading to her next class. It all worked against her.

The headmistress came to apologize while we were sitting in Dr. Butterfield's private quarters. He was digging some very old ice from the back of his tiny English refrigerator to put on my eye. She assured us that Sylvia had gone "beyond the pale" (yeah, they still said that in Jolly Olde England) and had wasted the last of many second chances granted her.

Whatever that meant, it didn't mean Sylvia returned to Neighborlee High for the rest of our junior year. Unfortunately, she did come back for our senior year.

I couldn't wait to get home and report to the "We loathe Sylvia Grandstone club." It wasn't really an *official* group, although a number of people in our graduating class confessed they had looked into voodoo dolls and sending requests to the State Department to keep her from coming back into the country.

No, that wasn't very mature of me. It also wasn't very mature that I let Mum and Pop praise me for not using my powers to slam Sylvia into the wall, or through a window, or just hold her up in the air and spin her around like a WWE wrestling champion. I didn't use my telekinesis because I didn't get a chance. Ten-plus years of self-imposed "never use our talents where other people can see" made me hesitate. Even when it came to a chance to work out my frustrations on Sylvia Grandstone and get payback for all my friends at school.

So I really didn't deserve any of the kudos I got. Sympathy for my black eye, yes, I earned that. Praise for *not* slamming that spoiled brat snot into a greasy makeup smear on the stone wall of the chapel? Nope.

~~~~~

We got home in early December. Just enough time to make up all the tests and quizzes I missed before Christmas break. Yes, Harry and I had homework we had to do while we were globe-trotting. I also got to cheer for the girls' varsity basketball team as they headed for the Lake Erie League championship.

I had lost my sports reporting job between the school newspaper and the *Tattler* because someone else had to fill in for me. Conrad Severidge, my friend and the owner's son, apologized. He was the head sports reporter, and offered me a chance to hang around with the college sports reporter and do fill-in jobs, especially with all the tournaments that would take place between Thanksgiving and Christmas, and then at New Year's. I took it. I got paid, since I wasn't doing the sports reporting for a grade.

I stayed on the school newspaper staff, but the editorial side, fixing grammar and spelling, typesetting, and figuring out the computer programs. They kept getting changed and improved and upgraded without any input from the people who actually had to use the wretched, convoluted, totally illogical software. Yeah, they did that to us a lot. Usually in the middle of putting together the next issue, meaning we had to redo half the paper.

While I was away "across the pond," Kurt got more involved helping out as a big brother/graduate at Neighborlee Children's Home. It only made sense for me to come along and help out, even though technically I wasn't a graduate, since Mum and Pop adopted me. Besides, I was still in high school. They usually asked
~~~~~

graduates to return once they were in college or had established careers or businesses of their own. Not that anyone met me at the door, thumped Gandalf's staff on the threshold and boomed out, "You shall not pass!"

I got the feeling Mrs. Silvestri was especially pleased, and not just because the homework helping team had lost the only person with truly decent English language and writing skills. I'm not talking about big, convoluted issues such as who vs. whom, or gerunds, or past perfect tense versus simple past tense, or object vs. subject questions. The kids and tutors were having problems with things like switching and misusing their, they're, and there, or accept vs. except vs. exempt, or affect vs. effect, it's vs. its, etc.

So that was how I became a tutor, twice a week. I was busy for the rest of my junior year of high school, between stringing for the *Tattler*, running track, youth group activities at church, and tutoring at NCH.

And that wasn't taking into account my duties as a guardian with Felicity and Kurt. Three nights a week, rain or shine (well, technically not shine, because it was at night, although maybe moonshine would count?), we took to the skies and patrolled our town. We parked at the edge of town, where Kurt could hide his truck among the trees, and went straight up and out of the sight of anybody who might be looking up. Kurt had traded his car in for a truck because it was easier to haul his equipment for his growing repair business, along with any small appliances and lawn equipment to work on.

Once we got airborne, we flew the perimeter of town, then spiraled inward, so we covered as much territory as we could without too much overlap. Kurt cobbled together a set of long-distance lenses, to gather evidence if we witnessed any suspicious activity. We snapped still shots, and then later moving pictures, with night-vision lenses so important details like license plates and identifying characteristics were clear. Fortunately, we never needed to figure out how to get that evidence to the authorities to ensure someone faced justice. Still, it was better to be prepared.

Neighborlee had a reputation, so other than big incidents of stupidity, such as the wannabe gangsters we once ran into at the quarries, there wasn't a lot of invasion from other towns and counties. Most outsiders heard about the weird things that happened to people who tried to sneak into our town to do some B&E or harass kids at Halloween or indulge in some vandalism. Not very many took that reputation as a challenge. When we patrolled, we didn't stay out very late. Felicity and I were both still in high school, after all. We managed to harass the would-be crooks and vandals into tripping up or giving up and fleeing town. When we needed to, Felicity could be prodded into an EM burst that fried car engines and electronics, to keep the jerks in place, usually arguing with each other until the police or park rangers arrived.

The truth be told, we weren't really protecting Neighborlee from the outside world, but protecting the rest of the world from Neighborlee and the weirdness that might slither through weak points and invade Earth from somewhere out there.

Life was good. We liked feeling necessary and helpful, enough that the approval of my folks, Angela, Stephanie and Mr. Longfellow was really all we needed. That was a good thing, because it would be kind of awkward and a little dangerous to take public credit for some of the trickier stunts we did. Such as zapping the engines of the drunks who decided they wanted to drag race from one side of the county to the other, and then yanking the keys out of the ignition and making their phones go nuts when they tried to call for help from more of their drunken buddies.

That incident with the drag-racing drunks taught us the value of anonymity. We could have been sued. No way was my allowance and my newspaper salary enough to pay legal fees. Two of those idiots were the sons of powerful people with a big, fancy, nasty stable of lawyers. The kind who did everything but devise a new branch of quantum physics to twist the law to convince the authorities their clients were totally within their rights to drive at three times the posted speed limits, without headlights, while hitting mailboxes and newspaper boxes and turfing front yards.

Not only were their clients within their rights, but those big fancy lawyers had prepared counterclaims, with paperwork four inches thick, trying to sue the people who had interfered with their clients' simple little need to get some fresh air and take a break from the strain of studying. That was probably the smallest of the lies. The drunken drag-racers had been kicked out of Cleveland State University three weeks before, should have left the state of Ohio, and had no classes to study for. The temperature was hovering at three degrees above zero, so what fresh air were they looking for? Sleet with a side of frost bite?

Carr, Cooper and Crenshaw, Neighborlee's resident lawyers, saved the day. They countered every single argument, each holding a briefcase behind their backs. Every time a twisted piece of proof and another lie crossed the clerk of court's desk, CCC untwisted it.

Of course, those big fancy lawyers lost a lot of ground and time trying to find the parties responsible for stopping the cars just feet away from crashing through the plate-glass walls of the front lobby of Eden, the name finally chosen for the community center in the old Bucksby Factory. They wasted a lot of money with accident reconstruction experts and subpoenaing the cell phone records of everyone who had been in the lobby that night.

That was the biggest strike against the drunken bozos. A group of middle school and high school kids were having a lock-in that Friday night to paint and decorate and personalize the small gymnasium that had just been finished, and celebrate the new name. With five meeting rooms renovated and equipped, two gymnasiums, a first aid/infirmary room, an office, the lobby, and kitchen, along with a daycare center, it deserved an official name. There were a lot of kids in the lobby, having just washed up from painting the new gym. All those cell phone records also proved the drunken bozos tried to get into the party two hours earlier.

They made a lot of noise, including trying to pry the doors open. Emphasis on *try*, because they were already lubricated enough to lose all coordination. They scratched the glass and metal of the doors with their tire irons, but never managed to get the wedge end of the tire iron into a hinge or between the door and central post, to pry it open. When they realized most of the kids and their chaperones were recording their fumbling and stumbling and all the filthy language they were spilling, they got defensive and even more offensive. For some reason, they decided their privacy was being invaded, so they threatened to call their lawyers down on the party organizers and the kids when nobody would open the doors for them or stop recording them.

If they didn't want to be recorded, as was pointed out during the first hearing, then they shouldn't have been trying to destroy public property, in public, and making a lot of noise.

What part of lock-in didn't they understand? It meant the

doors weren't opening for anyone, and if Gabriel came blowing his trumpet for the final judgment, he would just have to wait until 7 the next morning when the lock-in ended.

Them were the rules, folks! We done follows the rules in Neighborlee, by gum.

Well, most of the time. Magic seems to have slightly different rules that apply in slightly different ways from the laws of nature.

The drunken drag-racers hadn't even heard about Neighborlee until someone among their party animal friends mentioned the fight-the-ice painting party. They thought it'd be fun to crash the party. They thought it would be easy to convince some "hot" high school girls to go party with them. The drunks decided their rights were being violated, when they couldn't get to the under-age girls who were their targets.

Long story short: a bunch of arrogant snot rich kids put in a whole lot more work in one evening than they had expended all year in college, organizing themselves as best they could despite the alcohol messing up their brainwaves. They were really into technology, texting and emailing back and forth, so the plan to break into the party was well-documented.

Carr, Cooper and Crenshaw got hold of the text messages between the bozos and their friends, discussing what they were going to do to get into the party and make everyone pay for denying them what they wanted. Crashing through the front wall of the lobby with their cars was supposed to be the climax of the evening. First, they raced through town, vandalizing lawns and landscaping. All this was documented in videos they sent to each other, comparing the damage they had done.

Funny, how CCC was able to get all that electronic documentation, but the fancy out-of-state lawyers ran into trouble getting it. Maybe their tactics worked fine in normal towns and big cities, if there is such a thing as "normal." They were dealing with Neighborlee, where some natural laws don't quite…cooperate.

A lot of time and money was spent trying to figure out how the three drag racers' cars stopped just feet away from crashing through that plate glass window and into the lobby. Somehow, five decorative cement planters moved from the far right and far left of the doorway and ended up in cars' front grills. The question was *how* those planters moved. There were dents in the ground where the cement planters usually sat, and chunks of snow and ice had been visibly displaced. Also, some rusty chunks of metal had broken off the inch-thick staples that should have held the planters in place. Those were ripped out as easily as pulling smaller staples out of stacks of paper.

The next question the expensive lawyers and their experts and engineers couldn't answer was what killed the drag racing cars' engines. According to several videos, balls of green and blue sparks dove down into and through the hoods of the oncoming cars and then erupted out again.

Some people theorized a freak lightning strike. All right, one lightning strike *might* have been believable on a sleeting, cold, dark night full of black, churning clouds. Yet the evidence from weather satellites and weather monitoring stations around the country showed there had been no lightning all night. Okay, one lightning strike, not caught on the meteorological equipment, might be believable, but three? Striking at the same time? Hitting only those cars, but nothing else?

The truth? Felicity got furious-scared enough to blast those three drag-racing bozos with the biggest EM burst she had ever produced. Furious, because she had seen a few of the videos and comments posted online by friends inside Eden at the party. Scared, because I had just mentally pulled those planters up from a thick layer of ice and fought those rusted iron staples holding them into the cement, and it was pretty clear the cement planters weren't going to stop the cars.

Oh, yeah, and the fact that I put so much energy and concentration into the effort that we all fell, from about one hundred feet up in the air over the building. We should have landed on the roof *before* I tried that, but time was of the essence.

Kurt controlled of my kinda-sorta flying ability long enough to get us down to the roof. I collapsed with the worst headache of my life, bleeding from my nose and ears. We were stuck up on that roof, huddled together against the cold, for about three hours while the police and EMTs and tow trucks and news trucks from every station in Northeast Ohio dealt with the crash. Felicity was kind of worn out from the humongous EM burst she generated, but I was in the worst shape.

Kurt huddled with us, out of the worst of the storm. I was so wiped out that he couldn't even borrow my telekinetic talent to ward off the wind and snow. He called my folks, but they couldn't get near the building, let alone get to the back door to climb up to the roof and help us.

Angela got into the building with emergency supplies, and no one saw her. She climbed up a ladder to the rooftop entrance, with blankets, waterproof canvas, and a big insulated jug of one of her miracle-working teas. It soothed my headache and drove away that sick, twisting feeling that made me afraid I would tip right off the surface of the planet and go hurtling out into space. She sat with us, helping us get warm in our impromptu tent, with a lovely gold-tinted oil lantern.

To distract us, she told us about some crates she had decided to open up that evening, to restock the store, and all the surprises she had found. In the morning, when we had all recovered from our very stressful Friday night, she wanted us to come over and help her decide what to put out on the shelves. We would have first pick of anything that caught our fancy. Guardians deserved a reward.

Chapter Four

I couldn't fly or move anything telekinetically for about two weeks after that. It worked out fine for all of us, since the weather for the rest of the month was so bad, we couldn't have flown to patrol anyway. I was glad to spend the evenings curled up in front of the fireplace, reading through some of the lovely old first editions I found in those crates Angela "just happened" to find in the cellar of Divine's Emporium.

Of course, my evenings weren't all spent at home. This was my junior year of high school and there were social events like sledding and skating parties, and get-togethers for the church youth group and rehearsals for the spring play, and tutoring nights at NCH.

Miss Abby, my former housemother, moved up to counseling duties. She approached me one night after tutoring and asked me to sit and talk. How could I refuse, when she had a plate of mint Milano cookies and mugs of peppermint dark chocolate cocoa, heavy with whipped cream?

"You're starting to apply to colleges, aren't you?" she said, after wisely waiting until I had taken my first sip of cocoa.

"A couple, but I'm really planning on attending WB. Conrad and his dad both want me to stay on and cover college sports at the *Tattler* after I graduate." I shrugged, and couldn't help grinning. "Kind of nice that they expect me to still be stringing for sports next year, and into college."

"You're reliable, you're a local, and you're a good writer." She sat back and looked me over, her smile widening. "It's probably silly, since I didn't have you very long, but I feel kind of proud of you. You're still one of my girls, Lanie."

"Thanks. I don't think it's silly at all."

"Okay, here's the thing. You're good with the kids, tutoring them, and your command of English, and being able to communicate what you know. You should go into teaching."

"But I want to be a sports reporter."

All right, that was kind of a stupid response.

"You also want to play basketball and run track, right? You

can't do it all. You're good, but not enough for scholarships. There are scholarships for future teachers, though. Especially if you plan on teaching at Neighborlee High, or the middle school."

I opened my mouth, ready to tell her that I wasn't worried about scholarships. My folks were, as Sylvia had so crassly pointed out, very secure, financially. Besides, they had been putting money aside for college since the day they adopted me.

"You're already a hit with the kids. In fact, haven't you been talking with some of them about starting up an in-house newspaper? Using your experience at the *Tattler* and the school paper? That will all work in your favor. You'll have teaching experience. All that will look great on your resume. You can teach English, take over the school newspaper and the yearbook, and coach basketball and track, if you've got your heart set on it. Even with an athletic scholarship, you'd have to go for a degree anyway. What would it be in?"

So that was how I got talked into declaring teaching as my major, with minors in English, journalism, and sports. It made sense. I did like working with the kids. The thought of going back to Neighborlee High with some authority had a kind of appeal.

Besides, it would keep me in town, low to the ground, so to speak, with my finger on its pulse. Much easier to protect the town if I could hear what was going on, via the kids. Teachers were invisible, in some ways, and expected to be all over town.

My future was a little more solid. Now all I had to do was survive my senior year of high school and come up with a good prank for Senior Prank Night, before settling into life as a college student. I'm not ashamed to say that I looked forward to living at home and going to college. Granted, I already knew freshmen were required to live on campus in the dormitories, but once that requirement was met, I could live anywhere I wanted. Felicity and I talked about becoming roommates once she got out of high school and took care of the freshman requirement. It was going to be great.

Or not. Remember, we lived in Neighborlee, Ohio, weirdness capital of the United States, possibly the world.

Angela never came out and said it, but we just understood that we had been somewhat sheltered from the really big, nasty, messy, painful, scary aspects of being guardians of our town. We were growing up, and the nastiness from outside our world had been quiet, licking its wounds and gathering its strength for several years now. Next time something tried to come through, we might be called upon to stand in the gap.

But hey, we were semi-pseudo-superheroes, even if we didn't have funky names and costumes. What could go wrong?

Yeah, that statement was the cue for everything to implode in *The Incredibles*. Thank You, God, it didn't happen that way for us. Or at least, it didn't happen right away.

Granted, Sylvia Grandstone came home from England in time for our senior year at Neighborlee High, but I can't by any stretch of the imagination say she was an invasion from another dimension of reality. She had actually toned down. Her jerk-face cousins were somehow managing to stay in college and not get in too much trouble. Translated: in so much trouble that when they got booted from one college, the next college in line refused to take them. Chances were good they would even end up with degrees. On the six-year plan, rather than the standard four.

While I was busy with community service, building up my resume and making myself very attractive to the admissions board at Willis-Brooks College, Sylvia also did her own version of community service. It came in the form of leaving town almost every weekend, and sometimes not coming back until Monday morning. Sometimes she was so exhausted, she sleepwalked through her classes, which kept her from causing trouble. I was tutoring at NCH, playing basketball and then running track, patrolling and regularly reporting to Angela. Then in my alleged free time, I worked yearbook and the school newspaper and covered sports for the *Tattler*. All Sylvia did was act. Well, that was what she claimed, when she declaimed in homeroom and the cafeteria about her weekend activities. Reading between the lines, she was doing a lot of modeling work or walk-on, non-speaking, crowd scene work. Her family bought her an agent/manager when she came home from England.

Nobody got hold of any usable details, but there was a lot of speculation as to why she came home. Maybe the private school network in Europe had a good communication system, so no private school would take her, no matter how much money the Grandstones flashed in front of them as a bribe. My guess was that her family needed to keep a closer eye on Sylvia. Or they just gave in and accepted the inevitable: the only way she was going to snag a rich husband was to do the Anna Nicole routine, maybe land herself a reality show, and outdo all the egotistical useless-for-anything-except-gossip-magazine-fodder glamour-chicks.

All anyone at Neighborlee High cared about was that Sylvia was too busy with her "career" to torment us for not adoring her. She was easier to get along with, because she got enough ego-stroking during her weekends away to make her semi-pleasant during the school week. Plus she was constantly wearing all sorts of high-fashion clothes and new makeup and experimental hairstyles. The girls who cared about those things hovered around her, stroking her ego, eager to learn about the life. Having people turn to her for advice and looking up to her as an example was good for her ego and made her easier to live with.

However, as we got to the end of the school year, Sylvia wasn't quite so happy with her "career." It was finally dawning on her that most of her roles were non-speaking, background, crowd scenes, relegated to the gorgeous assistant to the game show host, pointing dramatically at the next prize. Whenever she did get to the front of the camera shots, she still played the part of decoration, usually a slave girl who wiggled or slithered her way to the side of the evil mastermind threatening to destroy the world. She handed him his remote control or a steaming goblet of some vile potion, and then wriggled or slithered over to the side of the set. There she would gaze adoringly at the evil mastermind while he gave his reveal-all monolog and threatened the hero, the heroine, the planet, or whoever else was available.

She wasn't getting speaking roles. She wasn't getting her name in the credits where it counted. How long could a girl coast along on "Slave Girl 1," "Gun Moll 3," or "O'Reilly's Bimbo"? Yeah, those were actual roles she played. Besides, non-speaking actors got peanuts for wages, compared to bit players who actually said just a few words, even if it was just to scream for help before the monster bit their heads off.

Sylvia was restless and unhappy as graduation and all the attendant senior activities approached. Her adoring crowd of sycophants was melting away. Even the girls suffering brain damage from overdosing on makeup and hairspray were busy getting ready for college of one kind or another. About mid-April, she went into a public melt-down when the realization hit her that she should have been preparing for college.

Considering the bullet we all dodged, the prayers during Youth Group meetings on Wednesday night at Neighborlee Gospel Church or in Sunday school must have been heavy-duty. Those of us townies who were staying home and going to WB were terrified that not only would Sylvia be inflicted on us for four more years, but one of us might get stuck being roommates with her. Or in the case of the guys, their girlfriend might be stuck as Sylvia's roommate. Grandstone-speak for live-in body servant.

Then the problems and questions of our dorm assignments pushed fears of having to live with Sylvia out of our minds. Temporarily. The housing department at the college was rumored to have been working with the psychology and sociology professors for several years, manipulating the roommate assignments and dorm groupings. This was more than the usual PR statements about making the freshman year easier for students by giving them supportive, friendly living arrangements. Translation: letting friends and classmates room together.

Clarice O'Donnell and I planned to room together at WB. We lived in dread that Sylvia would revert to her Kindergarten tactics, and insist that Clarice wanted to be roommates.

Two miracles happened. Or maybe just one miracle, and something so utterly strange that even a year later, we weren't sure if it was supposed to be a good thing or a bad thing.

First, Sylvia's agent/manager quit, and a much hungrier one snatched up Sylvia's contract. This one, though, had an actual spine, to stand up against all the Grandstone family interference. Think all the trouble Art Modell gave the coaches for the Cleveland Browns, how he interfered with all their decisions and overrode their plays, so people wondered why anyone would commit career suicide by working for him. This new agent/manager took charge of Sylvia's career, determined to turn her into a star before she hit twenty. Some people figured the guy planned to marry her the day she turned eighteen, tie up her career and her fortune, and maybe brainwash her into the bargain, to make her easier to live with.

Yeah, we were nasty. So sue us. In our defense, we were sick and tired of Grandstone arrogance. We were also seniors, running on fumes, desperate to get through graduation and collapse for a couple weeks before starting summer classes or summer jobs. More important, we were gearing up for the requirements of Senior Prank Night. As I mentioned previously, there was an implied touch of nasty mischief involved in choosing our pranks. Granted, most of us were merciful to the safety forces and city maintenance personnel, or school personnel. We chose pranks that everybody would enjoy and wouldn't make too much of a mess to clean up. Most of the time. However, with the approach of Senior Prank Night and graduation and everything else involved, we weren't the nicest people in town, much less the county or state.

Back to what I was saying earlier. The miracle? Sylvia's new agent/manager got her a speaking part in a low-budget scream-fest. She had to leave for two whole months of filming on June 1. She would miss Senior Prank Night, to the relief of the team whose prank she had been trying to commandeer for the last two weeks. Well, it was their fault, meeting in the open, where everybody could guess they were plotting, and talking loudly enough that those passing by could overhear what they were saying.

Sylvia didn't have anything to do with Senior Prank Night.

She didn't walk through graduation with us.

She smirked for a few days about how everyone would miss out on the blowout graduation party her parents had been planning for months. Seriously? She thought people *wanted* to come?

One benefit she probably never considered was that she wouldn't have to go through that don't-let-the-door-knock-you-on-your-teeny-tiny-butt-on-the-way-out humiliation, emphasizing how much she was not adored by the entire town.

Sylvia announced, and frequently, she wasn't going to worry about college. She was going to be a star. What would she need a college degree for, anyway?

Incoming freshmen at universities and colleges throughout the world were breathing a sigh of relief.

The other miracle that might not have been a miracle? That took some time to realize what had happened. It rested with the aforementioned housing department at Willis-Brooks College and its ongoing partnership with the psychology and sociology department. The miracle/un-miracle lay in the fact that the only students it really had any control over were the incoming freshmen. Sophomores and higher grades had the option of choosing their dorms, their roommates, and living off-campus if they wanted, either at home or renting apartments in town or other towns.

More about that later.

On to Senior Prank Night.

Considering all the rumors and giggling and teasing about preparations going awry, it was a given that Kurt, Felicity and I were going to be really busy on Senior Prank Night. That wasn't fair, considering it was *my* Senior Prank Night, and I had something of a right to enjoy it. Am I right?

I assembled a team, mostly by going around and asking some of the kids I trusted, who I liked, who I knew would want to get the prank done fast, make it simple, and not do too much damage, and then be home before midnight. What's the fun of being allowed to sleep in the next day if we *needed* to sleep in from exhaustion? As seniors, we didn't have to go to school the last two days of school.

Along with finding a fun, harmless prank we could brag about, I had the added criteria of needing to get it over with fast. I had to join Kurt and Felicity on patrol, to stop other pranksters from blowing up the town or trying to repeat Jinx Longfellow's prank. Or worse, Reggie Grandstone's attempted prank.

Gordon Priebe, who was working part-time for the Neighborlee PD and working through the criminal justice program at WB, came up with the idea. Not intentionally. Those of us who had foiled previous stupid, messy pranks gathered at Miller's Diner to gripe and reminisce and brainstorm about Prank Night. Gordon remarked on the abundance of flagpoles in our town. Multiple sets of flagpoles, in some places. In front of Eden, the Post Office, each school, the Board of Education Building, City Hall, the police department, and the fire department. Tall flagpoles. Not the skyscraper poles, but tall enough to defy the tallest ladder in town, other than the extension ladder on the new truck the fire department had just bought. Gordon mentioned catching a bunch of kids from Darbyville trying to take down the rope used to raise and lower the flag at Eden. Their excuse was that they were getting ready to go rock climbing in the old quarries, and they realized they didn't have enough rope. They swore they were going to give it back when they were finished. (Yeah, right.)

Gordon caught them. He figured it would be smart to put a watch on all the other tall flagpoles in town, in case the same stupid kids or their buddies still needed rope. Especially since the section of quarries where they wanted to go rock climbing was closed to the public. After the Reggie Grandstone fiasco, Chief Tanner had learned to listen to Gordon's hunches. They asked officers and other city workers to keep an eye on the flagpoles. Sure enough, the same Darbyville juvenile delinquents tried to "borrow" the rope from the Post Office and police department flagpoles. That was dumb, but Gordon figured it was a matter of pride by that time. They needed to prove they were smarter than the cops who stopped them from taking Eden's flagpole ropes.

Anyway, Gordon was talking about the trouble of re-stringing the flagpole rope at Eden without breaking out the extension ladder truck. Kurt sketched a design for a gizmo that could be used to remote control climb the flagpole, taking the rope up there, restring it through the metal loop at the top, slide down, and reconnect the ends of the rope. Then he got to laughing. Bryce Engle, another senior and fellow cleaner-upper who tried to stop idiots before they made their messes, caught on first. Bryce was so mechanically minded he had no imagination when it came to magical, fantastical impossible-yet-real things. I considered inviting him to join us in guarding Neighborlee. He had a real knack for gizmos, just like Kurt. In fact, over the last couple years, he had teamed up with Kurt in fixing gizmos that refused to work when he wasn't around. Bryce made things work for real, and he and Kurt were talking about being business partners, inventing things like security systems. Bryce was going to WB to study engineering. He also belonged to our Star Trek club, because he liked the challenge of making all the impossible futuristic technology of Star Trek work for real.

Bryce and Kurt got the idea of stringing things on the flagpoles all through town. Clarice and I came up with the criteria of something big, easily visible, a challenge to get to the top of the flagpole without Kurt's gizmo. It had to be not too messy to remove. It had to be cheap to obtain. Free would be good, as long as "free" didn't translate as "stolen."

We went to the landfill in Darbyville and got old tires. Really old tires. The kind without steel belts or any of the fancy-schmancy technology to help them hug the road and resist punctures. Messy, smelly, old black tires, some of which threatened to disintegrate as we dug them out of the landfill heaps and hauled them home.

Those tires were heavy. Even the really old, disintegrating ones. Kurt worked on his gizmo for lifting the tires up the flagpoles on the flag ropes. The gizmo worked for everyone, up until we put about ten pounds of weight on it. Kurt got it to work with any weight of tires when he was controlling it, but that was the problem. We needed multiple gizmos to carry tires up flagpoles all over town. At the same time. Kurt worked and fiddled and scratched his head and tweaked, to the point of wanting to sling his gizmo across the room. It worked fine, taking any burden he put on it, as long as he was there. However, Kurt's "field of influence" over the gizmo faded before it had climbed to the top of the tallest flagpole in town, when we tested it, at midnight, two days before Senior Prank Night. The silly thing froze up just a few inches out of Kurt's influence zone. I had to float up and unstick it from the flagpole and bring it back down. We did it eight times, tweaking and testing and me going up to retrieve it, before we gave up.

That gave us the solution, actually. Bryce and others took the sets of flagpoles that the gizmo could handle without any special attention. Kurt would be with the team on the second tallest flagpole in town, to get the climbing gizmo to the top after the weight of the tires interfered. I would be with the team doing the really tall flagpole, where the weight of the tires would halt the gizmo before it was even halfway to the top. I would have to give it a little boost with my telekinesis. If that didn't work, I would depend on Felicity to distract my teammates while I physically hauled the tire to the top and dropped it down.

We got our prank done twice as fast as planned, and we were home and most of our team was in bed before the patrolling teams of police and school and town officials got to work. Bryce had the honor of making sure enough people heard him talking about all the tires he found in the Darbyville landfill about a week before Senior Prank Night, and how many he was able to load in the trunk of his car. Word got all around town before we even performed the prank, so people would know our prank had to do with tires.

It wouldn't be worth all the trouble we went to if people didn't know we did it, after all. Of course, our "clever" PR work backfired, meaning we couldn't change our prank at the last minute. Which explained our panic when the day drew near and Kurt's flagpole-climbing gizmo refused to work.

Of course, later, when the fuss and flurry of graduation had subsided, it occurred to us that the best prank of all would have been to build up expectation and some small portion of fearful anticipation, and then done nothing. Zippo. Zero. Nada. Zilch. People would have been looking over their shoulders, looking at the sky and around corners, wondering what we had done.

Thursday morning after the town woke up and people started either laughing or cursing, it was a simple matter of getting the chainsaws from the city maintenance shed and cutting those old tires off. Over and done, minimal debris to clean up, less than half an hour of work total, and people were still chuckling over the simple, clever, fuss-free prank ten years later.

Looking back, I'm so glad I was part of the group that made people smile. When I needed it most, that good reputation came in handy. People were willing to step up when I needed help and encouragement the most.

~~~~~

Three weeks before our freshman year at WBC was to start, we had our class assignments and textbook and equipment lists, so we could go to the college bookstore and get whatever we needed. Problem: we didn't have our dorm assignments yet. Those of us staying in Neighborlee for college formed a support group, going through the checklists of preparation and comparing what we had bought for our dorm rooms and where we got it. Clarice and I had requested to be roommates, and we hadn't gotten even that confirmation, let alone the dormitory we were assigned to. Forget about the floor in that dormitory. What was going on?

We discussed the problem at our last Star Trek club meeting before the school year started, two weeks before freshman orientation. It was kind of funny, ironic, and a bit of kismet, because at that time we were meeting in one of the smaller rooms of the WB Student Center. Boxes stacked at the back of the long room had labels such as "dorm assignments," "meal program vouchers," "student ID supplies," and other pieces and parts of the packets we were to get the day we showed up. Out of the twenty-three members of our club, six of us were freshmen, two were sophomores, two were juniors, and three were seniors at WBC. The older members were a little concerned, because the ones living on campus already had their dorm assignments.
~~~~~

Finally, Gabe Kelly, our captain and a senior, announced he had made an executive decision. He walked over to the boxes marked "dorm assignments," and with the help of the command crew, turned the boxes around to see if they could find any clues.

The boxes were marked by alphabetical groupings and by college year. Sophomores, juniors and seniors. No freshmen. The same with the other piles of boxes and whatever paperwork and supplies they contained. Sophomores, juniors and seniors, just waiting to be assembled into packets. Nothing for freshmen.

"Maybe we don't exist?" Clarice smiled, but her lips trembled a little bit. She had a good sense of humor, but it was hard joking about something as vital as having a place to live on campus. Looking back, we wondered why we were so worried, because we were the loco locals, meaning we had a place to stay: home!

"Who do we know who works here?" Gabe said, after he and the command crew put everything back pretty much the way they found it. Unless someone was suspicious and looking for signs that people had been digging around, it wasn't obvious. We didn't break the thick packing tape seals on the boxes and look inside.

We sat around discussing what connections we had with people who worked at the college. The nice thing about Willis-Brooks was that it was still pretty much run by "family," meaning the founding families of Neighborlee, and they always tried to steer job openings to locals. Every once in a while, some teachers group or union organizers tried to tell the administration how to run things. Strong-arm tactics never seemed to work out.

Neighborlee took care of its own. Troublemakers who tried to come in from other states and advocate for big changes and disrupt the family atmosphere of WBC suffered the same discomfort and increasing "go away, we don't like you and we don't want you here" pressure that unfriendly residents experienced. That didn't mean that everyone who didn't exactly fit, or fully accept the everyday weirdness and slight touch of magic in the atmosphere got driven away. Lots of people who lived in Neighborlee and attended WBC never noticed the odd and wonderful things that happened. They also didn't go to Divine's Emporium. Some people have sworn over the years that those people didn't even know Divine's existed.

My point here is that everybody at our meeting knew a couple people who worked at the college, either staff or faculty. After all, how else could we have snagged the great meeting room? Figuring out who to ask, and the right questions to ask was the tricky part. We came up with names, and each volunteered to make some calls. By that time our meeting was ready to adjourn to Miller's Diner.

Our usual cluster of tables and booths were waiting, and Stephanie waved to us as we came in. By the time we were settled in the booth, she came out with the first pitchers of iced tea and soft drinks, with Bethany scurrying after her, carrying a big stack of plastic cups. That kind of impressed on me how much time had passed. Bethany was five now. I felt a little weird, a little old. It wasn't like I was leaving and going far away for college, but everything kind of crashed down on me. This was my last Star Trek club meeting where I would drive home afterward. Next month, I would walk from whatever dorm I had been assigned, and walk back, since the smart thing to do would be to leave my little beater car at home instead of paying the parking fees. WBC sat in the middle of town, with access to activities and shopping, so I really didn't need my car to get anywhere on campus.

Chapter Five

We had our usual post-meeting snacks, sharing plates and plates of appetizers. We discussed the newest SF and fantasy books coming out from our favorite authors, or what season of which favorite SF show had just come out on DVD. Kind of routine, kind of expected. Maybe the realization that hit me had also flattened the moods of the others, too. We didn't stay as long as we usually did to gab and brainstorm new stories for our club fanzine.

Mum and Pop were still up, working on galleys for their next book, when I got home. They asked about the meeting, and I didn't see any reason not to tell them how we had tried to find some clue to the mystery. It wasn't like we had opened any of those boxes. Granted, there was the implication that if we had seen a box labeled "Freshman dorm assignments," someone might have found a way to look inside. For instance, knocked the box off the top of the stack, so a seam split, and in picking it up very awkwardly, allowed some papers to spill out. That sort of thing.

"You know..." Pop's eyebrows drew so close together as he thought, it was like he had a bushy uni-brow for a few seconds. "I do know someone in housing, now that you mention it." He chuckled when I muffled a demand to know why he hadn't told me earlier. Well, duh, I hadn't asked, had I?

Paige Armenghast was my Sunday school teacher all through middle school, and she worked in the housing department at the college. Once Pop thought of her, I remembered how she had acted a little odd the last few Sundays, when we met up at church. More accurately, we didn't meet up. As in, she would see me, or any of the other incoming freshmen who attended Neighborlee Gospel Church, and run the other way. Kind of conspicuous behavior for a woman as big as she was. Once, she was standing in line to get her hot dog at the Sunday school picnic. She saw me walk up with Clarice, carrying trays of condiments and buns, put down her plate right on top of the grill, and scurried away. It just showed how distracted I was with getting ready for the big adventure of dorm life that her peculiar behavior never registered.

Pop went to see her the next day. That was more proof that something weird was going on. It was Saturday and the administration offices at WBC should have been closed.

So that was how we were reminded of those ridiculous and puzzling and strangely confusing questionnaires we had to fill out last spring, when we got our acceptance letters and started the process of choosing classes and meal plans and requesting dorm assignments and roommates.

The questionnaires, which no incoming class before us had ever had to fill out, asked about details in our lives. Every detail imaginable. Some of them made sense, such as allergies, sleeping habits, if we smoked or drank, if we were morning people or night people, if we studied with music or the TV playing or needed complete silence. Then they turned odd. Did we work ahead on assignments or leave everything to the last minute, or just keep up? What were our favorite movies, TV shows, books, sports? What kind of hobbies did we have? What was our life philosophy? Fortunately, there was an explanation that life philosophy didn't refer to religious beliefs, but what we considered our purpose in life. Did we have control over our lives or were we victims of fate? Did we have a hopeful view of the future or a pessimistic view?

Huh?

At the time, those of us comparing notes just laughed about it. Someone had inflicted their idea of "creating a level playing field" on the administration. Knowing Neighborlee, those nosey weirdos would be gone soon enough. We didn't worry about it, at the time.

Maybe we should have.

The questions went on and on, asking for the slightest details of our lives, our bodies, our minds, our hearts. What organizations did we belong to? What kind of jobs had we held? What was our dream job? What job did we want to avoid most strenuously, to the point we would rather starve in a cardboard box on the banks of the Cuyahoga River? If we didn't have to work for a living, what would we like to do with our lives? What did we think of recent legislation and socio-political movements? What political offices would we like eliminated? What changes did we want to see in the government on the local and state and national level? What countries would we like to cut off all relations with? What did we think of genetic screening? What did we think of the recent actions of foreign governments in the news? On and on, until final exams and figuring out what to do for Senior Prank Night were a walk in the park in comparison.

As soon as we finished answering those thousand questions of doom, and sent the packets back to WBC, we forgot about them. Kind of a survival skill. Give our aching brain cells a rest.

Behind all that brain-strain and strangeness was a surprisingly simple explanation. The psychology and sociology professors at WBC got permission to run a little experiment on the students. They didn't lock us in rooms and inflict all sorts of sensory stimulus on us. They weren't allowed to slip psycho-reactive drugs in the food or the water, or pipe subliminal programming into the dorms at the sub-audible level. However, they were allowed to manipulate our living conditions in the dormitory, as in determining who would be our roommates, our floormates, the people on the floors above and below us, the people who would share the floor lounge and dormitory lounge with us, what cafeterias we would eat in, and the people we would encounter at meals. Then they would observe us. All our Residence Advisors were seniors in the psychology and sociology programs, and half their grades for the year rested on careful observation of all our activities and interactions, and then reporting in fine detail.

The delay in giving us our dormitory assignments came from the nitpicky process of analyzing our questionnaires and then determining what living combinations to create. Did they want to put people together who had the most in common? Did they want to set up the dormitories for the maximum possible conflict and contrast, so roommates would be fighting each other from day one? Did they want to try to set up a psycho-social version of a chemical reaction and cause an explosion? Did they want to see who would change and adapt the fastest, and how people would react to uncomfortable situations?

There were fewer than three hundred incoming freshmen. Two dormitory buildings, with four floors, including basements that were half laundry room. The dormitory lounge and the Residence Director's apartment took up half again the square feet of the residence portion of the first floor, meaning the RD apartment and lounge were an extension annexed onto the front of the three-story-tall dorm portion of the building. The dorm floors were divided neatly in half by the central stairwell, with fire doors on either side. On each side of the stairwell, ten rooms on one side of the hall and seven rooms on the other. The space of three rooms were lost for the bathroom. So seventeen dorm rooms on each half of each floor. The room directly across from the bathroom was the only single-occupant room, with the Residence Advisor stationed there. Think: spy in the concentration camp. Double agent. So that left thirty-two rooms on each floor with two to four students in each, with one or two sets of bunk beds, and a dresser-desk combination attached. It really was an efficient furniture design, taking up the least amount of floor space and granting us a big general floor space where some girls were able to create a pretty comfortable lounging and entertaining area. Those of us who were locals were lucky, because we could go home and get things like rugs and tables, bean bag chairs, skinny shelving, and all the supplies and decorations we wanted to make the dorm room more personalized and more like home. The people who came from far enough away that they couldn't drive home on the weekends were kind of stuck. They had to make do with what they could find in town, as cheaply as possible, or hope they got assigned roommates with bigger budgets or who were townies.

Third floor of Wickslow Hall (named for the Wickslow Chapel founder) was assigned to the artsy-craftsy types. The theater students. The art and dance majors. The undeclared students who didn't quite fit in anywhere and were still trying to figure out what they wanted to do when or if they ever grew up. So why were Clarice and I both put on third floor, when I was an education major and she was an accounting major? Maybe because we asked to be roommates. Maybe because the floors assigned to our majors were full. Maybe because third floor was clearly for the misfits. We all liked science fiction and fantasy and role-playing games.

On move-in day, it got really loud and crowded in the hallway. The fire doors on the stairwell were open, so the guys on the left side and the girls on the right side of the stairwell could go through the stairwell and walk around and meet up with people, and everybody was admiring everybody else's posters. We spec-fic fans loved our posters for our favorite TV shows and movies and books, and just imaginative things like pegasoids and unicorns and spaceships and ray guns and nebulas. Everybody was loudly admiring everybody else's decorations and asking about borrowing or offering to loan their books and jokingly threatening lives if models and decorative weapons were taken without permission.

Keep in mind the psychology and sociology professors' grand experiment. Why they decided to put in one place all the creative, active dreamers, the ones who not only believed in magic and aliens and other dimensions of reality, but *wanted it to be real*, I have no idea. Think about it. These professors lived in or near Neighborlee, the weirdness capital of the United States. If something strange was going to happen anywhere in the country, it would happen in Neighborlee. Our professors should have been aware of the power of belief and the greatly increased chances of the odd and wonderful and bizarre happening here. Despite that (maybe because of it?) they put all the freshmen with strong imaginations and a passion for the magical on the same floor anyway.

Some of what happened was their fault. Yet, knowing what I know about enemies trying to invade from other dimensions, I can't completely blame them.

I still say they should have known better.

At first, the Neighborlee effect left us alone. We were busy settling into our dorms, meeting the other kids on our floor, learning the rules, figuring out how to use our key cards. We had one key card for getting into the dormitory between midnight and 5:00 a.m., another key card that let us get into the stairwell and then from the stairwell onto the floor, and a third key card to get into our rooms. The cards were color coded, so that helped us avoid the frustration of swiping a card multiple times before realizing we were trying to open a door with our library card, for instance. However, there was a technique for using the cards, and three people on our floor alone made the mistake of putting the cards too near electronics that demagnetized the magnetic stripe. Lots of people asked, multiple times, why we had to have three cards. Didn't we have the technology to code the cards to handle all three doors we needed to get through? The answer was yes, but then if the card was demagnetized, we would have to go through the complicated and tricky process of recoding the card for all three doors. Major pain. Another major pain was how to get hold of someone on the inside to open the door for us if there happened to be a power outage, or we forgot our cards.

Some of us speculated that the cards were deliberately made fussy and complicated to give us a sense of camaraderie, so we would pull together. Kind of like castaways on a desert island, or prisoners in a concentration camp. It worked, whether done deliberately or not. The newbies stuck together as we made our way to the cafeteria for our first meal as official college freshmen.

Through all this, Clarice and I, and the other freshmen from our Star Trek club, had kept our mouths shut about what Mrs. A. had told us about the dorm assignments experiment. She had asked us not to spread it around, because while she hadn't been asked *not* to tell anyone, there hadn't been any statement giving permission to talk about the experiment. She thought the housing department wasn't supposed to know anything beyond the official instructions to leave the freshman assignments to someone else. Clarice and I kept our mouths shut about it on the walk to dinner. The others from our Star Trek club were with us. We had identified a handful of floormates who might want to come to our next meeting, and were talking to them. Finding out that they belonged to Star Trek or role-playing clubs back home encouraged us.

It was loud and crowded in the cafeteria, but also fun. I had been on campus for different activities related to school or church or sports. I had eaten in the cafeteria. Being a student instead of a guest felt different. I liked it.

Before we left the cafeteria, the Freshman Orientation team got on the loudspeakers and offered us options of what to do that evening. It was a free evening. The official activities started in the morning, including competitions and times for visiting our advisors and checking out different departments, in case people changed their minds about classes once they saw their schedules.

Our group filed out of the cafeteria, and there in the lobby were tables filled with flyers and coupon books for local businesses, and little introductory goodie bags. I felt like I was cheating, getting a goodie bag that was supposed to persuade me to come visit. I knew all the stores in town, after all.

"Divine's has a coupon!" Clarice announced.

Okay, that was too good to pass up.

"What's Divine's," Babbie Winslow asked. She was three doors down from us on the floor, and stood behind us now, looking through her coupon book.

"It's no good telling you. You gotta experience Divine's." I shared a grin with Clarice and we turned around to see if our gang was still in the cafeteria lobby. "Hey, guys, if you haven't heard yet, Clarice and Tyrone and Zach and Aldo and I are from Neighborlee. Instead of going to a movie we've all seen before, how about a walking tour of town before it gets crazy?"

"And use our coupons before other kids get to the stores, and the good stuff is gone?" Sheri Carter said with a chuckle. She riffled her coupon book, and others laughed.

"You can do whatever you want, but you need to find Divine's Emporium before you do anything else. How you survive your first year here will rest on your first impression of it."

"Think they'll be able to see the Wishing Ball?" Clarice asked. Tyrone laughed. Zach and Aldo laughed louder, trying to sound mysterious, when a few people asked what the Wishing Ball was.

"Just come on along and see, okay? I'm not going to tell you anything more, so you're not prejudiced," I added.

That got the interest of some people who didn't look all that thrilled with taking a long walk after an exhausting day getting moved into the dorm. It seemed like a third of the entire dorm came with us as we headed down the sidewalk.

In the end, twenty-some people went to Divine's. As we passed through town, Tyrone pointed out places of interest, such as Miller's Diner and various shops where they could use their coupons. We lost some people. Clarice and Zach made note of who stayed with us for the walk of several blocks. Every single one was a fandom person of one kind or another. The freaks and geeks, as some of the arrogant jerks referred to us. We basically left the art and dance and music students behind—unless they were also science fiction and fantasy and horror people, too. Had to wonder if that was accidental. After all, there was already something strong building up on our dorm floor, with all the fandom gear people had brought with them to college.

When we got to Divine's, it was brightly lit. Usually Divine's wasn't open after the dinner hour, but Angela made an exception for the start and end of the school year, and during Christmas shopping season. She had hung lights on the wrought iron fence that ran along the sidewalk. They looked like strings of Christmas tree lights, until we got close enough to see something spinning slowly inside the tiny glass globes. Stars and comets and planets.

The gate hung open, and as I started up the flagstone walk, the front door swung open. A couple people noticed there was no one visible in the doorway, and they made "Huh?" and "Whoa!" and other sounds. Nobody freaked out. Maybe they were such movie geeks, so used to special effects and watching behind-the-scenes specials, they just assumed that was another special effect.

Nope, just Divine's Emporium welcoming the new students. I took that as a good sign. The door probably wouldn't have opened automatically like that if there was even one person in the group who didn't quite fit with the spirit of Neighborlee.

I was relieved when the reactions of the people spilling through the doorway into Divine's and immediately spreading out through the rooms were completely positive. No freaking out. No mutters or frowns of disdain. No one giving the telltale signs of discomfort that meant they were already getting hit with the subliminal "go away, you don't belong, we don't want you here" message. Divine's Emporium liked these kids.

The best sign? No one flinched or got wide-eyed or even blinked when Angela just seemed to appear from nowhere. One minute the area behind the counter was empty, the next she was there. Maybe they just assumed she had been behind the counter, bent down and working on something.

Looking back, the signs that everyone belonged should have been a warning. Angela sensed something unusual about us, and I can't fault her for not warning us of impending trouble. All she sensed was the potential, and she spilled out the welcome from Divine's. At that point, the very first day we were all in the dorm, everything was potential and possibility. The choices we made going forward would refine our path for the rest of the year.

"Aren't you supposed to be busy with college activities?" She stepped up and rested her arms on the thick marble counter.

"All moved in and free for the evening." Zach fluttered his eyelashes at her and made his good-doggy-begging gesture, with his hands curved up under his chin.

Angela laughed and reached back for one of the enormous old-fashioned candy jars, where Zach's favorite candy waited. Semi-hard diamonds of salted black licorice. Yeah, sounds kind of yech, doesn't it? I finally gave in and tasted some. Surprisingly good, but still an acquired taste. That broke the ice. Angela got everyone's name as they stepped up and spotted a jar of the candy they liked the best. In all the noise and laughter and chatter, nobody noticed when she reached for a jar before someone asked for it, or knew someone's name before they told her. She asked a few questions and directed people to various rooms where "you might just find something you'll like."

"Very interesting," she commented as she settled down at the little bistro table with me and Clarice and Tyrone after about twenty minutes.

Voices rang through the shop, people calling out to each other that they just had to come see something. I was positive at least one new room had appeared since the last time I was at Divine's, a week ago, looking for a really cool backpack for going to class. Of course I found it, a combination of army surplus olive canvass with colorful embroidered patches all over it, looking like I had been all over the world. I had the hope that it would turn out like Mary Poppins' bag and hold everything I wanted and needed to put into it. Hopefully with the added benefit of not being any heavier.

"Do I want to know how you gathered so many like spirits in just a few hours, before orientation even officially started?" Angela nodded her thanks as Tyrone took over to empty the tray of our floats made with caramel ice cream and cream soda.

"They're all on the same floor with us," Clarice said.

"Really? What are the odds of that?"

"Pretty big odds," I said, meeting Clarice's gaze. She nodded. As if I really needed permission to tell Angela?

I went on to relate what Pop had learned from Mrs. A, and shared with me, because I had a right to know what people were doing to me and my classmates. Even if that knowledge might skew the results of whatever research the psych professors were doing. Maybe lab rats didn't know what was happening when they ran through mazes and suffered through all sorts of tests and experiments, but we weren't lab rats.

Our club members among the freshmen had discussed the experiment, whether it was weird or dangerous. I thought about pretending to be an anonymous tipster and let the *Neighborlee Tattler* know what was up. We agreed not to tell anyone before school started, because honestly, what could anyone do about it?

Demand to change floors within the dorm? Try to get into different dorms? We basically, and vaguely, agreed to wait to see what happened with the people on our floor and in the dorm before we said anything.

However, this was the perfect time to take the conundrum to Angela. As a guardian of Neighborlee, I had a responsibility to take questionable circumstances to her, or at least present them to other known guardians. Just in case weird things happened from fiddling with demographics, and I was too close to the middle to notice.

"Okay, now that we can see what they did to us, it's kind of weird," Tyrone said. "They sure weren't putting us together with the other geeks and nerds to be nice, so what do they think will happen? Why not other statistics or similarities or whatever you call it? Other than the art and drama kids, we're not grouped together by our majors, like on the other floors and the other dorm. Is it just me, or do you feel like we're being singled out?"

"If you are..." Angela's gaze went unfocused and her eyelids half-lowered.

I could almost hear that sound I sometimes caught just on the edge of sleep, or when it got very quiet inside Divine's Emporium.

Sometimes it was the hint of wind chimes playing in some incredible, vast garden in the very core of the house, as if the walls were thinner than paper, thinner than air. If I turned at just the right angle, I might finally see the garden, and wind chimes made of incredible jewels, with sunshades made of tapestries woven to show otherworldly, ancient scenes. Other times, like now, I had a sense of music being played somewhere far away, just below the audible level, on instruments I had never imagined. This was basically the sound of Angela thinking very hard, and the magic of Divine's Emporium coming into play.

"I must believe that if anything is to come of having so many similar, imaginative souls gathered in one place," Angela said slowly, "then Neighborlee itself might be very glad that several of our own are among them."

She glanced at me, her eyes full of warnings and so many silent messages I couldn't catch any of them. She didn't mean townies, or maybe even our club. She meant people who could see and feel and sometimes even taste the magic that flowed through Neighborlee. Sometimes it was lightning, sometimes it was music, sometimes it was an otherworldly perfume. Sometimes it was an earthquake and a sense of a menace that made Godzilla seem cuddly.

Guardians. Maybe that designation had expanded to include some of my generation who had held onto our childhood belief in the wonderful and weird. The ones who still put our hands on the Wishing Ball when we went to Divine's, even though we didn't need a stepstool to get up to the counter to see it.

Then the moment passed and her usual slightly mischievous smirk returned to brighten her face. She counseled us not to share our suspicions and what we had learned with the others on our floor. At least, those who weren't Neighborlee residents, and especially those who we couldn't trust to keep their mouths shut.

"Why should we interfere too much with the experiment? Who knows what the administration might learn?" She met my eyes. "Who knows what we might learn?

I got that shivery feeling that went straight from my backbone into my gut. I had the momentary sensation that if I could blink hard enough, I might clear something from my eyes and see another layer deeper into reality. Not like having prophetic visions, but just a little more sensitivity. I had done enough reading to know prophecy was not a gift to desire by any stretch of the imagination. Prophets either got tortured or made fun of and ignored. Until something awful happened. Then everyone got all upset and beat up on the prophet who had been warning them all this time, even though the trouble had come *because* they refused to listen. No thanks. Nuh uh. Not this little gray duck!

Just a note about our Star Trek club. It wasn't just Trek, and wasn't just science fiction that drew us together, or that we read or talked about. It was all wonderful and weird and "otherness" that we loved. We just used the Trek label because people automatically expected Trekkers to play with weird toys and sometimes wear bits of costumes and talk about futuristic science and other planets. And yeah, it was kind of fun to use bits of made-up languages to communicate around the mundanes, or at least irritate people who thought we were weird anyway.

So those who belonged to our club had open, alert minds, and a willingness to believe that just because something happened that violated so-called natural laws, that didn't automatically make it evil or dangerous. Nor did we create "Welcome to Earth" signs, like those idiots who got incinerated first in *Independence Day*. Know what I mean? We were cautious. We had a lot of training, through books and movies and just discussing possibilities. We knew better than to assume that superior technology meant superior cultures and morality. Pointy ears didn't guarantee logic. Just because E.T. was friendly didn't mean all squashed monosyllabic critters were. Look at the gremlins.

Bottom line: if anyone in Neighborlee was a candidate to be tapped as defenders when the interdimensional monsters arrived, and not mess their pants and run screaming for Mommy, or curl up in a fetal ball, it was the members of our Star Trek club. So of course, Angela was willing to trust us and let us know we were the psychological equivalent of rats in a pretty complicated maze. Just as long as we didn't warn the other rats.

Chapter Six

About that point in the discussion, our little group had to break up. Our dormmates were trickling toward the cash register with the treasures they had found. Angela did some classifying and sorting of our dormmates as they came up to the counter with their purchases and the discount coupon. She sorted them with questions, with comments about what they had found, vintage clothing or jewelry or books or movies or CDs or whatever caught their interest. I tried to make mental note of who smiled, who gave her weird looks, who offered bits of details about themselves, who asked questions in return. It would be interesting to see who came back to Divine's, how quickly, and who avoided that side of town after that night. Maybe even who left at the end of the semester and transferred to another college, rather than staying in Neighborlee.

We found out later that Angela did go to talk to the administration, as high up in the food chain of politics and power at WBC as anyone could go without calling in lawyers. Then the scurrying, panicking, comparing notes, and denials among the officials and administration and departments began.

After the dust had settled, we learned some people in the administration of WBC had no idea a psycho-social experiment was taking place. Key people who had supposedly given their permission either claimed they never saw the requests and the explanation for what the professors wanted to do, or they saw the paperwork and sent a memo saying they advised against it. Some gave suggestions for changes, or voiced concerns that the college could be sued. Very few approved of it, and those who did were way down in the hierarchy of authority and blame.

Yet when the documentation was pulled out and examined, all the papers and permissions and approvals were signed by the appropriate personnel. However... The ink wasn't the standard navy blue the college stocked. Some said it was black with a hint of red, others said it was a muddy kind of purple. Plus, the dates on all the documents were Saturdays and Sundays, when no one in the administration came into the office.

The investigators found it hard to believe that someone would sneak into the offices on the weekend to forge papers and process miles of documentation to approve an experiment with no clear goals or theories. The professors were just setting up situations to see what would happen. They were oddly vague about what they would do with what they learned. If they learned anything.

My opinion? Curiosity is a lame excuse for doing something that disrupted a lot of lives, frightened a lot of people, and required Angela to get involved. And the guardians, of course. Maybe we should have just chosen that as our semi-pseudo-superhero names? It sounded like a rock group or pop group from the eighties.

Angela and the Guardians?

Nah.

Bottom line: it was too late to make changes. Moving everyone around, reassigning dorm floors and roommates, and changing out the Residence Advisors would raise questions and cause too much suspicion and disruption. The powers-that-be decided to leave things exactly as they were, but they were to be given copies of all the reports the RAs turned in. Anyone who wanted to change roommates, dorm floors, or even dormitories, would be allowed to do so, without the fines or waiting times that were standard policy.

The professors in the program were put under surveillance, with monthly assessments throughout the school year. Rumors said they could face severe disciplinary actions, including losing tenure. There were rumors of shakeups in the administration, in security, and new policies for processing paperwork.

All this added up to make me think things were a whole lot more serious than what Angela and my folks and Mr. Longfellow told us.

Yeah, my folks were involved. Think about the old ST:NG episode, *Who Watches the Watchers?* Well, there were multiple layers of people observing the people who were observing the people under suspicion, who were still observing the students whose lives they had been manipulating. At the top of the heap were ordinary, inconspicuous people in town, who could get on campus and listen and observe and take notes without anyone observing them. Then there were people like my folks, who came on campus to work with students and do the guest lecturer routine.

The Longfellows found excuses to come on campus and invade

the library or areas where equipment needed repairs, or talk with researchers who needed help finding obscure books. Mrs. Longfellow was a librarian and schoolteacher, and Mr. Longfellow had a lot of connections when it came to finding hard-to-find items.

Stephanie Miller kept watch on students and professors alike when they came into the diner, which was conveniently close to campus. She talked her husband into agreeing to the regular requests of the food service department at WBC for Miller's Diner to run the Student Center snack bar. Felicity took an after-school and weekend job at the snack bar. Kurt made sure everyone on campus knew he was available for repair jobs.

We had the campus covered. Then we learned the hard way that there *is* such a thing as being so much on the alert that we can't see what's happening right under our noses.

September flew past before we came up for air and relaxed a little bit. Those of us on the geeks and freaks floor, as some dorm groups referred to us, were especially busy adjusting to the whole dormitory life situation.

Part of the psycho-social experiment was to see what alliances and rivalries and conflicts developed when people with many shared characteristics and common interests lived with each other. Nobody gave us weird looks when we referred to people in books, TV shows and movies, using their lives and adventures to illustrate what we were going through, and sometimes even applying them to lectures or homework or some activity on campus.

Then the fun and camaraderie got to be the normal thing, and the honeymoon feeling lost its energy. Rivalries in fandom crept onto the floor. The age-old arguments of hard science fiction versus soft SF, and what exactly were the definitions of each. Fantasy versus science fiction. The lexicons developed by various groups of fans, arguing over whether the "facts" stated in the TV shows were more "factual" than what was said in movies based on the TV series. Then there was the question of TV episodes versus the novelizations. Kind of like the discrepancies hard-core fans found among the Star Trek TV series, the novelizations, and the movies. Which was lexicon and which was apocryphal? Don't even get me started on fan fiction...

Yeah, at this distance of years and experience, it looks a little silly, a waste of time and energy, but our fandoms were our way of coping with all the stress and trauma of learning how to handle the real world. The changes in our lives. The pain and inconvenience of having to grow up. And figuring out just what "growing up" was supposed to mean.

Clarice and I invited our new neighbors to our Trek meeting, and word got around. More kids than just the ones on our floor showed up for the September meeting. A lot of people liked Star Trek, or just hanging with geeks in general. People who didn't fit the misfit label. We were so jammed together in our assigned meeting room on campus, we took it outside where we could breathe. Our last item of business was to assign some people the job of finding us a new meeting room, because a room that could hold twenty comfortably was not going to work if we had fifty people show up every month.

By the end of September, the joking comments, like, "Hey, our Dr. McCoy can beat the snot out of your Dr. McCoy," didn't get more than a grin or a groan. Seeing the T-shirts worn by the people involved usually helped interpret such remarks. In this instance, Dr. Hank McCoy, aka Beast, from the X-Men comic books, versus Dr. Leonard McCoy of the starship *Enterprise*.

We had to feel sorry for the art and drama and dance folk who didn't have time for fantasy and science fiction. Most of the time they could evade being drafted into or witnessing our games and loud discussions about the actual technique of fixing a warp drive engine or how Sauron actually forged the nine rings in Mount Doom. When fandom feuds started, they pretty much hid in their rooms with the doors locked or found other places to spend the daylight hours.

I caught Mercedes, the RA on the girls' side of the floor, capturing the first screaming argument with a micro-cassette recorder. I really, really wished I had Felicity's talent for EM bursts, just to kill that little gizmo she kept pretty much hidden in the kangaroo pouch of her hoodie. Since I couldn't kill it with a handy little explosion, I tried to mentally yank it free.

Mercedes must have felt the recorder sliding out, because she wrapped her hand around it. Kind of hard to make the recorder jump out and hit the floor and shatter. I couldn't let her hurt anybody, even second-hand, to earn a grade. I just didn't need the headache from a tug-of-war between telekinetic power and those big hands that were made for basketball. She was wasted as a psych major. Seriously.

So, since I couldn't get the cassette recorder out of her hand, to self-destruct on the floor, I had to go with Plan B. The fight had gone past mockery, comparing the pseudo-science and weaponry design of one SF universe against another.

"Mercedes?" I had to fight a grin as she flinched and caught herself looking down at her recorder. Yeah, I did call out louder than necessary. Of course, my chances of drowning out the screaming argument at the far end of the hall weren't that good, but I could interfere with recording it.

"Not right now, Lanie," she said, and turned sideways to me.

"Don't." I mentally pressed down on her foot as she tried to walk away from me, to get closer to the fight.

"Don't what?" She looked down at her foot. I tried not to hurt her. Just sort of glue her foot to the floor.

"Don't record it. Don't report."

"Record?" She tried to jam the recorder further into her front pocket. "I don't know —"

"Yeah, but I do. I know about the research program. I know that your profs are in so much hot water, they're gonna be shriveled up until summer."

"What are you talking about?" Mercedes pulled the recorder out and turned it off.

"I know a lot of the signatures giving permission for this whole research program were forged, and a lot of people at the top didn't even know about treating all the incoming freshmen like lab rats. Don't rat on them, okay?" I gestured at the end of the hall where the fight had devolved into screaming criticism about each other's taste in clothes. At least they weren't fighting about props anymore.

"How do you know?"

"Do you know who my folks are?"

"Ah…no."

"First of all, I grew up here. Neighborlee is home. Second, go to the library and look under my last name. My folks are writers. They do research. They know how to ask questions, and they taught me to ask questions. They also taught me how to recognize when something feels or looks weird, and then figure out why."

"Uh huh. Who else knows?"

"Do you think everybody would still be here, if they knew they were lab rats?"

"I wish you wouldn't say that." She hunched her shoulders and looked down at the recorder still cradled in both hands.

"Just don't embarrass everybody, okay?"

"That's not what I'm here for." She gestured with her chin at the dying argument. "Do you even understand what's going on?"

"I'm a freshman. What would I know about all the pressures and changes and junk everybody's going through? I'm going through it myself. You know. Too close to see what's what."

"Yeah, right," she muttered, narrowing her eyes at me. The corners of her mouth twitched, visibly fighting not to grin.

"You're the psych major, not me."

"What are you going to major in?"

"Gonna be a teacher."

"You're going to need to figure out all the pressures and changes kid go through, then." She jammed the recorder back into her front pocket and leaned against the wall next to her door. The two combatants had retired to their individual rooms.

~~~~~

That night, Kurt, Felicity and I went on patrol. He wanted to do a flyover of the campus. He was getting the buzz-hum sensation that indicated power of some kind building up, as opposed to the different frequency he felt/heard when a semi-pseudo-superhero was about to emerge. He said this energy was kind of along the lines of the nasty things we sometimes sensed, slithering around underneath our town. Of course, since it was an interdimensional threat, could we really call it "underneath" Neighborlee?

I wasn't in the mood for philosophical and semi-magical or pseudo-scientific discussions. I had a test first thing in the morning. We needed to do the flyover, scope out the vibrations, and let me get back to my dorm to study for another hour, then sleep, then wake up early and study again.

We drove to our usual place to park Kurt's truck where nobody patrolling the Metroparks would find it. Then we linked up with our harness. I turned on my kinda-sorta flying and Kurt took over, so it really was flying. We tugged up our hoods and put our night-vision goggles in place. At about eighty feet up, the breeze got chilly enough we paused to put on our gloves. When we were ready, Kurt
~~~~~

took us up higher, just to the point where we couldn't make out details of the people in the cars below us. Then we flew straight to the center of campus.

Kurt could sense energy, but even after years of refining his control he still only had a general sense of direction until he was nearly on top of the source. He hadn't been sure I was the one humming with energy until I had been released from the baby cottage at the orphanage. He also had to make sure we could be alone for that first confrontation. Protecting what we were had always been first priority.

Protecting Neighborlee also fed into protecting what we could do, what we were. If something was going to break through from some nightmare dimension into Earth, using Neighborlee as a doorway, we had to stop it before enough weird things happened to attract the attention of the rest of the world. Especially the military. Yes, we had someone in the military protecting the town, but Col. Hayward could only do so much without destroying his career. At least, we had never asked him to distract people and lie to his superiors, to the point of destroying his career. I didn't want to reach that level of need. Or more accurately, desperation.

So we were up in the air at eleven on a weeknight, following the ripples of energy, and discovering just how much activity there was on campus this late at night. We could make out clusters of students walking between the classroom buildings and the dorms. Was the library open that late? Or had some late-night study groups just broken up? Plus there was the traffic from cars or groups walking back from the restaurants and cafes in town that were open late, such as the Sipping Post, or Hunky & Dory's. We made out four Neighborlee PD patrol cars weaving through the streets where town and campus converged, with campus housing on one side of the street and businesses or residences on the other.

"It's a good thing you don't have an astronomy program," Kurt whispered as our gliding speed slowed.

Felicity and I just grinned and muffled chuckles. We had learned the hard way that sound carried very well at night, and the colder the air, the clearer the noises. We had also learned that despite a tendency not to look up most of the time, when noises come from out of nowhere, a lot of people's first reaction was to look up. Still the general weirdness of Neighborlee seemed to work in our favor. People *expected* something strange to happen in Neighborlee, and they just ignored the funny twitches out of the corners of their eyes.

Kurt increased our height and slowed our speed more. His frown of concentration told me he was focusing in on the siren call of energy coming from campus. It had taken him a week to determine the energy did come from campus, and then narrow down the section. He had taken advantage of a repair job in the theater to walk around campus and try to get closer to the source of whatever energy made his fingers itch and the hair on his head stand up. What worried him was that the vibrations or energy resonance or whatever it was didn't broadcast continually. It flicked on and off, sometimes utterly quiet for days at a time, sometimes broadcasting strong and loud for ten, fifteen minutes, sometimes starting out soft and lasting for an hour of humming and tickling. Sometimes it went slightly out of key and built up to an itch that made him want to stick his hands in boiling water to make it go away. Kind of hard to track the source when it quieted every time he got near.

Like whoever was broadcasting sensed Kurt's approach, and stopped doing whatever generated the energy, to duck back into their hole and hide.

Yeah, we discussed that possibility a few times. It's always easier to do our job as guardians when the bad guys don't know they've been detected. That way, they aren't on the alert, and they aren't ready to set off the equivalent of a bomb or come tearing at us with a billion razor-sharp claws and teeth when we get within a mile of them.

Kurt hissed and flinched away, which naturally meant all three of us jerked back. Or, since we were airborne, jerked upward.

"What?" Felicity whispered.

"Power spike. With a strong flavor of majorly pissed off." He tried to grin, and gestured with his chin.

He had to gesture with his chin because even though we were securely linked together with our flying harness, we made it a rule to hold onto each other, arms linked. Felicity and I could gesture, since we each had a hand free. With Kurt in the middle, he had no free hands to speak of, or with.

I got about ten degrees colder when I followed the angle of his chin. We were now hovering about forty feet above the flat rooftops of the two freshmen dormitory buildings. Specifically, he had flexed his jaw at *my* building.

Remember the scene in the first *Mummy* movie, where the trio of mummy warriors dropped their jaws about two feet and roared at Branden Frazier? Remember how he kind of froze for a second, then dropped his sword, said, "Uh uh," and got out of there? Yeah, that was how I felt right about then. My dormitory, which made it even more my responsibility. It was in my best interests to stop whatever was going to happen, because what if an enormous sinkhole leading into another dimension of supernatural nastiness opened up and swallowed my dormitory? Those were my friends, my floormates, my roommate, about $200 in textbooks, and a really cool bomber jacket I had just found at Divine's, that could pass for a pilot's coat in the Star Wars and Battlestar Galactica universes.

"Closer," I said. Kurt kept us hovering until I got my priorities in order.

The pressure of making important decisions and having people's fates resting on me was exactly why I refused to let people nominate me for captain of our Star Trek club. I would have to get over my dislike for leadership if I was going to be a teacher, though. Was one month into my freshman year too late to switch majors?

Kurt lowered us slowly toward the roof of the dormitory building. I got an idea and looked at Felicity, and even though we had plenty of proof that we had no conscious telepathic connection, she seemed to catch my idea.

"If we land, we can all separate and walk around, and it'll be easier for you to do your Geiger counter thingy," she said, gesturing at the roof.

Kurt rolled his eyes, but his mouth twitched, fighting a smile, and we settled down a few seconds later on the gritty, slightly slanted surface of the roof. He flinched as soon as his feet touched down, and for a second there I thought we would go up again. An image of a 747 coming in for a landing and then trying to get airborne again, then crashing, filled my head. Not fun. Especially when I knew that any odd noises coming from the roof were going to get investigated. If anyone spotted us, I was the one facing expulsion.

"What?" Felicity whispered, as we worked to loosen the straps of our harness. We had quick release latches Kurt had devised, so we could separate easily once we landed, but not too easily, in case we hit some turbulence while in mid-air, and accidentally hit or tugged too hard on the straps.

"Contact just makes it stronger." Kurt bent over to look at his feet. I could almost hear the buzzing in his brain as it went into high gear, analyzing this discovery.

For the next twenty minutes, we spread out and walked around the roof, trying to get a sense for the epicenter of whatever the odd energy was. Kurt paced back and forth, going from one side of the roof to another, kind of marking it into a grid with his feet. His shoulders hunched a little more with every pass, and his fists stayed jammed into the pockets of his jacket. I imagined him clenching them to fight the irritation of the itching in his fingertips. His shoulders hunched in a subconscious effort to muffle the humming in his head that had nothing to do with audible sound.

"Something freaky," Kurt finally said, when he had walked back and forth across the roof from east to west, and then from north to south.

"What is?" I shuddered a little when I looked around and decided I was standing almost on top of my room. Had Clarice come back to our room yet? She had a late study session, trying to learn her lines to help one of our Trek club-mates with her theater directing class assignment.

"I'd swear it's the whole floor."

"Think we can get away with circling the whole building?" Felicity said after we stood and digested that bit of unhappy news for a few seconds. She gestured, making a swirling motion with her gloved hand. "You know. Circle the third floor, then the second floor, then walk around the first floor, see if the energy levels change?"

"She's smart." Kurt winked at me. "Must come from hanging around with us."

Felicity just rubbed her fingers together on both hands, her silent warning of impending EM bursts, which usually erupted from her fingertips or the ends of her hair. It was an empty threat, because she was grinning, and her power surges usually burst out when she was scared or seriously pissed. We had learned how to trigger them at need, but that usually involved some kind of peril.

While Kurt had developed some skill in harnessing that energy and directing it where we needed, that tactic was usually a last gasp effort to deal with whatever problem or danger we faced.

We strapped ourselves together, and on three we jumped up, I activated my kinda-sorta flying, and Kurt took over. Fortunately, this late at night, most of the lights were off on my floor. The few rooms where lights were on, the curtains and blinds were closed, so even the streaks of light that leaked out and touched us didn't reveal our presence. I muffled a chuckle as we passed Mercedes' room, and I thought about how she would write up a disciplinary report on me if she caught me flying. However, there was no rule about flying, period, much less flying after closed dorm hours. The only thing she could report me for was being on the roof.

Remembering the rules, I said a quick, silent prayer that our investigation wouldn't require Kurt to come inside. After ten at night, non-students weren't allowed in the dormitories. After eleven, non-residents of each building had to be gone. Between midnight and six, girls stayed on their side of the dividing line of the stairwell, and likewise for boys. At least, those were the rules for freshmen. When we had some choice in where we lived on campus, if we lived on campus at all, we could choose different dormitories with different rules about quiet hours and who could be in the building, on the floor, and in someone's room, at what time of the day or night.

We circled my floor, and then dropped down to circle the second floor. Kurt dropped us to the line where second floor met first and went around again. He frowned so intently that Felicity and I stayed silent. When we landed, we let him think while we undid our flying straps. The silence remained while we walked around the building once. Kurt came around to the main sidewalk leading to the front door of the building and leaned against the railing for the first of three shallow flights of steps, with his head tilted back and gazing up at the third floor. Was it too much to hope that he was focused on the sole window with any light slipping out from behind the blinds? That room belonged to Laci and Charmaine, both theater students, both ready to pull each other's hair out until neither one got the starring role in the Christmas production. We had a guest theater teacher that year who wrote for off-off-off Broadway, and he wrote a script for WBC. I don't remember the title, but it had something to do with an evil faerie trying to destroy a Christmas festival. There was no happy ending for play or cast or guest artist. In fact, I think he left campus early.

Considering what I had learned about the Fae from Angela, chances were good some real Fae had heard about the play and decided to punish him for slandering them. If I remember correctly, that was the year Will and Phil came back to visit at Christmas, so maybe they did something. If they were Fae, as I suspected.

Getting back to the dormitory…

My room was next to Laci and Charmaine's, and the light came on, meaning Clarice had returned from rehearsal. The night was getting late. I wasn't worried about me, but Felicity had to get back to the orphanage and into her cottage without anyone noticing she had been gone.

"Verdict?" she said, as I turned and opened my mouth to remind them of the time.

"Whatever it is, the energy envelops the whole third floor," Kurt said, still looking up. "It's like it's soaked into everything, the metal and brick. The prickling I'm getting goes down about a third of the way into the second floor."

"Can you tell if it's growing? Like, if we don't figure out what's up, it'll soak into the second floor and then head for first, and then the basement?" I shuddered with a half-formed image that kind of exploded in my head.

Chapter Seven

"What?" Kurt finally took his gaze off the third floor.

"What if that's the goal? To get down to the bedrock, go down deep enough to touch whatever keeps trying to come upward?" I hated my theory, but I had learned never to keep things like that to myself, just so we had a chance to analyze the chances and try to do something to prevent it.

"It's been long enough since anything weird and freaky-strange happened," Felicity said. "We're about due."

"Okay, first thing in the morning, I'm ..." Kurt shook his head. "Ford hasn't contacted me yet, but that doesn't mean he isn't sensing anything. It just isn't strong enough, so he doesn't have anything specific. If we get together, maybe it'll trigger something he's noticed, solidify it, whatever."

"Stephanie has the morning shift at the snack bar," I said. "I'll meet up with her, see if she's gotten anything."

"Please don't tell me it's my job to talk to Miss Angela," Felicity said. "How about I write up a report on what we did and give it to Mrs. Longfellow, to give Mr. L?"

We had to laugh at that. It wasn't that any of us were afraid to go to Angela. She was M, if we looked at ourselves as secret agents. Very junior Double-Os. She was our coordinator. Felicity just had a very tight schedule, between school and her job at the veterinary clinic with the vo-ed school, and then the snack bar on campus, so she didn't get back to NCH until dinner, and sometimes not until long after dinner was over. As one of the older kids there, she had responsibility for overseeing study time and tutoring. One of the perks of being the oldest in her cottage, especially with the population dwindling at the orphanage, with fewer than sixty children, was that she had her own room. That made it much easier for her to sneak out and join us on patrols.

"We'll all go talk to Angela tomorrow afternoon," Kurt said. "Once we have a better idea of what's going on."

~~~~~

Stephanie Miller had Bethany with her when she came to open
~~~~~

up the snack bar in the Student Center the next morning. She asked me if I would mind walking Bethany over to the theater building, to wait for Ford Longfellow, who was bringing Athena up for some experimental Kindergarten program run by the drama department. I kind of shuddered, visibly, when she said "experimental."

She laughed and assured me that nobody from the sociology and psychology departments were involved. It was all drama and playing with costumes and props and letting the children's imaginations go wild. I was glad to do it. Any excuse to spend time with Bethany. She chattered nonstop about her friends in the theater and the games they played and how she got to be a "sojer" and run around with a sword and protect the "pinsess" and the "keen." I couldn't figure out if she meant queen or king.

We reached the main entrance of the theater building just about the time the Longfellows showed up. Ford saw us, and instead of taking his truck around to the parking lot on the side, he pulled up to the steps and let Athena jump out to join us while he parked. No contest between the two five-year-olds, they were both my favorites. Getting hugs from those two little girls worked like a good strong inoculation of magic for the rest of the day.

I needed it. We all did. Not that any of us realized it when we started off on our errands that morning.

When Ford joined us, I let him know Kurt was going to try to catch up with him on his rounds at the college. I wasn't surprised they hadn't made contact yet. For all his love of gizmos, Kurt didn't like using his cell phone. Maybe he didn't trust what passed for security on anyone's phone. With something building up on WBC's campus, he was especially touchy about the wrong people (or things, or forces, or entities) accessing or interfering with messages. Since I had time, with no classes until just before lunch, I agreed to get the girls into the program, so Ford could look for Kurt.

Stephanie thanked me with a hug when I returned to the snack bar. The team of students who were supposed to close up the night before had left a couple messages about problems with inventory and changing the oil reservoir on the fryer, and she needed to get those problems taken care of before the first hungry customers of the day showed up. Heaven forbid she be unable to deliver baskets of fried cheese sticks and batter-fried veggies within seconds of being ordered. Miller's Diner had a reputation to uphold, after all.

I told her about our fly-over of the dormitory and what Kurt had detected, what we had theorized, but it took me about five installments between customers. She was alone for the first hour the snack bar was open, but once the first shift of work-study students showed up, the traffic trickled down to almost nothing, and she could step out from behind the counter. We went over to a quiet corner of the snack area, partially hidden behind some particularly pitiful silk fig trees, to talk.

"Whatever you three picked up on, I'm not getting any warnings," she said, after we had settled down with berry smoothies. "No dreams, no vibrations, no sickening smells, or even smells that don't belong wherever I am." She muffled a chuckle, and I guessed that my expression showed just how confused I was by that last bit of information. "When I was pregnant with Bethany, every sense seemed to cross over into a smell. Noises that were too loud generated a smell like the dumpster behind Punderson's grocery last summer, when it was so hot and they dumped that entire order of dairy that had gone bad before it even arrived." Another chuckle bubbled out of her when I reacted.

That was one of the most noxious smells I had ever endured. It put texture in the air. Since Punderson's was near the offices for the *Neighborlee Tattler*, those of us who worked there had to put up with the stench that clung to it even after they had the dumpster steam blasted clean and sanitized. Some of us swore the light changed in that area behind the grocery store. If anything truly evil was going to tear the fabric of reality and invade from another dimension, that would be the weak spot, where reality had been scorched thin.

"Anyway," she continued, "it's been quiet, all around. Maybe we've all been concentrating so much on the problem with those professors..." She frowned, eyes going distant.

"What did you just think of?"

"Just gossip." She shrugged and took a sip from the tall paper cup, her eyes hooded, her gaze pensive. "Despite every effort to keep that whole mess covered up, it's impossible to keep secrets on a college campus. Other departments know. Especially when the head of the psychology department looks daggers at his underlings who forged his signature and claimed they got approval and permission from him, even though he and the other leaders of the department never met to discuss the experiment."

"So you've overheard other professors talking about the mess when they come here, or come to the diner?"

"Diner. They don't talk about school politics here on campus. You have to admire them for that. It's best to put on a united front for the students." She took another sip. "What comes to mind now, and I have to wonder why it didn't register at the time, is that the two ringleaders in the whole mess, Tudderman and Winghast, have been seen making regular visits to a house in Darbyville. The street straddles the border with Neighborlee. It's near a main street, so the professors who live in Darbyville and take that route see them on a regular basis, coming or going, and never together. Someone finally remarked on it, and someone else said they had seen it, and I guess they started asking questions and..."

She shrugged, her lower lip sticking out as she visibly thought it over. "What made it memorable is that the house has had a for sale sign in the front yard for more than a year. The grass is high and some of the windows are boarded up. If either of them were planning on buying the house, maybe they don't know the other is looking at it."

"Maybe they're waiting for the price to go down more?" I shivered as I said it. It sounded stupid, but Stephanie didn't react, still deep in thought.

"Something strange is going on. I know that I've heard people talking about it, multiple times, yet none of those times... I don't know, the incidents didn't stick in my memory until just now." She sat up and looked around the Student Center. "Do you have time for a field trip?"

Ford Longfellow drove up as I was walking to the corner, to wait for Stephanie. She had to take care of the students working the snack bar and then get her car and come meet me. He was on his way to meet Kurt, after picking up keys to get into the dormitory through the service entrance and go straight to the roof, to see if he could sense anything. When I explained the things Stephanie overheard and remembered, he got that too-quiet, thoughtful look I had seen him wear the first time we faced something nasty in Neighborlee together.

"Yeah, kind of the same thing for me. I didn't remember dreaming about the dormitories until Kurt mentioned what you three found." He shook his head, and his lips worked for a second like he was getting ready to spit out a bad taste. "Something tells me you two shouldn't go out there alone. Abandoned houses are always bad news. Especially on that side of Darbyville. Ever been out there?"

I shook my head. He tipped his head up a little and looked past me, and I turned to see Stephanie pulling up in her Jeep.

"If you ever need proof there's a defensive dome surrounding Neighborlee, that's the place for it. Like night and day, different sides of the street where the border between our two towns runs down the middle. Do me a favor, and wait for me and Kurt to catch up with you? And stay on our side of the street until we get there?"

I agreed. He tipped a salute off his eyebrow to Stephanie and drove off. I got in her Jeep and told her what Ford had told me. I hesitated to suggest we go get Angela and bring her with us. The thought of taking Angela to a place Ford Longfellow didn't like made me feel kind of queasy. That's the only way to explain it.

"We might need more firepower than we have with just the four of us," Stephanie said, as she signaled for a right turn.

We were heading for the border of Neighborlee and Darbyville. A right turn would take us toward Divine's Emporium. How come I wasn't relieved that she decided to go get Angela?

When was I going to learn to trust my instincts over what people said? Granted, I was only eighteen at the time, and I was a little tired after flying patrol in the cold and all the running around I had done that morning. Plus I was a teensy bit distracted by the growing certainty I was going to miss my upcoming class. Did I have a quiz scheduled, or just another lecture? Who in the class would loan me their notes? More important, who among those friends took really good, coherent, usable notes?

See? Lots on my mind at the time.

Angela was outside, sweeping leaves off the flagstone sidewalk in front of the wrought iron fence when we pulled up.

"Is it—I don't know—safe for you to leave?" I had to ask, after Stephanie gave the bare bones of what we had discovered and what we were planning on doing with Ford and Kurt.

"You've seen me away from the shop before," Angela said, with a chuckle. "I'm not needed to anchor it down and keep this place from blowing away." She gestured with her broom at the front door. "Let me get a coat and leave a note."

"That's not what I was afraid of," I muttered, as she glided up the walk and went inside.

"Believe it or not, Angela has left the city limits, and the county, and even the state from time to time." Stephanie smiled, but her voice didn't sound as carefree as I would have liked.

When Angela came out again, it finally occurred to me to get out of the front seat and slide into the back of the Jeep, to let her have the front. She winked at me as she swept down the walk again and through the gate. Everything felt wrong, and that made no sense. She closed the gate and hung a laminated sign on it, stating she would be back by two. That reinforced Stephanie's statement that she did indeed leave the shop, because who would have a laminated sign lying around if they didn't use it?

Angela wore a tweedy-looking coat in a deep shade of lavender, and she had changed her slipper-shoes for some stylish, light brown ankle boots. What did she expect to be doing, just going to the border of Neighborlee and Darbyville to get an impression of a suspicious house there? I wasn't planning on getting out of the Jeep. That realization just struck me at that moment.

Funny, how the position of being a guardian of Neighborlee had never felt so serious as it did right that moment, when I had no idea what was going on.

The ride went quickly as we caught up Angela on what Stephanie had observed during her time on campus, all the bits of gossip she had gathered, the people she had observed. Then I told them about the examination we had given my dormitory building the night before, and the really weird fight that had broken out over prop weapons from two different TV series.

"Did I just make things worse?" I had to ask, after confessing how I had let Mercedes know that other people knew about the experiment and we didn't much like it. Plus asking her not to record and report on the fight.

"Never doubt your instincts, Lanie," Angela said after a moment of quiet. Stephanie made the last turn onto the street where the border between our two towns followed the center yellow line.

"At least they can't say they weren't warned," Stephanie added. "And if you think about it, the students who are doing the observing are being treated unfairly. Their professors know they're in trouble, that they've acted without official permission, but the students doing all the hard work of observing and writing up reports think it's all legitimate. Until now, they also think nobody knows what they're doing. Anonymity gives some security and some boldness."

"Yeah, just look at all the superheroes who wear masks," slipped out before I thought how that would sound.

Fortunately, that got smiles from both of them.

"I'm sure Mercedes will pass on word to the others that people know what they're doing. They might write their reports with a little more thoughtfulness," Angela said. "The possibility of losing their invisibility has a tendency to slow down those who might otherwise gleefully run around playing pranks and causing havoc."

That reminded me of a story I had read, just because one of the girls in my first period Tuesday class had recommended it. The heroine turned invisible in the moonlight, but her clothes didn't. To support her destitute family in Victorian London, she had to strip naked and steal jewels and coins that she could keep others from seeing, because unlike a lot of fantasy stories, the things she touched didn't turn invisible. The problem was that the phases of the moon affected her invisibility. When the moon waned, she became visible again, sometimes sooner than she liked. I snorted, remembering the story. Stephanie and Angela both wanted to know what amused me. That took up the little bit of time we had to wait between parking on the Neighborlee side of the street and when Ford and Kurt pulled up behind us.

I have to admit that I avoided looking at the house in question. Instincts again? Who knows?

On first glance, it didn't look menacing or dangerous. However, when we got out of our cars and really looked at the place, a chill that had nothing to do with the bright fall day passed through me. It was an Indian summer-warm day, even with all the scarlet and gold leaves showering from the trees around us, thanks to a really strange cold spell just the week before. Well, that's what makes this time of year Indian summer, a warm reprieve after the first hard taste of the winter weather to come.

Then I realized just what I was seeing. The trees on either side of the house were utterly bare. The house didn't have any trees in the front yard, and while the grass was tall, proving no one had done any maintenance in weeks, maybe months, it was brown and patchy. I swear there were matted spots that looked moldy. It made very ugly contrast to the emerald velvet lawns on either side of the house. Except, of course, right along where the neighbors' yards touched the abandoned property. Spotty patches of brown extended into the other yards, like mold or the way dirty water wicks up into paper towels set on the edge of the puddle.

I decided to listen to my instincts, since Angela had just told me not to ignore them, and told the others what I saw. Just in case they didn't. No one looked annoyed. I had the feeling they were noticing other things, besides the evidence of how bad neighbors could lower property values.

"What do you feel?" Ford said, finally turning his gaze off the house long enough to glance at Kurt.

"Nothing." Kurt kind of frowned, kind of pouted, and those creases formed around his eyes, meaning he was concentrating hard enough to give himself a headache. "If anything is going on here, if there's something dangerous about those professors, it's not here. It's just an ugly old house."

"Perhaps." Angela tipped her head toward the house. "Shall we?"

I wanted to ask if we could all hold hands as we crossed from Neighborlee into Darbyville. The words clogged up in my throat, because I realized how much I sounded like a Kindergartener. Again, I should have listened to my instincts.

We crossed the yellow line together in slow, steady, almost synchronized steps. Kind of like the scene where the team of sheriff and deputies walk down the center of the street to meet the outlaw gang. We stepped up onto the curb, and crossed the tree lawn in two steps. Actually, the strip of grass between the crumbling sidewalks of Darbyville and the equally crumbling curb, glopped up with asphalt, didn't really count as a tree lawn. We lost our unified steps on the sidewalk. Ford and Kurt put one foot onto the lawn of the abandoned house about a second before Stephanie and I did.

Angela wobbled and her knees folded a little bit. She was in the middle of our group, with Stephanie and Ford on either side of her. They both looked back at the same time and reached for her. Angela let out a breathless little chuckle and took two steps onto the patchy, matted grass, and this time did go to her knees.

"Get her out of here!" I shouted, and didn't wait for anyone to respond. Looking back, that wasn't smart.

When I mind-lifted Angela, they were still holding onto her, and naturally they resisted when she rose up in the air and sort of went into a reclining/seated position. The couple of seconds of mental tug-of-war *hurt*. Something kind of reach up through the power I had wrapped around Angela and dug claws into my brain. I had a nosebleed by the time we all got back across the street. Kurt yanked the back door of Stephanie's Jeep open and they got Angela inside.

I leaned against the back panel, my hands pressed against my temples, trying not to be sick. I had never worked myself into a strain headache like that before, and certainly not so quickly. Kurt ran around to the other side of the Jeep and found my emergency stash in my backpack. Dark chocolate studded with raisins and almonds, and a backup slab of fruit leather. By this time, Ford saw I was in bad shape. He pulled out his enormous blue cotton handkerchief to deal with my bloody nose. Stephanie saw the chocolate and snatched it out of Kurt's hand before he had it unwrapped, broke the bar in half, and pressed her half to Angela's mouth before tossing the rest back to Kurt.

"I felt something," Kurt said, after I had inhaled my half of the bar.

Ford pulled out his pocketknife and sliced the slab of fruit leather in half, passing one piece to Stephanie for Angela before pressing the other into my hand.

"Whatever hit Angela..." I swallowed hard against a wavelet of nausea that came from a flicker of memory. Honestly, the whole tug-of-war had happened so fast, I had to think back over it before I could sort out the impressions. "It was trying to hold onto her."

That made a whole lot more sense than Ford and Stephanie being strong enough to pull Angela from my telekinetic hold.

"It was a surge, or maybe more like a flash of light when a door opens, before someone inside turns off the light." Kurt shuddered and put his hand under my chin, making me raise my head and meet his gaze. "Black light. Not even black. Colors I've never seen before."

"Angela?" Ford went down in a crouch in front of her and caught hold of one of her hands.

The other hand was holding that strip of fruit leather to her mouth. Angela had inhaled the chocolate bar, but she was sucking on the dried fruit. Her head was bowed, her hair hanging loose like a curtain so we couldn't really see her face. What little I could see, her color looked normal. Ford was really the only one who could see enough of her to know how she was.

"I should hate to think that the rivalry between our towns has extended this far," Angela said after a few seconds.

"Huh?" Kurt said.

Stephanie chuckled. "It isn't the town attacking you, and you know it." She glanced over her shoulder at the house, and I looked too.

Weird. The house looked less menacing now. As if the attack on Angela, the attempt by something to drag her down, maybe keep her in the yard, maybe even suck her into the house, had used up whatever inimical energy it had.

"Or it sucked something out of you and kind of…" I stopped, a little stunned to realize I had been thinking aloud and everybody was looking at me.

"Kind of what?" Angela sounded almost normal, but her smile seemed thin.

"I don't know, maybe whatever it took from you kind of inoculated it? You're a really strong influence, and your power, your magic, kind of stunned whatever got hold of you?" I groaned and slid down to sit on the bumper of the Jeep. "That sounds totally stupid, even worse aloud than when I was thinking it."

"No, it makes a little sense." She sighed and offered us something close to her usual knowing smirk. "I hope you'll forgive me if I hesitate to act as a massive dose of penicillin or a bandage soaked with antibiotic ointment."

"You're not going anywhere near that place ever again," Ford said, with a hint of growl in his voice. "We're going to recruit some folks we can trust to keep an eye on it, watch whoever goes in and out, see if anything weird happens. Me and Kurt here, we'll stop by every once in a while to see if we get any leaks from wherever or whatever. It's quiet now, but who knows? When it recovers, it might decide it likes the taste of you, and come back for more."

"I will be safe inside the shop on the other side of town." Angela reached to brace herself on the sides of the door, to stand up.

The fact that she overpowered Stephanie and Ford when they tried to make her stay in the back seat, and just turn her legs to sit so they could close the door, encouraged all of us. Angela didn't even need to brace herself on the Jeep as she walked around it to get in on the passenger side. When we pulled away, I looked back to see Ford and Kurt leaning against Ford's truck, arms crossed over their chests, frowning at the house.

"I wonder why those two professors never seem to go in the house at the same time?" Stephanie murmured, once we had put that residential section of Neighborlee between Darbyville and us.

"Maybe we should ask them?" I said.

"That might start a chain reaction that none of us are ready for." Angela turned enough to meet my gaze, and her knowing, mischievous smirk was back to full power. Then she looked at the strip of fruit leather in her hand, which she had eaten down to the last two inches. "I have never eaten one of these before. Very good choice. I'll have to stock them from now on."

Something flickered in her eyes, and for a moment I could have sworn she wasn't there. Or rather, the Angela I had known most of my life wasn't looking out at me.

"I remember...someone..." She sighed and clenched the last piece in her hand and turned to face forward again. "Someone I knew, long ago, I don't know if he favored such things or he simply had such food with him when we met."

"You're not all right, are you?" Stephanie took her hand off the steering wheel to rest it on Angela's arm for a moment.

"I wonder if this is how horses felt, when they used to culture vaccine in them."

An exasperated sigh escaped Stephanie, and even though I couldn't see her face, I knew our Angela was back.

When we got back to the shop, she let us gently bully her into going upstairs to her apartment to have one of her infamous herbal teas and lie down for at least a little while. I followed her upstairs while Stephanie stayed downstairs to check messages on her cell phone. I knew better than to even try to support her on the climb up the stairs. On the second floor landing, movement along the wall caught my attention, and I nearly stumbled when a closer look showed the movement was *inside* the wallpaper. The abstract pattern sort of melted together, turning into shadows for a few seconds. I thought I heard night birds singing, and the shimmer of wind chimes coming through the wall. For just a second there, the lavender turned into moonlight and shadows, and I was looking at an ancient kind of garden, with pillars and latticework and trees draped with moss, and a tiny sparkle of water trickling over stone in the moonlight.

The sound of Angela's apartment door clicking open cut off the sounds and the lavender swirls replaced the moonlight and shadows. It was just wallpaper again. Shivering, I hurried after Angela. She was in her kitchen, plugging in the electric kettle.

"Whatever that is, hiding over the border..." She sighed and closed her eyes and rubbed at her temples instead of reaching for a tea canister. "It isn't coming from underneath us. It isn't the usual threat we face. The power it feeds off, the power it generates, the echoes it creates, aren't..." She reached for the tea. "They just aren't what we expect or usually face."

"So how do we face it down and get rid of it?" I stepped over to the cabinet, to reach down one of her enormous, brightly painted teapots. This one was big enough for the five of us to have at least two mugs each. I assumed Kurt and Ford were joining us soon. I had already decided I could skip my morning class, even though we had returned in plenty of time for me to get to the lecture hall.

"I have had dreams." She offered me a smile that was ninety percent normal and ten percent weary. "The kinds you can't remember when you wake, but you know you've had them."

"Where you think you've been fighting the War of the Roses in your sleep?" Stephanie said, stepping into the kitchen with us. She snorted and patted me on the shoulder. I must have given them both a weird look. Maybe one of fear or apprehension. "Don't worry, Lanie. If the boogieman underground isn't strong enough to impact on our dreams enough for us to remember, he isn't strong enough to break through. So he isn't strong enough to fight us. We have time."

"We always have time." Angela scooped tea into the big infuser that barely fit into the teapot. It was full of dried fruit and flower petals, spices and chunks of barley sugar. "I have lived so long...or maybe I have lived many lives...at least, I believe so. There are things I have chosen not to remember, because remembering gives those things and people and events power over us."

Frowning, she closed the lid on the canister. "What was I saying? Oh, yes. I have faced so many times like this, I can speak with certainty that there is a pattern. We will have warning. We will have clues. We will always have a chance to overcome, to do our duty and stand in the gap. However, sometimes," she said, her voice softening just on the edge of being a whisper, "there is a price of some kind to pay."

"Is the threat to you?" I blinked, feeling a little dizzy, and just as surprised as they were that the words came out of my mouth. "It's not Neighborlee or the college, you're the target?"

"It is possible." Angela blinked slowly, as if she were waking up. "When you have stood against the darkness as long as I have, when you have stood in the gap, enemies are expected." She shrugged, and gestured at the electric kettle, which was rumbling now with the water on the edge of boiling. "Enemies with long memories."

"There's a garden, trying to come out of the wallpaper out in the hall," I said, as I lifted the kettle and then remembered to flick the toggle to turn it off. I figured, in for a pound, right? Then I saw how the color left Angela's face, and I regretted that. "It's not there anymore. Just for a second. It's not real, is it?"

"Who knows what real is? I have dreams of a garden and a man, dark and strong, scarred, yet sweet enough to make me cry. Whether he is my past or will be my future, or perhaps even a future that will never be because of choices I have made and doors I have closed, who knows?"

"You need to sit down." Stephanie gave me a startled look when Angela let her lead her to the table in the next room. No resistance on her part.

Kurt and Ford showed up about then. They reported that nothing had happened when they crossed the yellow line into Darbyville for a second time. No reaction. They had flagged down Gordon Priebe just a street away, and asked him to keep an eye on the place, whenever he happened to be in the area. Gordon was always willing to go the extra mile, after we had supported him with the whole Grandstone mess during Senior Prank Night. When Ford told him it had to do with the experiment on the freshman class, Gordon said he knew at least ten other officers in the Neighborlee PD who would help keep a watch on the place.

Angela was her usual self by the time the tea was ready to pour. She even remembered that I had a class to go to, though I had never told her my schedule. She insisted that I go. Skipping a lecture so early in the school year, as well as so early in my college career, wasn't smart, according to her. It would start bad habits, and besides, how could I expect my students to show up for class and on time when I became a teacher, if I skipped classes now? Yeah, Angela was definitely herself again.

I was pretty sure she wanted to talk to Stephanie and Ford without me around, and without Kurt, because she asked Kurt to take Ford's truck and get me back to school. What difference would it make? Ten minutes faster by driving. Stephanie asked me if I would get Bethany from the drama program, and Ford asked me to take care of Athena. We agreed I would get the girls lunch and keep them at my dorm room until they came to get them. That made me feel a little better, since I had important things to do besides go to a class I couldn't have cared less about.

Chapter Eight

On the way out the door, I took a detour into the main room of the shop and pressed my hand on the Wishing Ball. Maybe I was too old for my wishes to be valid, but I would never be too old to believe in the magic of it. I stared into the dark, multi-colored, glossy depths for a second. Kurt was still upstairs, talking with Ford on the landing, so I had time.

"If there's anybody there, anybody listening, we need help. Angela talks about the Fae, so I figure maybe you are real, or at least something close enough to the Fae, or maybe just magical people period." I groaned. This was turning into a mess, and I was running out of time. "Look, if Angela reports to anyone higher up, can you send help? I don't know what's going on, but something or someone we've never faced before is gearing up for something. I'm scared it's an attack on Angela, specifically, not just the town. Please?"

The ball hummed softly under my hand. Not exactly an electric buzz, but there was a sense of warmth through the cool, smooth stone or glass or whatever it was made of. A vibration. No change in the colors, but a sense of light. Maybe someone had heard, or maybe my own willpower had forced a reaction.

Then Kurt came banging down the stairs and I had to go.

How anybody expected me to get any good out of class, I don't know. I took notes, but only time would tell if those notes would be worthwhile when I had to study for a test.

I really wished I had a cell phone. Back then, they were still kind of expensive, and I honestly couldn't justify getting one. Texting hadn't become a big thing then, and cell phones didn't have wireless and Internet access, so all they were good for was talking. I was satisfied to use the payphones on campus. The phone booth on our floor didn't require payment, although we did have to use our student ID numbers to make calls outside city limits. So when I left my class, I ran out the closest door and down the sidewalk to the Student Center, which was closer than my dorm. It occurred to me that I could call in a lot more support than whatever magical beings might be on the other side of the Wishing Ball. First step was calling my folks.

I was almost there when *Ode to Joy* blared out, nearly knocking me off my feet. I almost ran out of my shoes as I turned, looking for our van. There were my folks, pulling into the driveway to the main parking lot of the Student Center. Maybe they heard me thinking about them? Parental radar had nothing to do with genetics, and everything to do with love.

I ran, and Mum laughed and reached out the window to hit the latch for the sliding door, so I was able to dive inside almost before our VW had come to a full stop. They were just passing by and saw me making a break for it and Mum felt sure something was up. "Up" wasn't quite the word for it. We drove over to the theater building and sat in the parking lot, waiting until the drama program ended, and I told them what had happened. Pop pulled out the long, thin reporter's notebook he kept in his pants pocket. He wrote down the address of the house, the name and number of the realtor on the faded for sale sign, and all I could tell him about the two professors who visited the house, but never together. I felt a lot better just knowing he was going to pull every string possible to dig up information.

"Something else on your mind, honey?" Mum said.

"We need more reinforcements. Can you ask Pastor Rocky to maybe get some people praying about this? I mean, yeah, sometimes what's going on here sure looks and smells not right, but who says magic is automatically evil? It's not like Angela bursts into flames when she attends church, right?"

"The Pharisees accused Jesus of consorting with demons," Pop muttered. He winked at me. "Nothing wrong with asking for all the help we can get for Angela. I'm sure on judgment day, there are going to be a lot of people stunned speechless, when they see who is counted on the side of the light." He snorted. "And who isn't. The people who put words in God's mouth are going to be pretty surprised."

"Never a good idea to put your fingers near something liable to bite them off," Mum added, eyes sparkling. She reached back to pat my shoulder. "Think about this, though. What makes you think we don't already have people at church praying for Angela? There are lots of us who can see what's going on, who are aware of the vital role she and Divine's play. Just because she doesn't wear the uniform or speak the lingo doesn't mean she isn't one of us."

"Babe," Pop said, "we don't wear the uniform, and we don't use the lingo most of the time."

"You know what I mean," she said, shaking a finger in his face. Pop leaned forward, snapping as if he would bite that finger, and we laughed. Then Bethany and Athena appeared in the doorway of the theater, and it was time to go get them. Definitely not the kind of topic to continue in front of little girls.

We had more than enough proof that the weird and wonderful was real, but we also knew the power of prayer. Pastor Rocky never hesitated to agree to set up a prayer vigil to protect Angela and Divine's and the dormitory.

~~~~~

Our visit to the house on the border of Darbyville triggered some kind of reaction. Or else whatever was building up on my dormitory floor sensed the three of us flying around the night before. Whoever or whatever was controlling the portal of energy or the faucet or whatever it was (Kurt labeled it a sphincter, but we voted him down) essentially panicked. At least, that was my interpretation.

Mum and Pop and I took the girls to lunch in the cafeteria. Bethany and Athena were big-eyed and suitably awed by the very different scenery, so they were quiet and easy to control. Not that they were ever trouble to begin with, but that day they never strayed more than a foot away from us. They both thought it was cool that they could pick out whatever they wanted for lunch. Within reason, of course. What Kindergartener wouldn't love being allowed to make her own sandwich, and put strawberry, lime, and grape gelatin cubes in the same bowl as her chocolate pudding? They decided my sandwich was cool and copied it, although I expected them to make faces when they bit into it. Hey, I had a semi-pseudo-superhero's metabolism, and I could get away with loading up on fat and sugar. My sandwich was three slices of oat-nut bread, with peanut butter, honey and cranberries on one side of the divider slice of bread. On the other side, mayonnaise, bologna, swiss cheese, salami and spicy-sweet mustard, in that specific order. It might sound gross, but the sweet and salty and spicy kind of modified each other. The mayonnaise greased the
~~~~~

track so the peanut butter didn't stick quite as much as it should have. What was funny was that the girls loved it. Mum warned me about repercussions from the Longfellows and from Stephanie, when their girls demanded those sandwiches at home. Pop just laughed and said he wouldn't be surprised if my gloppy sandwich creation appeared on the menu of Miller's Diner eventually.

When my folks dropped us off at the dormitory, I fully expected to see either Stephanie's Jeep or Ford's truck waiting outside, and one of them inside, to pick up the girls. Nothing, though. We trooped upstairs and I planned to pull out a pad of blank paper and colored pencils to keep the girls occupied while we waited. I didn't have a class until three that afternoon. What was I going to do if Stephanie didn't show up by then? What would that indicate about Angela's reaction to our field trip out to the house on the border?

There was a note on my door that Stephanie had called just five minutes before, saying she was on her way. Reprieve! We took a walk to the bathroom, because I knew how little girls' plumbing worked after a big meal and an invigorating walk up two flights of stairs. And big girls' plumbing, too.

The lights flickered, not quite going on and off, but dimming and brightening past the normal level, as we came out of the bathroom. The door from the stairwell opened, and Stephanie walked through.

That was weird, because I expected her to call from downstairs, asking to come up. Closed dorm hours and all that. While non-students were allowed in the dorm during daylight hours, somebody still had to let them through the big fire door between the lounge and the rest of the dorm until about three in the afternoon. Stephanie paused two steps away from the stairwell and looked up at the ceiling. She must have sensed something, even though the lights were back to normal. Then Bethany saw her mother and shrieked and ran to meet her.

"What?" I asked, after we got the girls' coats back on them and herded them toward the stairs. Bethany and Athena were having one of those best friend arguments, where they disagreed on something that happened in the theater, but laughed about it every time they corrected each other. Adults, especially politicians, could have learned something from them.

"I don't know." Stephanie glanced at the door that opened off the stairwell into the boys' side of the floor. "It's like when you're in the house and you can hear something, but you don't know what it is. Then you go into a room and the TV is turned on, but the sound is on mute."

"Yeah. Know that feeling." I rubbed my arms. She had that look in her eye, as she glanced at my T-shirt-clad arms, so I cut her off before she could lecture me about dressing warmer. Stephanie was a mom, after all. "How did you get in this far? The doors aren't unlocked for another hour. Did someone use their key card to let you in?"

"The door was hanging open." She paused, one foot lifted to go down the next step. Then we just nodded and herded the girls down the stairs.

"What about the one on my floor? Did it do anything when you tried to open it?"

"The stairwell went completely black, just for a second. I didn't feel or hear anything when I touched the door."

There was no door at the bottom of the stairwell where it opened onto the first floor. When we went through the fire door between the first floor rooms and the lounge and lobby area, it buzzed just like it was supposed to. The pneumatic hinges took over and pulled it closed once we were through. Stephanie looked at me and shook her head. She hadn't sensed anything that time.

Why was the door hanging open? It made no sense. Unless something wanted Stephanie to come inside?

"I'm not saying I felt anything, but that muted TV feeling seemed to come from the other side of the floor," Stephanie offered as she pushed the lobby doors open and the girls scampered outside. "Do you have any reason to go on that side of the floor?"

"Eww, the guys' side. Like, I'll catch some ghetto diseases or something, just breathing the air." I shuddered, exaggerating, and that helped both of us grin and relax a little more.

"Any reason for Kurt to go there and do his divining rod trick?"

"If I have to go break somebody's popcorn popper or that mini deep-fryer or the laser show projector they keep bragging about, yeah, I'll find a reason."

Stephanie hugged me and then she had to hurry to catch up with Bethany and Athena, who were chasing leaves around on the sloping front lawn of the dormitory. Funny, how those swirls of blowing leaves looked like dust devils. I stayed in the doorway, watching, laughing with them as they scampered around, snatching at the leaves that twirled upward and then away.

Athena let out a giggling shriek and darted after a clump of leaves that bobbed and wove, staying just out of her reach. Stephanie called to her, then bent to pick up Bethany to put her in the car seat behind the driver's side. Yes, there was a seat for Athena in Stephanie's Jeep, and one for Bethany in the Longfellows' truck, since the girls spent so much time together. Sometimes it was like they were twins.

I had been told enough times just that day to listen to my instincts, and they told me to stay there in the cold entryway, watching Athena while Stephanie had her back turned, taking care of Bethany.

That dust devil—leaf devil? debris devil?—whatever it could be called, that mini tornado leaned forward just like in the cartoons with Taz and Bugs, and zoomed out across the lawn, heading for the sidewalk. Something between foresight and instinct had me leaping down the steps, shouting for Athena to stop before her little sneakers hit the edge of the sidewalk. She followed the leaves across the sidewalk, across the tree lawn, right into the empty street.

Or at least, what had been an empty street five seconds ago.

I flew the forty feet or so, and made a sonic pop. Not quite a sonic boom. Yeah, I broke the most vital rule Kurt and Felicity and I had, to hide what we could do, especially in daylight. But an even more important rule put others first, especially their lives, especially the lives of little kids.

Stephanie screamed. Not one of those stupid damsel in distress screams of utter helplessness, that did nothing but distract the hero. This was a scream of warning.

I was too busy to hear her exact words, zooming in on Athena and reaching for her, just as her sneakers crossed the broken yellow line in the middle of the street. From the corner of my eye, I saw the car racing straight for us. I heard the rising shriek of the engine. It was *gaining* speed. I grabbed hold of Athena and boosted us up, still hurtling across the street. The car fender hit my foot and knocked me sideways. I curled myself around her as we tumbled across the lawn. Thank goodness it was dry and sloped upward a little, and there was no garden in our path. It was gardening day, meaning if the flowerbeds around campus weren't mulched, they were watered. Ugh.

The car didn't stop until the driver missed the corner. Maybe it would be more accurate to say the car missed the turn and hit the corner with near-precise aim. We were still rolling across the grass when the scream of the engine died. When the car went up over the curb at the corner, the angle deflected and slowed it, so it only knocked over two campus newspaper boxes and dented the third, squishing it up against the mailbox that was next in line. Except for scratches from the newspaper box hitting it, the mailbox wasn't damaged.

Stephanie reached me, just as I managed to sit up. Athena clung to me, big-eyed and white and shivering like a drowned kitten.

"Stay still," Stephanie said, when I tried to get to my knees to stand. Not very easy to do with a five-year-old clutching at me, but I wasn't in any mood to let go of Athena any time soon. Then she reached out a tissue and touched my forehead.

"Oh, yeah." Aching shot through my head, at the curve above the outer end of my right eyebrow. Like a delayed reaction.

The tissue came away smeared with blood. When I'd gone sideways, I tipped down, head-first, and hit the curb before Athena and I went rolling.

Didn't anybody have classes right after the cafeteria closed? It felt like everybody who lived on that side of campus came pouring out of the dorms and the nearby classrooms.

Gordon muscled his way through the gathering crowd. Did I mention the guy is huge? Kind of a mix of Bigfoot and Godzilla, but clean-shaven and all marshmallow goo inside, with a heart as big as Lake Erie. He was also in uniform. In fact, he had just located Professor Tudderman for his first shift of watching him, as Ford, Angela and Stephanie had requested. That was convenient. Maybe an answer to prayer.

Because the guy in the car that nearly hit me and Athena was Professor Tudderman. Gordon had seen him coming out of the building where he was supposed to be lecturing all day, staggering and holding his arm against his chest, looking like he had had a seizure or a fit of some kind. Before Gordon could get through the maze of dividers and little islands of grass and trees in the parking lot, Tudderman got in his car and zigged his way out of there. Sometimes going over those little tree-and-grass islands. Gordon got some of it on camera, and he said the professor slumped sideways in his car, and didn't go more than ten miles per hour until he turned onto the street that ran in front of my dormitory. Then the car roared and leaped forward and burned rubber, before it screamed down the street about three blocks, never slowing and never wavering off course until his fender clipped my shoe.

I learned all that a short time later. Gordon could bellow like a whole corral of bulls, and got people away from the car, where Tudderman wasn't moving. He waited for me to tell him I was all right, that I could get up, and he made sure I did get to my feet. Then he left Stephanie to take care of me while he stomped over to the car to check on the professor. Stephanie finally persuaded Athena to loosen her grip enough she wouldn't tear my T-shirt, and then transferred the little girl to her hip, so she could offer me a hand to help me stand.

By this time, Bethany had managed to work her way out of her car seat and down out of the car, to the pavement. She was smart enough to stay right there by the Jeep and wait for us to come back to her. Alysyn, our resident director, met us there and insisted we all come into her apartment. I was ready to, because I finally felt the cold. Usually my semi-pseudo-superhero metabolism kept me warmer in the winter and cooler in the summer, but maybe I had strained it too much, or maybe it was shock, but I was cold.

I've said it before, and I'll probably say it a couple thousand times before I'm dead and gone: when it comes to superhero powers, I was shortchanged. Gypped. Robbed. Cheated. If God was going to give me the ability to kinda-sorta fly, wouldn't it make sense to make me invulnerable? Okay, I'm not talking about bullets or nuclear bombs, but would it be so unfair to make my skin tougher and strengthen my bones, so I didn't get cut and bruised so easily? Granted, that afternoon I didn't even need stitches, but there have been other times when I smacked my hand or foot against something and broke a small bone, or I wore bruises for weeks after a really rough rescue attempt. And then there was the biggie that changed the entire direction of my working life.

More on that later. Much later.

Alysyn produced cups of chocolate pudding for the girls, and settled them down in front of her TV to watch cartoons. Athena's color was back to normal and she squealed with Bethany and giggled when the first spoonful of pudding revealed gummy worms buried inside. I felt better just knowing she was going to be okay. Then Alysyn got to work on my head, inside and out. Aspirin, antiseptic wipes, anesthetic spray, styptic pen, and a big square bandage to cover it all. After that Stephanie and I got our own pudding cups. Kind of hard to eat pudding when one hand is devoted to holding a plastic bag of ice cubes to my throbbing head.

Gordon showed up about the time I debated asking for seconds. The EMTs on the scene said Professor Tudderman's eyes were unevenly dilated, he had dried blood in one ear, and the arm that he had been clutching against his chest was still in that position, as if frozen. The general consensus was a stroke of some kind, or an aneurysm, a broken blood vessel, which explained the blood in his ear. Considering what Gordon had seen before the professor got in his car, chances were good the attack, whatever it was, happened before he started the car. So why was he driving?

"Some people don't realize anything is wrong," Alysyn said, as she came back from the refrigerator with pudding for Gordon and a second one for me.

Which just confirmed what a number of us in the dorm had already theorized: Alysyn could read minds.

"Their wiring is so tangled, they think everything is fine, and they don't realize that what they're doing is wrong or dangerous," she continued. "I'd be interested in knowing what he thought he saw, just before he hit you."

Gordon muttered a couple things under his breath. It sounded like Klingon. Remember, he was in my Star Trek club. That was what made him such a great guy, and we could trust him with the weirdness of everything going on with the experiment and the dorm, and now Professor Tudderman.

"Whatever happened, it's gonna be a while until anybody can ask him anything, much less him being able to answer," he said.

Charlotte Longfellow came by to get Athena before Stephanie was convinced that I was okay and she could leave me under Alysyn's care. Mrs. L heard about the incident while she was bringing her fourth-grade class in from a game of kickball. Her grandmother instincts kicked in. She left her class in the care of the gym teacher at the elementary school and hurried just down the street two blocks, without even knowing that the little girl who nearly got hit was her granddaughter. She hugged me a long time and promised she would have a long talk with Athena about chasing leaves when she wasn't in her own backyard.

"It wasn't Athena's fault," Stephanie said, resting a hand on Mrs. L's shoulder to give a little emphasis to her words. "Ask Ford what we were working on today. I'm afraid it was some kind of backlash." Then she glanced down at the floor.

"Ah. Of course." Mrs. L settled Athena more securely on her hip.

"They were probably coming after me, or testing me or something," I offered. "Maybe the kids should stay away from me, or maybe this place, until the whole mess gets cleaned up."

"Hmph. Just as likely targeting Athena for Ford's part in it, as you," she said, with a brisk nod. Then her eyes got sparkly and I felt sick with the dread she would start crying. Mrs. L reached out and hugged me again. "One of these days, Lanie Zephyr, you're going to go so far out on a limb for someone, you'll run out of limb. Then what are the rest of us going to do?"

"Pray a lot harder?" Yeah, that was lame, but I was getting kind of choked up, mentally and physically. I got one of those shivers through the center of me that had nothing to do with temperature. If anything, Alysyn's apartment was downright toasty.

Curtis, one of the geekiest guys on our floor, was sitting on the bench that ran across the wall at the top of the landing, when I got back upstairs. Granted, I only say he was the geekiest guy because the guys from my Star Trek club said he was. He came to our meeting, along with about two-thirds of our floor, and then sat in the back and just grinned and didn't say anything the whole two hours. Tyrone later told me Curtis had never been to a convention or a club meeting his entire life, and all his exposure to fandom was through the Internet. It was overwhelming for him to be with real live people talking about the things he loved.

He got to his feet so fast he lost his balance. "How come you're hurt?" I thought he was going to lunge at me, or go hurtling down the stairs.

I am ashamed to admit that I took a step to the right to get out of the way. My head was still throbbing, despite liberal doses of chocolate and aspirin and anesthetic cream. I wanted to lie down. I was pretty sure my folks would be calling as soon as they heard what happened, so I wanted to be near the phone booth. Maybe it was time to give in and get a cell phone? The last thing I needed was to have to catch a clumsy guy who was about ten inches taller than me, but probably weighed a good eighty pounds less than me.

"Uh, where were you an hour ago?" I headed for the door to my side of the floor.

"I saw it." He gulped loudly enough to almost qualify as Gollum. "I saw you fly. So you can't get hurt."

"Hate to burst your bubble, but yeah, I can get hurt." I tapped the blood smear on my shirt. "That's proof."

"But you're a—you can—you shouldn't get hurt if you can fly." His mouth and eyes puckered up for a moment, so I thought he might cry.

Honestly, I wanted so much to agree with him. Correction: I wanted to sit down with him and gripe and get a little sympathy. If God gave me superpowers, how come He didn't give me the whole package? See my previous grumble.

I couldn't do that, though. Rule number one: hide what we were, what we could do.

"Seriously, I was running pretty fast. And I'm on the track team, I'm good at jumping. It only looked like I flew," I said, and reached for the latch for the door.

"You flew. You're the reason I'm here."

"Here for what?"

Okay, part of my moronic half of the conversation could be blamed on the adrenaline still seething through my veins, and my aching head. Part of that could be blamed on practice conversations Kurt and Felicity and I had over the years, preparing for the day we got caught by the Men in Black. Or maybe Agents Fox, Preminger, Gerard, or Mulder and Scully, or even that moronic reporter, McGee. Whoever would finally prove immune enough to Neighborlee's weirdness quotient that they would see what was really there, and yet not freak out.

Curtis just stood there, giving me that earnest, slightly sweaty, ready-to-break-into-a-seizure look. It occurred to me that he might be working for the people in the dark van. The ones who made other Lost Kids with semi-pseudo-superhero powers vanish.

"Willis-Brooks doesn't have a flight school, and Neighborlee doesn't have an airport of its own. You have to go to Cleveland Hopkins if you want to learn how to fly."

Granted, not my most snappy comeback. I needed to learn to have snappy comebacks and think really fast on my feet if I was going to be a schoolteacher. See the paragraph above about my headache and all that adrenaline buzzing my brain cells.

"Magic," Curtis whispered.

"What about it?"

Then something cut through the throbbing. Something that should have bothered me all along.

Curtis had gone with us to Divine's that first night when we were getting settled in the dorm, but doggone if I could remember seeing him actually go inside. He certainly hadn't gone along on any of the spontaneous hikes across town. Usually when someone said, "I'm going over to Divine's to replenish my (whatever). Who wants to come?" she would get at least four heads poking out of their rooms, like slavering hound dogs picking up the scent of the fox. Amazingly, even if the proposal to visit Divine's originated at one end of the dorm floor, people on the other end, even through the airlock of the stairwell with two heavy fire doors, would hear and come running.

There was something odd about people's need to go to Divine's in groups, rather than solo. None of us who were natives felt the need for company, but like girls need to go to the restroom in schools like fish, our dormmates needed to go to Divine's in groups of two or more. I didn't think about it right at that moment, but going over the series of events later, that thought occurred to me. The best theory we could come up with was that being from outside Neighborlee, they could sense the power, the thin veil between Earth and Otherness that Neighborlee and Divine's protected, and they were wisely cautious. Kind of like when dealing with Aslan. Just because he was good didn't mean he was safe.

Yeah, kind of like dealing with Angela, too.

"This place is magic," Curtis said, after backing away half a step, then leaning forward, then backing away again, to the point of generating enough breeze to waft his scent to me. He smelled oddly musty, like he had been locked up in some slightly damp, yet dusty place. Maybe it was his breath. Or some exotic cologne.

"Are you on drugs? There's no smoking allowed on campus."

"I'm not on drugs!" he shrieked, and lunged at me.

I yanked the door open with my brain and got through it before he got his hands with those dirty, broken fingernails anywhere on me. Using telekinesis after banging my forehead on the curb? *Not* a recommended plan of action. Not even to get away from a guy whose eyes were about to go spinning in opposite directions.

Curtis banged on the door. I had an image of him slamming his face into it. So sue me. I laughed. Just once. It hurt my head. The phone rang as I started down the hall. I needed to get into my room before Curtis managed to get the fire door on the stairwell open.

Come to think of it, how come he couldn't get it open? The timer on the lock should have clicked over now that open dorms had begun. Maybe I messed up something when I opened it with my brain, in panic?

"Mum?" I said, yanking the phone off the hook. I really needed my mother.

"Ah…no," Pop said. "What's up, Lanie? Harry called us from school and he said you got hit by a car. Your mom is dealing with the school office and him being out of class, while I get to check on you. Do you need us?"

I slid into the phone booth and settled on the triangle bench set in the corner. Yeah, we had a real phone booth in the middle of our hallway. Someone got whimsical during a renovation about forty years ago and went whole hog with the folding door and the overhead light that came on if the booth was occupied, and changed color if we stayed in it too long. Define "too long" for college students? I closed the door just enough to block most of the sound, but not enough to flip the switch to turn on the light.

Then I spilled. My folks had taught me how to tell a story well, and how to present details so people wouldn't keep interrupting me to ask questions. It didn't take long, since he knew most of the details already. I reminded him about the two professors who visited the house on the border in tag-team fashion, and ended with the revelation that one of them had nearly run down Athena and me. According to Gordon, he was nearly unconscious, kind of drooling, his eyes glazed, and in the hospital. Too bad Neighborlee didn't have its own hospital, we had to share with three other cities. Right then, I would have felt a lot more comfortable if Professor Tudderman was recovering within Neighborlee's influence.

"Does he live inside town?" Pop asked, when I shared that new thought with him.

"No. Gordon even said his route takes him past that house on the way to and from work every day."

"Somebody better check on the other teacher involved in this whole mess. Winghast?"

"Yeah." I had it on the tip of my tongue to ask Pop to make the call. I was supposed to rest, after all. Alysyn had promised she would check on me regularly, to make sure I didn't have any bad, delayed reaction to hitting my head.

"We've never really had a threat..." Pop sighed. "Rewind that. To our knowledge, we haven't had a threat that came from earthly levels, from people outside Neighborlee. Either the threats come from people inside our borders, people who turned against us, or they come from other realities, the spiritual dimension."

"Pop, I'm scared this is an attack directed at Angela. I mean, she acted kind of weird. Yeah, Angela is a little strange, but it's a good strange, it usually means she's about a dozen steps ahead of all of us and she's just waiting for us to catch up. This time, it was like she wasn't there for a little bit. It was more than just stepping foot into enemy territory that drained her."

He sighed loud and deep. His thinking sigh, Mum called it. "Makes sense to me, hon. As soon as your mom finishes bailing out Harry's backside, we'll take a drive over to Divine's, see what she needs us to do. What she'll let us do."

"Thanks, Pop."

"Will it embarrass you if we stop on our way home, maybe bring you some ice cream, or take you home for the weekend?"

"Please, embarrass me!"

Laughing made my head feel better.

I needed that little boost, because if things hadn't already grown past the normal background weirdness of Neighborlee that day, they were about to break a few records. Starting with the sound barrier.

Chapter Nine

When I opened the door of the phone booth, the noise got louder. It came from the stairwell and the not-nearly-effective-enough barrier of the fire door between us and the boys' side of the floor. I had been hearing giggles and running feet and some muffled shouting when I was inside the phone booth, but that was normal for our floor. Now I saw a few girls standing by the door, trying to look through the narrow window, about eight inches wide by two feet long. When I walked down to see what was going on, the shouting got louder and clearer. At the right angle, I could see through the window in our door, across the stairwell, through the window in the boys' door. A wrestling match was in progress, bouncing off the walls and falling to the floor and rolling around so much it was hard to tell who was involved. I counted four colors of shirts, but at least six heads. A guy's back regularly slid across the window enough to block the view. I figured at least two boys leaned against the door, blocking it. Just like, I realized, four of the girls on my side of the door were leaning against it to keep it closed.

"What's up?" I said.

That got a few shrieks and yelps from them. Everybody was so intent on watching the fight on the boys' side, they didn't notice me coming up behind them.

"Some jerk is out to kill you," Bonnie said, eyes wide, her face flushed with excitement.

"Me?"

"Near as we can tell, he was yelling about making you tell the truth, and proving something, and he just about broke down the door of some other guy's room to get a gun and come after you. For such a skinny little dweeb, he's pretty fierce."

"Khaleed stepped over to warn us, and Janie ran down to get Alysyn," Taylor said with a giggle. "Kind of exciting, you know?"

She was a theater major just so she could play with makeup on a scholarship. Go figure. She was good and would have a great future doing aliens or monsters for movies, but I was pretty sure she had inhaled too many weird fumes from aerosol cans or liquid latex remover. Jellified the brain.

"Nobody should have a gun. For one thing, it's against the rules." As soon as the words left my mouth, I realized how wrong I was. Three-quarters of the guys on our floor had weapons of some kind. Of course, so did I. Mostly movie and TV props to decorate our rooms. Some of the theater guys were into military re-enacting. Then there were the guys who were into paintball. They hung their guns on the walls over their beds, like other guys hung up crossed swords over their coat of arms. For full disclosure, I had Han Solo's blaster, a light saber, a Classic Trek phaser, and several weapons from the Men in Black movies, including the Noisy Cricket.

Maybe it was my headache, or maybe I had started to develop some unreliable, unpredictable precognitive abilities. Or maybe just all the weirdness of Neighborlee had broken through to new levels. I came up with some wild, crazy, yet weirdly logical conclusions.

What if the energy we felt surrounding the whole floor last night made it possible for prop weapons to become real?

What if that gun Curtis had snatched from someone else's room worked?

For about five seconds, I seriously considered going to my room for a weapon. Self-defense, right?

Logic also told me that I would look pretty stupid, and I would be wasting time. If my toys suddenly became workable and real, shouldn't I have noticed the change when it happened? For one thing, the hollow plastic should have turned into metal and fallen off the putty I used to mount them on the walls.

Maybe that was what gave Curtis the clue that the gun he went for was real?

Then there was the escalation in the situation I would be creating if I snagged a totally useless toy gun or my light saber, and faced down Curtis, who had a working weapon. He could claim self-defense when he shot me with a working gun, right?

My head really hurt.

Shouts became screams. I smelled something hot and kind of stinky-melty-plasticky-gross-synthetic. Then I saw the smoke. The girls blocking the door shrieked about a second after that.

The boys' door burst open as guys fled, screaming and swearing and some of them trailing smoke. Fortunately, I didn't see anyone on fire as they raced down the stairs. The girls nearly knocked me over, evacuating the doorway. When I got back to the window, the boys' door had caught in the dent in the tile where a doorstop used to be. I saw two figures rolling around on the floor. One was Curtis. He had been wearing that neon purple Incredible Hulk shirt when he confronted me earlier.

The other guy was at least two feet shorter than him. Kind of like Pippin fighting with Legolas. Weird how I could remember the guy planned on being a Hobbit for Halloween, but couldn't remember his name, only that he was on our floor. Even as I struggled to remember his name, Curtis rolled free and staggered to his feet and drew back his foot for a kick.

Curtis was wearing big old boots, a cross between lumberjack, military issue, and ski boots.

"No you don't!" I shouted as I slammed my door open and leaped across the landing.

Hey, praise me for being a superhero and putting my life on the line for someone. For some stupid reason, I just kept doing it. Enough to risk picking up the ghetto diseases that had to be hovering in the air on the boys' side of the dorm. Besides, I liked Ricky DeSouza—yeah, now I remembered his name. He was a cool kid, even not counting the sci-fi-type weapons he designed.

He clutched one of those weapons against his chest. That was what Curtis was going after. Lights flashed between Ricky's fingers wrapped tight around it. Green and red and a deep violet like black lights. Coming from the grip and out the muzzle.

The last time Ricky showed me the progress he was making on this new design, sleek and black, with ruby and silver highlights, he hadn't figured out the wiring or power source to make those lights work.

The pause I earned by startling Curtis ended. He snarled something under his breath and drew his foot back. Can I blame panic and my headache coming back? I swung my hands around, shoving physically as well as with my aching head. Curtis swore as he flew backward about twenty feet, until he hit a door that had been propped open, and got the breath knocked out of him. When he hit the floor, he went limp like a rag doll. I hoped he was just unconscious, and I hadn't broken anything. Like his idiot head.

"No no no no," Ricky moaned, finally uncurling. He held out

the blaster that he hadn't even named yet. He seemed to be a lot more green than the flashing lights could account for.

"What's it doing?"

"It's powering up—" Ricky yelped and dropped the gun. That melty-plasticky-scorched stink got stronger, and now little wisps of smoke were coming out of the muzzle. "It's hot! But it shouldn't be doing that."

"Pretend it can. What's it doing?"

"Those lights mean it's about to overload."

"Why do people keep insisting on putting doomsday programming into things?" I sank down in a squat and just looked at the gun. Doggone it, but the black plastic body (if it was still black *plastic*) had taken on a reddish glow all over. It looked as hot as it smelled. "How much time do we have?"

"I don't know!"

"Ricky." I reached over and just gripped his shoulders when I really wanted to shake him until his eyeballs rattled. "You designed it. You said you were working on programming for all sorts of special effects. You know it's powering up to overload, so you have to know how much time we have."

"Uh—uh—I think—" He held his breath and nodded his head to match the beat of the flashing red and green lights. "Yeah, we have about two minutes."

Fortunately, there was a muddy field to the right of our dorm, big enough for pickup football or baseball games and those stupid getting-to-know-you games we had to play during orientation. I could get down the stairs in thirty seconds. Out the back door of the dorm, and another thirty seconds to the field. That was the best I could do. We could worry later about the blast zone and radiation or whatever dangerous chemicals and fuel or whatever Ricky had imagined would be involved in the operation of the gun.

I picked up the gun—with my mind, of course—and headed down the stairs.

Yes, I know it would have been smarter to leap out a window and fly/float down to the ground, but most of my self-defensive programming was still holding. It kicked in more when I came out on the first floor and saw the lost-and-found desk outside Alysyn's door, with some laundry someone had left in the dryer long enough to be confiscated. I grabbed a towel and wrapped it around the gun and carried it sling-fashion the rest of the way.

Good thing I did, because when I ran out into the lobby and headed for the back door, beyond the pop machines and snack machines, the place was full of people talking and more people coming in the front door, probably drawn by the shouts of the guys who ran screaming like little girls. Come to think of it, the smell of scorched clothes and hair was pretty strong in the lobby. So, okay, they had some reason to scream.

Ricky was right behind me. For such a little guy, he was a good runner. Maybe he should have tried out for the track team.

I bombed out the back door. The lights were strong enough to bleed through the towel, and that scorching smell was under my nose now. The heat traveling through the towel was just at that point where I wanted to throw it down and blow on my hands.

Then a squealing-wailing sound came from it, kind of a *wee-doo-wee-doo-wee-doo*, up and down, just two notes.

"What does that mean?" I screamed as we raced down the wheelchair ramp. Fortunately, it was a straight ramp, no switchback, since it only had to go up six steps to the back door.

"One minute!" Ricky shouted, sounding kind of breathless. Maybe track wasn't a good choice after all.

The lights were now flashing fast enough to almost be a strobe effect. Increasing headache here. I wove between the cars in the side parking lot. Across one row, then the second. I let the towel slide further, just holding onto the edges now, and even that was too hot. My fingers were going to blister any second.

My foot hit the parking lot bumper at the edge of the muddy field. I stumbled and got over it, gasping at an awful image of going face-down in the mud with that scorching hot gun underneath me. Fortunately, not a precognitive moment. Two more steps.

The wailing cut out like someone hit a mute button.

I ran five more steps before Ricky let out a surprised yelp and I looked at the flashing bundle hanging from my hand, held out at arm's length.

Correction: *No flashing.*

Not taking any chances, I kept running until I got to within ten feet of what I hoped was the center of the field, tossed the gun to that target point I had eyeballed, and turned to run before it hit the mud. Ricky kept running past me. I groaned and slid to a stop. Just to show what a crazy, strained day I had had so far, my first thought was getting the mud out of the treads of my new sneakers. Then I thought about picking up Ricky and dragging him out of the danger zone.

Then my third thought was actually a question: *What danger zone?*

The gun had stopped flashing, stopped wailing, and other than the little wisps of steam rising from the puddle where it had landed, no one could tell from just looking at it that it had been about to overload a few seconds ago. Okay, the smell of metal and oil and plastic and other weird smells that I imagined belonged in a futuristic setting, like a spaceport in the middle of a battle zone, could be counted as a clue, too.

By the time Gordon showed up, a crowd had gathered around, but nobody put a toe off the parking lot pavement. Alysyn had called the fire department and campus security and the head of housing, and Curtis's academic advisor. Ricky and I had retreated to the edge of the parking lot too, just because it felt kind of weird to stand out there in the mud, with everybody staring at us.

Clarice got back to our dorm about the time I was heading out the back door. When she heard what had happened and where I was, she proved what a good roommate she was and how much common sense she had. She went to get my jacket. Yeah, I was shivering, but it wasn't all from the damp breeze and dropping temperatures as we stood there, staring at the lump of towel covering the gun.

Gordon met my gaze as he and his trainer walked across the parking lot. He kind of slumped, then he shrugged and gave me a crooked grin. I caught him gesturing at me as he talked to the other officer, and I said a quick, silent prayer of thanks that Gordon was in my life. All we had gone through together, the things we had in common, covered over a lot of disbelief and the problems that logic created in utterly incomprehensible situations like this. Well, incomprehensible in other towns and other college campuses. While Gordon wasn't a Lost Kid, which would have explained his ability to handle the weirdness so calmly, his mother had been a Lost Kid. History has proven that helps a lot.

His trainer got to work talking to Alysyn and Ricky and the guys who were involved in the fight. Gordon gestured for me to follow and we walked about halfway between the blacktop and the puddle holding the gun. Then he put me through a much friendlier interrogation than everybody else was bound to get. For one thing, he let me tell him the sequence of events and didn't even blink when I told him about Curtis's accusation that I could fly.

We were standing there, looking up at the dorm and everybody talking and laughing and pointing and generally having way too much fun, considering how close they came to a nuclear blast. Kurt's words from last night came back to me. Was it only last night we had done our flyover of the dorm?

The important detail was that the field of unrecognizable energy had only extended halfway down into the second floor. There were limits to the energy field. I tried to eyeball the distance on the building and compare it to the distance from the building to the muddy field, where the overload sequence on the gun just stopped. Chances were good that it wasn't mud or something in the ground itself that interfered with whatever made the gun real enough to threaten our lives. The energy field ended at the edge of the blacktop.

"Oh, heck, it's growing," I muttered.

"What is?" Gordon turned to look up at the building, probably wondering what I was staring at.

"I think it has to do with the whole stupid experiment and that house we asked you guys to keep an eye on. There's something on our floor ... Gordon, something is threatening Angela. Can we leave it at that?"

He looked down at me with those big, warm, teddy bear eyes in his Godzilla-with-a-shave face. I could almost read his thoughts as he analyzed and considered everything I had just told him, and everything he knew.

"Gonna have to tell Chief Tanner, at least," he finally said, and reached out to squeeze my shoulder.

"I'll talk to my Pop and Ford and Angela, and they can clear things with the Chief, how does that sound?"

"Perfect."

About then, I felt a clearing in the air. That's the only way to describe it. Gordon looked past me, and I turned to see Kurt walking across the corner of the field, from where he had parked on the street. That was the only place left to park, with the lot so full. He gave me a look about as close to scared as Kurt had ever looked. Scared for me. I almost didn't need the jacket Clarice got for me, I felt so warm and safe right then.

Gordon didn't even clear it with his trainer before he walked with me and Kurt out to where the gun still lay covered with the scorched towel. Kurt bent down and tugged aside the towel. The inside had brown streaks, and a big solid brown patch where the gun had rested in the center. He always carried a mini tool kit in his back pocket, and insulated gloves. He put the gloves on and squatted there and moved the gun around, just poking at it with one finger, then the tip of a screwdriver. It sounded like metal when he tapped it, and it was heavy enough to need some strong pushing to make it move.

"Okay, that's just freaky," I said. "I touched that gun a few times, when Ricky was working on it and he showed it to me. That shell should be a carbon polymer, light and strong, and a little flexible, so it won't shatter if it gets dropped, like plastic would. He put lenses and those light filaments in it, and a couple little computer chips for controlling the special effects, but most of it should be hollow."

"Doesn't feel hollow," Kurt said.

"How does a freshman get materials like that?" Gordon wanted to know. He shrugged. "Gotta ask all the questions, because Chief Tanner sure will."

Fortunately, I had the answer for that. Ricky was looking like a petrified rabbit about to get squashed by an oncoming car, under his interrogation. Granted, he was probably still all tangled up from his gun not only coming to life but threatening to blow up the dormitory. I couldn't imagine Officer Wong being that scary. He went to my church and he played in the retro band with Pastor Rocky, Ford, my Pop and Chief Tanner.

"Ricky's uncle works in the movies, designing props and stuff. He does a lot of science fiction and military movies, and lets him come out and work in the shop in the summer. He's getting his apprenticeship out of the way and by the time he graduates, he'll be in the union and have some film credits under his belt. Kind of cool, huh?" I said.

"Yeah, except how does a kid who builds props make something that works?" He sighed and closed his eyes. "Dumb question, huh?" He raked his big hands through his frizzy hair. "I'm still a trainee. The Chief trusts my gut. But the paperwork doesn't trust anybody's gut."

He turned and looked around. So did I, and there were way too many people standing there, watching us, nudging each other and whispering. Right then, I really hated the rule that freshmen had to live on campus.

That was the wrong attitude, I knew instantly. I was a guardian. What would have happened if I hadn't been in the dorm when Ricky's gun turned real and Curtis tried to…

That's where my reasoning fell apart. Curtis wouldn't have gone off the deep end if he hadn't seen me flying to save Athena, and if he hadn't confronted me and I hadn't denied it. Athena wouldn't have been in danger if she hadn't been on the dorm front lawn, chasing leaves that, in retrospect, sure were acting weird, because she wouldn't have been leaving my dorm if I hadn't been living on campus. Maybe Professor Tudderman wouldn't have had his seizure and tried to make it into NASCAR if I hadn't been there, and if I hadn't been part of investigating that Darbyville house.

"Any word on Professor Tudderman?" I asked, mostly to get my thoughts out of the spin cycle of guilt before I went too far in.

"What about him?" Kurt asked.

Gordon filled him in. The professor was still undergoing tests, but the last he heard he hadn't regained consciousness, or at least awareness of his surroundings. His eyes were open just enough to look really creepy, just about a quarter inch of white under his lids.

"Okay, there is something definitely causing trouble on your floor," he said, when Gordon finished.

Like, duh?

"I suppose blaming Communist spies isn't going to cut it," he continued, and turned to look up at the building again. "Somebody mean and nasty and up to no good is behind the whole problem. The experiment, the professor acting weird, whatever is going on in that house, and somebody tampering with that prop gun to make it real. Why did they just set it off now? Accident, you think?"

Both of them looked at me. Well, it made sense, since I had been there. Sort of.

I took a deep breath and plunged in, backing up to the beginning. Mum and Pop had taught me how to tell a story properly, after all, and I knew Kurt would interrupt and dig until he got all the details. I couldn't just say Curtis grabbed the gun and the wrong buttons must have gotten pushed when he was fighting with Ricky and the other guys on the floor. Kurt would want to know why Curtis wanted the gun.

I started with picking up the girls at the drama program and Stephanie coming to take them home after lunch, and Athena chasing the leaves. I put special emphasis on the leaves acting weird. Kurt's mouth flattened a little bit. He understood what I couldn't say in front of Gordon. He reached out and grabbed my arm when I told how I jumped out of the street and my foot got clipped by the speeding car's bumper. Yeah, he understood that I had flown. That was the only way I could have saved Athena. Then he just squeezed harder when I told how Curtis confronted me with being able to fly, and how I had to get away from him. Then he took Ricky's gun and there was the scuffle on the boy's side of the floor, then all the smoke. I stopped Curtis from kicking Ricky when he was down and we realized the gun was going to overload, so we got outside.

"So Curtis knew the gun was real," Gordon said, bending over to look at the gun. He nudged it with the toe of his boot.

"It's outside the field now," I whispered to Kurt. "The field's bigger."

He nodded, glancing up at the dorm with a look I had seen him reserve for really big repair job messes someone brought him. When it was very evident the person had been abusing the engine or machine. Kurt despised people who beat up on equipment that was only doing what it was built to do, or malfunctioning just like expected when something broke. He was kind of like a veterinarian who would call the police if he had evidence someone was abusing their dog. Unfortunately, Kurt couldn't call the police to report someone was abusing their lawn mower or toaster oven.

"Maybe Curtis is part of a Neo-Nazi plot to infiltrate the college and brainwash students," Kurt offered, when Gordon stopped muttering under his breath and scowling at the gun.

"Makes as much sense as anything else. But what do we do with him?" Gordon nodded at someone behind us, and I turned to see Officer Wong and Ricky walking over to join us.

"Where is he?" I had to ask.

Curtis was still where he had landed when I sent him sliding down the hall. Just the five of us went onto the floor, ostensibly to examine the scene of the crime. Alysyn stayed in the stairwell doorway, and most of our floor residents were either cramming into the stairwell or spilled onto our floor. Real good. Witnesses if something else happened. Officer Wong and Gordon went over to Curtis and examined him, while Kurt and Ricky and I went to Ricky's room, where the fight had begun. We had been warned not to touch or move anything, but Officer Wong didn't look too happy telling us that. It was all for procedure, he explained, in case he had to testify in court.

Court? This was going to go to court? Maybe campus court, dealing with infractions and such, but did it have to go higher?

I had the awful feeling Ricky and Curtis were going to be really unpopular soon. This whole mess could result in all the props and toy weapons and anything even remotely connected to geekdom and fandom being banned from campus.

Kurt whistled long and low when Ricky pushed his ajar door open all the way and we got our first look at the rack of supplies and tools on the far wall. Ricky and his roommate had stretched a pole from the end of their bunkbed to the top of the cabinet that served as closet and vanity. The entire wall over Ricky's desk had different sizes of baskets hanging from it, and free-hanging shelves. All sorts of gizmos for making models and modeling the carbon polymer and other materials. Gobs of wires and circuit boards, tiny lightbulbs, fiber optics, and enough tools and pieces and parts to make Kurt drool. It was Kurt's entire workshop in miniature.

"How come we haven't met before?" Kurt said. I swear he came close to putting an arm around Ricky's shoulders. "I'm introducing him to Ford."

"Good idea." I was still gnawing on the idea of court problems. It occurred to me that maybe we could build on the semi-joke of enemy spies causing trouble on campus, give it a serious turn. Maybe ask my folks to call Col. Hayward to give Ricky some protection. Maybe put some pressure in the right places and intimidate people into stopping their questions. I had no idea if that would work.

"I hate to say this," Officer Wong said, as he stepped into the doorway of Ricky's room. "I'm thinking drugs are involved."

"This was no hallucination," I had to say.

"Not the gun. Him." He hooked his thumb over his shoulder in the direction of Curtis. "Pupils are unevenly dilated, and Gordon says he's spazzing just like the professor."

"Does Curtis have a class with him?" Kurt asked.

Ricky didn't know. We kind of got pushed to the side as Officer Wong started his investigation in earnest. We couldn't really be officially involved, because we weren't part of the police force, but Ricky and I had to stay there, to answer any new questions that came up and offer any more details as we remembered them. Kurt had to leave. He would have left anyway, to go report to Angela and Ford.

Curtis's roommate, Mike, was a drama student. He had been in a couple dozen commercials for things like frozen snacks and skateboards and acne cream. He was kind of cool because he thought it was just funny instead of something to get all stuck-up about. He also proved what a good guy he was because he was right behind Alysyn on the landing in the stairwell, worried about Curtis. He let Officer Wong and Gordon into their dorm room and helped them search the room, looking for Curtis's class schedule, look through his textbooks, to find out if there was any connection between him and Professor Tudderman. The EMTs had arrived and finished tending to Curtis and got him downstairs on a gurney by the time the first cursory search finished. Nothing to indicate any connection between him and the professor. The next step was to question all the guys on the floor, to find anyone who linked Curtis and the professor. I had to leave then. My folks had arrived and there was no reason for me to be there. It was late enough in the day that they had Harry with them.

We huddled in my room, with the radio turned up loud and our voices low as we went over what had happened. Harry got over his excitement at being in a girls' dorm room and turned his curiosity to the gun. That had already been bagged and sent to the police station for evidence and examination. A three-foot-by-three-foot square of muddy field had been roped off with crime scene tape, until someone from a lab could come out and test for any inimical residue. Harry also thought that was pretty cool. Then Mum told me Chief Tanner and the administration wanted me and Ricky to get examined, to make sure we hadn't been exposed to anything while we were saving the dorm from imminent explosion.

"This is one of those times I wish I was totally invulnerable, like Superman or Captain America, or Wolverine, you know?"

"Yeah, but you'd have to tell people you couldn't get hurt by things like that, to avoid the doctor's exam." Pop settled down on the bed and wrapped his arm around me. Mum had been holding me the whole time on my other side. It felt really good. I was only eighteen, after all, and despite previous close calls, today had been kind of scary. The shakes didn't really settle in until I got away from all the questions and investigating and could totally open up with people who understood.

Sometimes Pop's logic could be really irritating. I stuck my tongue out and told him so, and we laughed. Then we got to work figuring out what was going on, and how to cover things up so the wrong outside people wouldn't poke too deeply into the normal, everyday, background weirdness of Neighborlee. Pop liked my idea of getting Col. Hayward involved, or at least notify him and ask for some advice. Mum liked Kurt's comment about getting Ford Longfellow involved in mentoring Ricky. He could probably avoid some disciplinary action, or at least reduce the potential for more weapons becoming real if his workshop was moved off-campus, and the administration knew he had some adult supervision.

"How did that gun become real?" Pop said, pacing. "That's the important question. It ties into whatever you sensed last night."

"Do you think our investigation triggered anything? Like maybe Curtis seeing me fly to protect Athena triggered something when I told him he didn't see what he saw?" I had to ask.

"Oh, honey, don't you go blaming yourself," Mum said.

Angela agreed, when we took dinner over to Divine's to have a conference. If we hesitated to do anything because we feared a negative reaction from potential enemies, we would never get anything done, make no progress in defending our home.

She was back to normal, but she wasn't willing to go into any detail over the cryptic things she had said while she was somewhat dazed that morning. Parr for the course. We discussed our battle strategy for finding out everything we could about the two professors experimenting on the freshman class, backtracking the plan from the moment it was a twinkle in their nearsighted eyes. Pop had talked Chief Tanner into keeping us updated on the examinations of Curtis and Professor Tudderman. The tradeoff was that Ricky and I had to submit to an exam ourselves. The college administration wanted it, and different authorities involved in the investigation, including the insurance company.

Other than some completely understandable and expected signs of stress in both Ricky and me, the physical revealed nothing. That was a relief, actually. No insights into being a semi-pseudo-superhero. Nothing anyone could use against me in the future, when more weird things happened, and someone besides Curtis saw something they shouldn't have.

The authorities interviewed Professor Winghast, the other half of the team conducting the experiment. We couldn't tell anyone about the house in Darbyville, and somehow Gordon and the other volunteers managed not to mention to their bosses that we had asked them to keep an eye on the activities of the twosome. Winghast didn't know anything about his fellow professor's activities and convinced the investigative committee that if drugs were involved, he didn't know anything about it. More in-depth searches revealed nothing to tie either professor to Curtis.

He and Tudderman stayed in the hospital for three days, and they both had gaps in their memories. Professor Tudderman's memory gap started the day before, when he drove home at the end of the school day. Curtis's gap started just before lunch. So I didn't have to worry about him trying to convince other people that I could fly, or lying in wait for me to mess up.

Chapter Ten

Things quieted down after that. Kurt, Felicity and I did flying checks of the dorm at least once a week. The energy was still there, but it retreated. Maybe that was due to about twenty-some freshmen whose parents relocated them, either into another dormitory or off-campus housing, or out of college. Eleven were on our floor alone. If the experiment was to observe us, or the energy was tied into the psycho-social aspects of our floor, then maybe the balance had been disrupted, or the power flow had been changed.

We expected an outbreak when Halloween arrived, based on our own experience with Halloween weirdness. That wasn't anything tied in with the time of the year or the fabled "thinning of the walls between Earth and the Otherworld." From our experience, and the things Angela had taught us, the power of belief simply made weird things more possible. The people of Neighborlee believed, even if mostly subconsciously, that strange things would happen at certain times of the year. Because we believed it would happen, the power of our belief, down through history, made it more possible, gave more energy to the weird and wonderful. Those bizarre and freaky and amusing events were recorded in public memory and sometimes in the town history records, which just bolstered belief, which just made more oddness possible. Vicious cycle.

So we were on the alert in the week leading up to Halloween, primed with the strength of our belief, and our fantastic record as guardians, that whatever happened it would turn out just fine. If anything happened, Neighborlee would be safe. Maybe even entertained.

The energy level around the third floor of our dorm increased. Kurt said the humming rose in pitch, the energy vibrating faster. We were positive something was going to happen. I recruited my Star Trek club friends to be on the alert. We flew patrol on Halloween after trick-or-treating ended and all the silly parties and the haunted house in the theater building had closed down. The sense of building energy had dropped so far that at first Kurt thought we had gone to the wrong building. Excuse me, but I knew my dorm, from all angles.

The question was whether something that happened on Halloween drained away that energy, or the energy had been building up to accomplish something specific, and that goal had been accomplished. We couldn't figure out the answer. We didn't have enough information to even start finding an answer. For all we knew, the energy was just being stored in our dorm, to be used somewhere else. Kind of a blow to the ego, finding out we weren't a target but just a battery. If that was what happened. We wouldn't know until we could look at the whole mess in the rearview mirror.

It gave us some ideas, though.

If the threat was against Neighborlee, and all the creative kids, the geeks and freaks, had been gathered into one floor in one dorm, maybe the power of belief, the unique energy of our group of freshmen, was the target? Or maybe we were the ammunition?

Despite knowing Mercedes was technically a spy for the enemy, we all really liked her. She was easy to talk to, even knowing she was a psych and counseling major, and she had been taking training to be easy to talk to. I trusted my instincts, and they said Mercedes was there for us. Maybe the problem with Curtis and Ricky's gun and Professor Tudderman had made her question the whole reason for her RA assignment. She cared. Maybe there was an undercoat of guilt, but we knew she cared.

She was also fun. She gave out prizes every week at our floor meetings. We gathered on the stairs and in the doorway of the stairwell, so we could all be together in one place, with incredible acoustics, where we could all see her. The prizes were usually small, usually inexpensive, like a package of Oreos or a couple candy bars, or a coupon to the snack bar, or pencils with funny erasers. Mostly there wasn't any real contest involved, but just a chance to be silly and hand out certificates for things like "most hours playing their music loud enough to damage everyone's ear drums without their neighbors killing them," or "most times mopping up after people who left the bathtub filling and walked away and forgot about it," or "most generous with care packages from home." That sort of thing. Official contests included decorating our doors, and clue hunts, where she would tuck folded index cards into tight places up and down the halls. We had to find as many as we could to solve a riddle or spell out secret words.

Mercedes was big on holidays. Every holiday imaginable, official school-sanctioned holidays and government holidays and observations of every possible spiritual and religious belief of the people on our floor. If that wasn't proof that we had been thoroughly analyzed, the fact she knew about our traditions growing up should have convinced the most skeptical. It was kind of fun. And just to prove how oblivious college freshmen were, none of us wondered until later where she got the money to buy the decorations and prizes, and how she even had the time she spent on all that.

So when Mercedes brought out the dream box the Monday after Thanksgiving, when we were all settling in for the big push with term papers and studying for finals, nobody really thought about it. Other than that it was another fun, slightly nerdy, slightly sentimental floor activity.

Looking back, I know I should have caught on sooner to what was going on. Maybe if Mercedes had called it the wishing box instead of the dream box, the light bulb would have lit. As in a flashing danger sign.

The gist of the dream box was to help us focus as we headed into the final stretch of the semester. We were all encouraged to write out on a piece of paper what we wanted to do with our lives, what we wanted to change about ourselves, big dreams for summer and Christmas break, things we wanted to explore, our careers, our love lives, whatever we had discovered about ourselves during our first semester of college. We could write as many notes as we wanted to fate or destiny or whatever we believed in, and put them in the box. She also encouraged us to just put our hands on the box and think about our dreams and hopes and goals. It was a wooden box, so it could stand up to a lot of touching and leaning.

The box had no visible lid, no hinge that we could see when Mercedes brought it out at the meeting that Monday night and showed it to us. I just assumed the top lifted off like those covers for square tissue boxes that the little old ladies made for Christmas craft fairs. Other than the slot in the top for putting our papers in, there was no visible way to get into the box.

First rule of objects with even just a hint of magical abilities: never assume anything. Usually the first three letters of that verb will kick, hard and painfully.

Mercedes had decorated the bench that ran along the wall of the landing at the top of the stairs, and set the box right in the middle of all that tinsel and poinsettia blossoms and brick printed wrapping paper. She didn't fasten it down, like with a chain, and she didn't put any kind of warnings around it, such as "Do not move on pain of death, dismemberment, or being expelled." Which, thinking about it, was really smart. Nothing like telling someone what not to do to make them want to do it, especially when they never thought about doing it until someone told them not to. I really expected to come back from classes the next day and find the decorations trashed and maybe even the box gone. We had some real jerks on the second and first floors. They made it their mission to mock what other floors were doing, and mess up what other floors had, just because they weren't included. It didn't matter if it wasn't something they wanted to do, the fact they weren't included meant no one else could enjoy it.

The continuing pristine condition of the dream box and the decorations around it should have been my next clue. In my defense, it was a very busy week, and I never really looked at the bench and box when I passed, other than to see everything was just the way Mercedes had left it. Usually I was climbing the stairs with others on the floor, comparing the progress of our term papers or griping about how the quality of cafeteria food was steadily going downhill. Others griped about the weather, which was incredibly wet and white. I never griped about the weather because I had grown up with the seesaw of the lake effect. Griping just wasted energy. We have a saying in Northeast Ohio: "Don't like the weather? Wait five minutes—it'll change."

That first weekend after Thanksgiving, we were essentially snowed in. Nobody cared about the football or basketball games or the movies in the Student Center. We scurried from the cafeteria to our dorms on Friday night and hunkered down. That had the effect of getting about ninety percent of the dorm's residents in one place at one time, which usually didn't happen until between the hours of 1 and 5 a.m. The big difference was that everyone was conscious and when we weren't trying to study and polish up papers, we were griping about the snow. So in some generalized ways, we had a lot of young minds focused in specific areas.

The next time someone advocates the benefits and wonders of a collective consciousness and a group mind, do me a favor and punch their lights out. Repeatedly. Until they change their minds.

All that energy. All that anxiety. All that griping. All gathered together under one roof. With the geeks and freaks and creative types at the top of the heap. Remember the *ka-whoosh* explosion out of the old firehouse in the first Ghostbusters movie? Not quite like that, because we didn't have the fireworks and sound effects until the end of the struggle. However, a plug had been pulled out and something was leaking. Maybe it was a pinhole at first, but the problem progressed geometrically as people noticed and focused their attention on it.

It started with Robbie the Robot. Yeah, the dome-headed robot with the twirly things on the sides of its head, from *Forbidden Planet.* Kind of a dark metallic, skinny version of the Michelin Man. He belonged to Nettie, who lived two doors down from me and Clarice. Her full name was Antoinette. She was small enough to dress as a Jawa for our dorm Halloween party, and she even went trick-or-treating on a dare. She had just about fallen over herself on move-in day at the start of the year, when she walked past our door and saw us decorating. On our ceiling we had printouts of nebulae and galaxies. We hung models of spaceships from different SF universes on threads from the ceiling panels. She had nearly burst into tears when she found out that not only were we fellow geeks, but we belonged to a Star Trek club and she could come with us to the next meeting.

Nettie had been taunted by her family and her class at school for her love of all things fantasy and SF. They had her convinced there was something wrong with her, and that when she got out into the "real world," whatever that was, she would discover that hardly anyone cared about "that weird stuff." Yeah? Then how come the SF and fantasy section at the bookstore was just as big, if not bigger, than the romance section or the mystery section or the finance section? Need I say more?

The funny thing was that her brothers always gave her SF and fantasy T-shirts and movies and toys, like Robbie, for her birthday and Christmas. They thought they were teasing her, but she loved it. She brought Robbie and a light saber and a gun from the Buck Rogers TV series and a few posters with her to college. Most likely to keep them from being confiscated and tossed by her interfering family, while she was away. Robbie stood eighteen inches high. He came in for a lot of admiration and envy.

Robbie was walking down the hall of our dorm when I came back from lunch Saturday. Everybody else was lingering in the cafeteria because nobody wanted to make the ten-minute trudge through gale force winds that were blowing perfectly horizontal at about thirty miles per hour, according to the Weather Channel. I came back early because Nettie was sick and her roommate, Rhonda, another geek, asked us to look out for her while she went home for the weekend. Nettie was sick enough she didn't even try to get up to go get something to eat. Clarice brought her breakfast, so it was my turn to bring her lunch.

I nearly dropped the bag with Nettie's toasted cheese and the cardboard tub of chicken noodle soup when I saw Robbie. While yes, he could walk, Nettie didn't put batteries in him. He was too old and too precious to her to risk breakage. She kept him on a stand on the back corner of her desk, where he was braced on two sides by wall. His dome head lights were flashing and the knobby things out the side of his head were turning. I didn't know they could do that. He took steps with a *grind-squeak-crunch* that had to be a sound effect, because it made him sound like he was about seven feet tall and weighed about a ton, and his joints needed oil.

"Nettie," Robbie said, pausing when I was about five feet away. He tipped back from his knees, and while he didn't have a face inside that dome, I got that chill down my back with the certainty he was looking at me. Maybe even glaring at me. "Needs."

"You're not supposed to talk."

Well, duh, like telling him that would do any good?

"Doctor," Robbie said. The lights got brighter, the twirly things spun faster, and he sort of tipped back at a bigger angle from his knees, to really look up at me. "Nettie. Needs. Doctor."

I did what any normal college freshman would do when faced with a toy from a classic science fiction movie that had suddenly come to life.

Correction: I did what any normal college freshman would do who had been raised in Neighborlee, the weirdness capital of the United States, when faced with a toy from a classic science fiction movie that had suddenly come to life.

I went to check on Nettie. Granted, I did nearly drop her lunch, but I didn't scream and toss it at Robbie. I also didn't try to kick him through the goal posts of the door to the stairwell. For all I know, I probably would have broken my foot, and he might have tried to shoot me with his laser beams, or grab my foot with his pincers.

The door was ajar. The room stank with that sick sweat smell, salt and vomit and pee. Nettie lay twisted in her bed, all her covers kicked off, shivering and drenched in sweat. I kicked aside three ginger ale cans when I went to her bed. Like I sometimes did when I teetered on the edge of panic, I focused on them for a few seconds instead of Nettie. Those cans shouldn't have been there because first, all the ginger ale in the pop machine in the lobby was gone. I knew that because I went to get some for Nettie, to help settle her stomach. Also, the pop machine stocked Cotton Club, and these cans were Canada Dry.

The only ginger ale in the whole dorm was the stash of Canada Dry belonging to Susan Hillary, who had already been voted most likely to become Miss Havisham. That's a reference to Dickens. The girl was a drama major and bored everyone within the first week of school, talking about the modeling she had done, the commercials she had been in, and how she had been a dancer in high school. Really? With those size twenty hips and flat feet?

She constantly tipped her head to the right and looked at people from her half-closed eyes and sneered at whatever other people said. Mostly because they didn't agree with what she considered valuable. She knew better, she knew the truth, and anyone who disagreed with her was only expressing their *opinions* while she knew *facts*.

Susan made it known that she had three twelve-packs of ginger ale in her room. In a spirit of camaraderie due to the blizzard conditions, she would gladly sell her precious commodity for a fair and reasonable price.

Nobody wanted to go near her to even ask what that fair and reasonable price was. Mercedes asked her to prove she was a decent human being and let Nettie have some ginger ale, and she offered to pay ten cents more than what it would cost in the pop machine. Of course, Queen Susan said no. Gee, maybe she was offended by the "decent human being" remark?

Anyway, I kicked aside those ginger ale cans that certainly

didn't belong there. I felt the heat radiating off Nettie when my hand was at least five inches away from her face. A little puddle of watery vomit lay on the mattress next to her. Not that I was a forensic scientist, but it looked like she had only managed to get down the orange juice and a little of the Cream of Wheat Clarice brought her for breakfast. She had also peed herself.

Most of what I knew of first aid came from books, but some of them were history or war novels. I had also seen every episode of *M*A*S*H* at least three times. My first thought was to try to lower her temperature. I picked her up. She was so small to begin with, but now she seemed to have wasted away just since Clarice and I checked with her after breakfast.

"Nettie. Need. Doctor," Robbie said from next to me. I nearly did kick him aside this time, just because he was in my way as I headed for the door.

"Robbie, get Alysyn or Mercedes."

I didn't wait to see if he obeyed me. What made me think he could even hear me, or that he was programmed to obey? I stepped over him and hurried down the hall to the bathroom with Nettie burning up in my arms. When I slammed through the swinging door, I had my plan pretty clear in my head. First, put her in a lukewarm tub, because cold water would be too much of a shock. Get her washed up, get her cooled down, then dry her off and haul her downstairs. Either settle her in Alysyn's apartment to wait for a doctor to show up, or hope Alysyn's car would start and we could get out through the snow to get to the hospital. Why didn't Neighborlee have its own hospital? Would the campus health center be able to handle Nettie?

She was small enough to cradle on my lap while I got the water running. It was dang cold, and so was the ceramic of the tub. When the water was just a little warmer than the air, but a lot cooler than Nettie's skin, I put in the stopper and then I put her in. Then I finally thought about what I would do once she was cooled down and cleaned up. Duh. I certainly couldn't leave her in the tub while I went back to her room for towels and clean clothes. Not very clear thinking. What kind of a semi-pseudo-superhero was I?

"Nettie. Need. Doctor."

If I didn't have to hold her up, I would have tried to drop-kick Robbie. Of course, I could have used my telekinesis to shove him away, but again, duh, why wasn't I using it on her?

"Robbie, get Nettie's quilt."

Then I saw towels that had been left to hang and dry in the bathroom, over the shower curtain rods and the sides of the toilet stalls. Hopefully they were dry enough to help Nettie. I mentally snagged a couple washcloths. Glory hallelujah, someone had left a bottle of herbal shower gel. The smell alone would help Nettie. Just getting her clean would certainly help me. Not that I had a weak stomach, but her aroma made me feel a little queasy. As I held her up with my mind and got to work opening up the gel and sopping a washcloth, I glanced around.

Robbie was gone. He had heard me? He obeyed me?

That chill washing over me had nothing to do with the cold tile floor and the cooler air.

I had Nettie stripped down and washed up, with the dirty water draining out of the tub, and was reaching for the first borrowed towel when I heard Robbie come back, *squeak-grind-crunch*. I wrapped a towel around her and lifted her out, to put her on three more towels on the floor, then turned to look for him. Alysyn was right behind him, her eyes big, staring at the robot and the queen-size quilt he dragged behind him with both hands, walking backward.

"Nettie needs a doctor. I was trying to get her temperature down," I said, and yes, I was babbling.

Alysyn gave me an incredible look of relief, like she was about to burst into tears, then took a couple wide steps around Robbie and came to kneel next to Nettie. We got her dried off quick and wrapped her in her quilt, and took her back to her room. Alysyn explained that she had come upstairs to check on Nettie, just in time to see Robbie coming out of her room with the quilt. He looked right at her and repeated himself. Those seemed to be the only words he knew. When she saw Nettie's room was empty, she took her sanity in her hands and followed Robbie.

"How did you get him to do that?" she asked as we finished getting Nettie dressed in fresh pajamas, then her robe, then thick socks and slippers, then wrapped her quilt around her again.

"I didn't. He was coming down the hall when I got back with her lunch."

"This is that mess with Curtis and Ricky's gun, all over again," she muttered. "Most of the time, I am so glad I live in Neighborlee, but times like this..." She shook her head, and stepped back as I gathered up Nettie.

"Neighborlee takes care of its own." I nearly finished on a screech, as I turned and there was Robbie, standing in the doorway. "Yes, Nettie needs a doctor. Go back to—" I couldn't exactly tell him to go back to bed. "Go back to your place on the desk, and wait for us to bring her back. Okay? We'll take care of Nettie. You did good, Robbie." I shuddered a little and swallowed down the urge to say, "Good robot."

Well, he was kind of like a guard dog, right?

The snow was still blowing sideways. We couldn't see the dorm on the left of us, or even across the street, when we got downstairs and looked out the big picture windows that took up two walls of the dorm lounge. It looked like everyone was stranded in the cafeteria for now. I had never been in the dorm when it was so quiet during the day. Alysyn had me take Nettie into her apartment. We got her settled on the sofa and Alysyn had me go get her thermometer while she called the health center. She was still on the phone, answering questions, when I came back. I put the thermometer in Nettie's mouth, and felt a little better when she closed her mouth over it. That meant she was aware enough to respond. Not like she was in a fever-induced coma or anything.

Another chill washed over me, when the plot of a half-dozen SF movies and books flashed through my mind. Maybe Robbie had come to life because he was draining the life and awareness out of Nettie? Or had her consciousness transferred into Robbie?

What kind of hallucinogens had they put in our lunch?

"Dr. Sloane is getting hold of Dr. Prescott, who has a snowmobile, and he's going to come over here to take care of Nettie," Alysyn told me, once she hung up. She took the thermometer out of Nettie's mouth.

"Bad?" I said, when she frowned at it.

"Not as bad as I feared. Lowering her temperature was a good idea." She shook the thermometer to get the mercury down, then put it on the coffee table. "What are we going to do about..." Alysyn pointed up. "How did that even happen?"

"Maybe just because Nettie needed him."

"If things happened in Neighborlee just because they were

needed, a lot of things wouldn't happen here at all. Not that that makes much sense, but you know what I mean." She tried to smile.

"Yeah, I know." I immediately thought of all the work that Kurt, Felicity and I had to do, patrolling and picking up the messes when odd things happened, just so people wouldn't freak out more than they already did, when Neighborlee took care of its own.

Right then, I wondered if I had studied myself into brain cramps or something. The commonsense thing to do when something really bizarre happened, that couldn't be explained away by mistaken identity or optical illusions or other things, was to call Angela. Alysyn got that "well, duh," exasperated look when I asked if I could use her phone to call Divine's Emporium.

"You'd think after all these years, I'd know to do that, myself," she said, when I got off the phone. "What are we supposed to do?"

"She's coming over with some tea for Nettie. We're supposed to think about anything weird, or maybe more weird than usual, that has happened lately. And ask everybody else in the dorm if they've seen anything, felt anything."

"It's nearly finals time and we're snowbound." Alysyn sighed as she got up and crossed her living room to the kitchen nook. "It sounds like the plot for a horror movie."

I agreed. Somehow, I had never imagined that the monster from the other dimension would try to come through during a blizzard, or that he or it or they would start their attack by animating a toy robot.

Angela arrived before Dr. Sloane did, and she came with Kurt in his truck. Of course, I should have realized that if anyone could persuade a truck to get through the blizzard conditions, it would be Kurt. Maybe there was something in the general atmosphere of the dorm that interfered with my common sense.

The scary part of that idea was that when I mentioned it, Angela took it seriously. That was later, once the dust settled and we could talk in relative security and privacy at Divine's.

Angela bustled into Alysyn's apartment with a bag full of supplies and directed me with a tip of her head to go with Kurt. Actually, I had to lead Kurt upstairs. He wanted to see Robbie for himself. His frown got fiercer with concentration as I told him what had happened. The lines around his mouth and eyes and creasing his forehead grew deeper and darker as we climbed. On the landing between second and third floor, he stopped and dug his fists into his hips and his head tilted a little to one side as he stared up to the landing for my floor.

"What is that?" he finally said.

"What's what?"

"That box."

"What do you see?" I shrugged when Kurt glared at me. I hurried to explain the dream box idea, which Mercedes had put out to help us focus as we geared up for the end of the year. Then it hit me. "You can feel energy, bad guy energy, coming out of it? Or going into it?" I caught my breath and clutched at his arm, which I usually didn't do because honestly, it was such a moronic, melodramatic gesture. Too-stupid-to-live twits in horror movies clutched at the hero's arm. "It's sucking energy out of Nettie?"

"I don't know. It's a vibration or hum or whatever, at a pitch I've never really felt before. The really freaky thing is I can see these lines going into it, or coming out, not sure yet. Just three coming from the left and two coming from the right." Kurt took a deep breath and headed up the steps. "I've got the awful feeling one of those lines is going to go straight to the robot."

Kurt was right. Even worse, though, he said he saw a line going from Robbie, down through the floor. From the angle he indicated with his hand, it was a good bet it connected Robbie and Nettie.

We found Robbie in Nettie's room, trying to climb up from her desk chair, onto the desk. Maybe it had been easier getting down from the desk to the chair and then to the floor, to help Nettie. Robbie didn't have the flexibility or length of reach to grab onto something and swing himself up, to go back to his stand in the corner where Nettie kept him. We stood there for a few seconds, watching, and I felt kind of sorry for the creepy little thing.

"Robbie." I started to step into the room, and Kurt stopped me. "Robbie, the doctor is coming for Nettie. She's going to be all right."

I had to say it twice more, then he just stopped, hanging there on the handle of the desk drawer for a couple seconds. Kurt let out a yelp and dove into the room, but he wasn't able to get there in time to catch Robbie as his pincer hands opened up and let go and he fell. Fortunately, nothing broke.

Kurt sat down and opened up Robbie right away. He confessed later he was half-afraid he would find all sorts of gears and gizmos and a whole bunch of melted stuff inside, just like the police lab and the bomb squad found inside Ricky's half-finished space gun. Fortunately for us, there seemed to be nothing inside Robbie the Robot that didn't belong there. In fact, there was less. No batteries. No visible sign of a power source. When Kurt looked up the specs for that highly valuable collectible toy, he learned that particular model did light up and move, but it didn't have sound effects. No crunching footsteps or creaking joints, and no voice synthesizer.

As if that wasn't creepy enough, as soon as I told Robbie Nettie would be all right and he turned off, Kurt said the visible line of energy going from the toy to Nettie died away. By the time it hit the floor, the energy linking the dream box to Robbie had faded too.

We walked down the hall, and Kurt indicated which rooms the other threads of energy led to. Lucky me, I would be responsible for getting into those rooms and talking with the girls, to find out what toys or props or other objects they had in there that could be imbued with possibly malevolent energy. Then we went into the boys' side of the dorm, and Kurt showed me which rooms and occupants I needed to investigate.

"Huh," Kurt said, as we stepped back into the stairwell. He went down on one knee and leaned in close, studying the box. With the movement of his right hand, I guessed he was tracing, maybe trying to touch the lines of energy that he could see.

Right then, I lost my envy for Kurt's ability to sense energy. It looked kind of strange, even knowing what he was doing. What did it look like for someone who didn't know Kurt's particular semi-pseudo-superhero powers?

"What's it doing?" I asked, as a door banged open downstairs, what sounded like the first floor. My guess was that some brave ones had made it back from lunch.

"A couple lines are thickening, getting brighter." He stepped back, against the railing side of the landing that looked down on the stairwell. Stomping, splattering footsteps soon grew louder. Kurt kept his back to the stairs as the people returning from lunch climbed. "One guy and two girls," he whispered, and gestured at the lines of energy that I couldn't see.

I played with the idea of lifting him, mentally, just enough to make him panic. Then I tossed that idea aside, because he would just hijack my telekinetic power and use it against me.

Sure enough, the first people to reach the top of the stairs included one guy and two girls from the rooms the energy threads led to, along with about ten other people from our floor. In the kind of weather we were having, common sense said to travel in packs. At the very least, large numbers provided some small wind break and shared body heat, and some safety if sudden white-out conditions hit. We got some weird looks, and I was scrambling to come up with an explanation for why this stranger—a guy, no less, who obviously was too old to be in the freshman dormitory—was standing on the landing. Then a couple guys from town recognized Kurt, and he came up with the excuse that he had come to check some of Ricky's manuals that he hadn't taken over to Ford Longfellow's workshop yet.

Chapter Eleven

Susan trudged up the stairs just about the time Kurt was coming back into the stairwell with the manuals. She looked him over, with that sly little smile that finally made something click. Now I knew why I disliked her from the moment we met. She reminded me of Sylvia Grandstone. The same assessing, judgmental look. The same rise of pheromones when a handsome guy showed up, like she was getting ready to go on the hunt. I wanted to grab her shoulders, shake her hard, and shove her down the hallway, with a warning not to drool on my friend who was like a brother. I knew better than to hint I knew Kurt, though. She was the type who would chase him down just to irritate me.

Yeah, no love lost between us. I think my crime was that I didn't care about the things she valued, like hair and makeup, the *Wall Street Journal* and *Vogue*.

Kurt wrinkled up his face and crossed his eyes at Susan's back, once she headed down the hall. The guys with him, who wanted to talk about his sled runner design and the possibility of adapting it to motorcycles, laughed. No love lost between them and Susan, either. They didn't pass her muster, because they were the geeks and freaks and creative types.

We stood in the stairwell, chatting a few seconds longer. I was mentally urging the guys to get out of there and get back to their warm rooms so Kurt and I could try to examine the dream box.

A horrific scream erupted from the girls' side of the dorm. Susan staggered out into the hall and pointed dramatically at her door, demanding to know who had done it. Who was the villain? Who was the terrorist?

"It" turned out to be a chunk about eighteen inches high and about six inches wide, cut through her door. From the dark substance edging the hole, my guess was that it had been burned. Come to think of it, I had smelled something that reminded me of burned wood and carpenter's glue. I was familiar with it because my folks would have bonfires in our back yard, burning up broken wood scavenged from renovations in our old farmhouse, including old doors. The doors in the dormitory were hollow core, meaning they weren't solid wood but layers of laminate. Lots of glue.

Kurt came down the hall when I gestured for him. As a side note: no thread of energy went into Susan's room. Remember what I said earlier about the power of belief? It tied into dreams and imagination. The only time Susan used her imagination was to come up with new and creative ways to mock those who didn't conform to her standards. The only dreams she had were of becoming a high-power lawyer and wearing the latest fashions. Oh, yeah, and convincing everyone that she was still the good dancer she had been in high school. She claimed she had fallen during a tricky dance move, hurt her ankle, and was still getting her strength back. Losing about sixty pounds gained while on her back for the summer wouldn't hurt and would make her story more believable.

Back to Susan and the hole in her door. Kurt came down the hall and got down on one knee and rubbed at the black edges of the door. I was right. Burned. The black was char. He estimated something very hot, very intense, and very focused. It could only come from a laser beam of a strength not available on our college campus. Maybe some experimental lab at NASA Glenn Research Center, or Cleveland State, or the University of Akron.

"Robbie," Kurt whispered.

Before I could even react, Susan shoved her door open and gestured across the floor at the mini-fridge tucked up under the window. It hung open. It was also empty. A trail of ginger ale cans marked the path between door and fridge.

Yeah, Robbie had burned his way into Susan's room. After all, Nettie needed ginger ale for her stomach, and the dehydration from all that sweating she had been doing.

I beckoned for Kurt to come with me, and we hurried down the hall to the stairwell, while my dormmates showed no sympathy for Susan, the ginger ale hoarder. No way was I confessing I had found ginger ale cans in Nettie's room. I made a mental note to get in there and clean things up before her roommate came back.

"Is Robbie supposed to have a laser?" Kurt muttered as we hurried down the stairs.

"We'll have to watch the movie again and see."

When we got downstairs, we found Dr. Sloane had arrived. Nettie was awake, sipping the tea Angela had made. We waited in the doorway of Alysyn's apartment until Angela could step away from the sofa. Then we took her to the hallway behind the lounge and the cluster of pop and snack machines, to the back door. It had to be the coldest place in the entire dorm, but that guaranteed no one would come there and interrupt us while we talked.

We talked fast. Comparing when different things happened, upstairs and downstairs, we decided that Robbie returning to a normal toy and Nettie waking up weren't connected. Angela had got some tea into her long before Dr. Sloane showed up, so Nettie being awake again had nothing to do with the connection between her and Robbie dying. Kurt didn't watch closely enough to tell if the connection broke from Robbie's end before the thread between him and Nettie died. He could confirm that the line of energy between Robbie and the box died after the link between him and Nettie. But what good did that do us?

"We need to sever the link between that box and the other students on your floor." Angela chuckled. "Sometimes the best way to build a plan is to state the obvious and work up from there."

"Obvious" seemed to be a good place to start. Maybe people weren't conscious of what was happening. If we pointed out something weird about the box, that might loosen the bonds or interfere with the connection. The power of belief and all that. Some of Mum and Pop's friends who wrote science fiction and fantasy postulated that the ancient gods' power wasn't born into them, but was generated by the belief of their followers. When devotees died out and worship became rote instead of an integral part of their lives and souls, then the ancient gods weakened and were overthrown by other gods whose followers still believed strongly in them.

Theory: if we could get modern college students to consider the possibility of something weird going on with the dream box, maybe their logical minds and the materialism of modern life would get in the way. They would pull back from the connection that powered the box.

"Problem," I said. "Everybody with a link to the box is a geek. Tell them there's power in the box, that'd be like handing Frodo's ring to everyone in the dorm."

"Which could be exactly what the enemy wants," Angela murmured. "The buildup of energy could be luring people in. The next step is to make them aware, make them active believers. While they're having fun, he or she or they are draining them dry."

"Is that what made Nettie sick?"

"Oh, no, she just had a severe case of the flu, thank goodness."

"Had?" Kurt said. "From what Lanie said, she was pretty bad just a little while ago. Is she cured now?"

"The crisis passed, perhaps brought on by making the toy act as her voice. She wanted help so very badly, and in her fever dreams, she spoke through it. No, your friend is going to be fine, and I wouldn't be surprised if she doesn't remember a single thing from the moment the connection began."

"So..." I wanted to close my eyes and put my hands over my ears and just block out everything while I tried to coax the nebulous thought up out of the swirling darkness at the back of my head.

Maybe they put something weird in our chili at lunchtime? Considering how people thought it was okay to experiment on the student body, I wouldn't have been surprised to learn they had been dosing us with all sorts of medicines to prevent the flu or give us extra alertness for final exams or some other justification. That would explain the decline in quality of food since Thanksgiving.

Angela and Kurt waited. Thank goodness we were all used to each other coming up with ideas that needed some fleshing out, and we all trusted each other enough to fix what didn't make sense at the beginning.

"So maybe when the link with the box breaks, everything goes back to normal? Or people at least don't remember something weird happened?" I finally said. That wasn't quite what I had at the back of my mind, but it was close enough for horseshoes and global thermonuclear war.

"Easier to break the box than the link, I'm thinking," Kurt said.

"Fine, you do it," I said. "If Mercedes catches me doing it, I'm dead meat. It's her box. It might even be an antique or something."

"Hmm, yes, and that's a factor we hadn't considered yet," Angela said. "There could be a link between her and the box, and if it is of long duration, she might be hurt."

Ugh. Hadn't thought of that.

We went upstairs with a vague plan, to be refined as we went along. Angela went to talk with Mercedes and find out the history of the box. Kurt went down the hall to talk to the guys who had threads of energy going to their rooms, while I went to get the girls. Funny thing: Curtis and Ricky's rooms *weren't* marked by the threads coming from the box. I would have expected them to be at the top of the list, since they were influenced at the start of the year. Later, we theorized they had been immunized by the blowup earlier in the fall. Or, the box and its energy had a completely different source from whatever made Curtis go a little crazy and turned Ricky's raygun real. Maybe a different enemy. Maybe someone else entirely was taking advantage of whatever power was generated by all the creative types clustered on one floor.

Not really a comforting theory, but Angela had warned us before, it was foolish to believe we had only one enemy, or that multiple enemies would take turns and attack one at a time. While the forces of evil had just as much trouble cooperating and sharing as the forces that considered themselves good, sometimes they pulled themselves out of the quagmire of selfishness and the quest for utter domination to work together.

While Angela talked with Mercedes, Kurt and I gathered the unwitting power sources in the stairwell.

I introduced him as a friend from town who sometimes worked with the college. It was the truth, but we left everyone to fill in the blanks with their own imaginations regarding just what Kurt did for the college.

"You've been chosen to participate in a little experiment," Kurt said. "The physics department is working with the psychology people to bridge the barrier between the mind and a bunch of stuff that would make the CIA drool, y'know?" He winked. "Your RA, Mercedes, is a psych major, and she's been taking notes on how you react to the ideas she gives you, on her teacher's orders."

Right then, I was wishing we had just blown the whistle on the whole stupid psycho-social experiment at the start of the year. Hindsight was always a lot clearer, right?

"We're doing some experiments with focusing mind power. You guys have been chosen for one of the test groups. We're not going to tell you if you're the control group or the ones who've been tampered with."

"Like how?" Rodney Shipton blurted, his eyes brightening.

Okay, he was going to be a problem. I could see him gladly picking up the ring of power and putting it on, even after watching all three Lord of the Rings movies and even cheering when Gollum went into the lava in Mount Doom. His roommate, Yuri, had the same look in his eyes, along with Rodney's twin sister, Rita, and her roommate, Colby Ashton.

I got that shivery feeling down my back as I made a connection among the four of them. What was it about them that made the alarms softly wail in the back of my head?

"The physics department has installed collectors and amplifiers in several buildings throughout the campus. Not going to tell you where." Kurt's words slowed as he frowned at me.

Whatever I was feeling, he was either picking up on it, or it showed on my face. I shook my head slightly and took a step back from the little group in the stairwell. We were all starting to shiver a little, but my shivers weren't entirely from the chill air.

"Mental energy collectors and amplifiers," he said, picking up the pace again. "You've been focusing on the dream box all week, right? That's been training you."

"How come other floors and other dorms don't have the box?" Yuri took a step back too, and crossed his arms, a typical *You're yanking my chain* pose.

"They don't have boxes, but who says their dorm leaders haven't done other focus experiments on them?" Kurt gestured at the box. "What I want you to do is focus on the box and think about something in your room that's part of the most incredible dream of your life. Something magic, something out of this world, that you would just about sell your soul to make it come true. Know what I mean?" He bared his teeth at me in a "so sue me" grin when I glared at his choice of words.

That was the problem when dealing with hopeful invaders from other dimensions. If they could get someone to sell their souls, thus giving them permanent rights of access into our world, they would. The language they used and the terms they employed were so convoluted and confusing, they would make the trickiest lawyer in our world look like a two-year-old who couldn't figure out how to make Jack come out of the box.

"Okay." Colby glanced at the other kids in the stairwell with us, not just the members of her foursome. "So we just think about a great wish, and focus on the box?"

How come I couldn't remember what tied them together? It

was important, I knew.

"Pretty much," Kurt said.

"How long?"

"Until it starts glowing and goes through the roof," I muttered.

Kurt snorted and shook his head. Most of the others laughed. A couple looked around the stairwell, probably looking for the amplifiers and collectors Kurt had mentioned. It was a decent lie or cover story. Blame something scientific and material, to take their minds off the weirdness quotient involved.

From the corner of my eye, I saw Angela come out of Mercedes' room. They went down the hall together to Nettie's room. I tipped my head, gesturing down the hall, and caught Kurt's gaze. He nodded, and I went to join Angela and Mercedes.

Robbie was back in his corner where Kurt had put him. Angela stood with her arms crossed, frowning at the toy while Mercedes gathered up Nettie's damp, sick-smelly bedding to put it through the laundry. She questioned me on what I had seen and done, which only made sense since she was in charge of the girls on our floor. We stepped out into the hall, and Mercedes went to her room to get the master keycard, to lock up Nettie's room. Angela caught her breath and turned, facing the stairwell, her eyes widening.

I saw something. A momentary flash. Colors I had never seen before and couldn't describe, because there was nothing to compare them to. Before I was conscious of what I had kinda-sorta seen, a loud crash echoed through the floor, followed by a thud and the rattle-clatter of wood tumbling down the stairs. *Then* everybody in the stairwell yelled.

Delayed reactions are always suspicious, in my book.

Angela and I hurried to the stairwell, followed by Mercedes. We got there just as Kurt went down on one knee amid the wreckage of the bench and decorations. A slightly scorched smell touched the air, but only Kurt seemed to react, wrinkling up his nose.

The dream box sat amid the wreckage of the bench: broken wood, torn decorations, shredded paper. It had fallen straight down. Still sitting in the same position it had been on the bench, with the cute little slate sign on the front proclaiming it the dream box, to deposit their dreams and wishes. A second look revealed a somewhat frightening detail. The bench was essentially squared-off two-by-two poles, eight of them, about eight feet long, with two braces about three feet in from either side. The jagged ends of the wooden bars put the dream box in the center of the breakage. The dream box broke the bench. The braces were metal tubes the same dimensions as the wooden bars of the bench, and they had been bent down, crumpled in several spots.

"What happened?" Rodney shook his head, blinking and then rubbing his eyes.

I didn't get close enough to him, or to anyone else, to see if their pupils were unevenly dilated. Quite frankly, I didn't want to.

Bottom line, nobody in the group could quite remember what had happened from about the time they left the cafeteria to come back to the dorm. They all had hazy fragments of memories, and a few could remember Kurt and me coming to their doors to talk, but not what we discussed, or how they got out into the stairwell.

Mercedes didn't quite believe anyone. She thought someone had done something stupid, pulled an idiotic stunt, and not only broke the bench but destroyed all her decorations.

"Notice she didn't say anything about the box?" Kurt said, when he, Angela and I gathered in Alysyn's apartment to talk.

We had included Alysyn in the conference because she understood the necessity of consulting with Angela. Chances were good she wouldn't be weirded out by what we were talking about. Funny thing, though. Years later, I learned Alysyn was also one of the Lost Kids. She was like Ford Longfellow and Mr. Wellington (now principal at Neighborlee High), with no superpowers. She eventually came back home to settle and work and, even if only subconsciously, help protect our town.

Alysyn blinked a few times, shook her head a few times, but she never argued and never looked even the slightest bit freaked out when we told her what Kurt and I had discovered. What Kurt had seen, as in the energy lines coming out of the box and going into Robbie the Robot and Nettie. And what had just happened when he asked the kids attached to those energy lines to focus on the box. Alysyn knew about the psycho-social experiment, but hadn't been told until after the first crisis occurred. To say she was major pissed at this new development would be putting it mildly. And to be honest, it was kind of comforting.

"I want that thing out of here," she said, once we had gone

through the entire chain of events and all our theories.

"That might not be so easy," Kurt said. "You saw how it smashed down on the bench?"

"I fear there might be a dent in the floor," Angela said.

The group in the stairwell had done just what Kurt asked. They focused on the box and thought about their dreams, what they had written on the papers they put in the box and what they wanted to have happen. Working off what had happened with Nettie and Robbie, Kurt then told them to think about something cool they had brought to college with them, that tied into their biggest wish.

"The box glowed like the northern lights, all in black light, and the lines of energy linking it to the kids got thicker than my arm, for about two seconds. Then the bench just snapped and the box hit like a ten-ton safe. I'm surprised nobody came running from the sonic boom of it hitting the floor," Kurt said.

"All I saw was a flash of light, and all I heard was the bench breaking," I said.

Angela said the same. Alysyn had heard nothing down in her apartment. She wasn't surprised that the kids involved couldn't remember much, which said a lot for how aware she was of the general background weirdness of Neighborlee. She was going to be a good ally in whatever we had to do next.

Since she wanted the box gone, we tried it the easy way first. We went back upstairs and made sure the stairwell doors were closed. Alysyn stood in front of the door to the boys' side of the floor and Angela blocked the window for the girls' side, then Kurt and I got to work. We tried lifting it with our hands. We managed to get our fingertips under the box where a few fragments of compressed, squashed wood provided space to slide under.

No luck. The thing wasn't so much heavy as it felt like it was part of the floor, fastened down securely, maybe melted into it.

Then we got to work with my telekinesis. I wrapped my mental hands around it as tightly as I could, then Kurt took over and augmented it with his talent. We worked until I got a bloody nose and I thought my brain would squeeze out my ears. Kurt didn't get any bad reaction, other than exhaustion. Alysyn looked kind of white, and later she said she saw something, she wasn't sure what it was. Like a glow but not exactly light, wrapped around the box. The same glow in wavering streaks went between it and Kurt's and my foreheads. Well, at least she didn't think we were faking it.

"Maybe something inside it is holding it down?" she suggested, after we were settled down in her kitchen again, with big mugs of deluxe hot chocolate and sandwiches to replenish us.

"That could be it," Angela whispered. "You said the other students wrote down their wishes and put them in the box. The physical representation of those wishes could be an anchor."

Fortunately, she didn't go into a lecture on principles of earthly magic or interdimensional magic. None of us were in the mood for it. I needed a nap, for one thing.

Alysyn came up with the first solution we tried, and it really was brilliant. If it had worked. She proposed that if the written wishes and dreams were the anchor, the physical representation of whatever belief power held the box down, then maybe we could just take the pieces of paper out, and break the force that anchored the box?

First problem: when we checked with Mercedes on how to open the box, we found out it was indeed very old, set up like I had envisioned. The outer box was the larger piece, the cover, and slid over the inner box, which was smaller. So lifting the top, larger box off the smaller bottom box was the challenge. Needless to say, it wasn't happening.

Our next attempt was to get some skinny tongs from Alysyn's kitchen and try to pull the slips of paper out through the slot. It was a decent-sized slot, maybe three inches long and about half an inch wide. Meaning it was wide enough to shine a flashlight beam inside to see what we were doing.

Kurt stuck the tongs in there to grab some papers, and something sucked the tongs down into the box. His forefinger got stuck between the hinge of the tongs and the box. It turned purple-red and white around the edges, and bled where the sides of the tongs cut the skin, by the time we managed to get our hands—and my telekinesis—on the tongs and pull up enough to slide his finger out. Then the box sucked those tongs down with a *clang-bang*. I swear, I heard a distant slurping sound.

Not good.

"Sorry, Alysyn," Angela murmured, as we all took a step back and just looked at the box. "I will replace those for you."

"Can't get anything out of there," Kurt said, just as softly, but the corners of his mouth were curving up just enough to make me shiver. Not an amused little smile. More of a nasty, *Okay, you think you're so smart? We'll see about that,* kind of smile.

"What are you thinking?" I said.

"Roaches check in, but they don't check out."

"You're not talking about a couple dozen cans of Raid to poison the thing, are you?" Alysyn tried to smile.

"That might be a good idea." He stepped back against the railing on the other side of the stairwell, between him and open air and a long drop to the first floor. "Of course, how do we get those cans in through that teeny tiny slot, and then light them up?"

"Explosives?" Immediately I regretted that suggestion, when Alysyn flinched.

"We have to break it from the inside, whatever we do," he said. "Kind of a one-way trip. What goes in will not come out. At least, not in one piece."

"We need to break the connection with the kids powering it."

"That could be a large problem," Angela said. "They've had a very visible demonstration that something is happening here, even though they can't remember all the details. I imagine asking them to stop thinking about the box will not work at all."

"How about when they're asleep?" Alysyn said. "Won't the link or whatever it is be broken then?"

"I've read enough psychology, helping my folks with research," I said. "Chances are good they're going to have their heads so full of what happened this afternoon, they're going to dream about it." I shivered, from more than the chill in the stairwell. "Chances are also good they could just be adding fuel to the fire, in their dreams."

"Then a distraction is in order," Angela said. "Distance might help. I hesitate to, in some sense, invite the spider into my parlor. However, taking the battle into my territory might weaken the link between the invader and those he is duping." Her eyes narrowed and she nibbled at her bottom lip as she stared at the box.

I thought back to that scary moment last fall, when Angela had stepped into the yard of the house in Darbyville, and something drained her.

"What if that's what it or him or they or whatever wants?" I had to say.

"That is very possible," she whispered. "I have made enemies through the years, standing in the gap. I have lost friends and I have put aside memories, because the pain of loss was so great. However, as they say, forewarned is forearmed." She reached out to clasp Alysyn's hand. "I hope you don't mind if we cause a little bit of a ruckus here?"

"Be my guests." Alysyn managed a brave smile, but she did look a little more pale than she had been when we came back upstairs, and even after the box swallowed her kitchen tongs.

"Kurt, I am depending on you to find something small but mighty, and fast-acting." She caught hold of his hand.

"Got just the thing." He grinned, still not a nice grin. "Don't worry, I'm going to get some advice from Ford. Putting things together means you have to know how to take them apart, too."

We ended up calling in the whole team. Stephanie dropped Bethany at the Longfellows' house, to stay with Athena and her grandmother. Jinx Longfellow helped his father and Kurt put together what looked like a string of firecrackers. A really long string, like a bandolier. It was a series of glass vials of different chemicals. Kept separate, they were relatively harmless, but once a couple of those glass vials burst and the contents mixed, the explosions would break more vials, causing more explosions, until there was nothing left. They wired everything together with a battery pack to power the whole mess, but just in case, they picked up Felicity from NCH on their way back to the dormitory. If something sucked the power out of the battery packs, we wanted her EM burst as a backup to trigger the whole thing.

Alysyn requisitioned a van from the college motor pool. She assigned Mercedes to take the "affected" kids from our floor, and anyone else who wanted to cram into the van that seated twenty, and go to Divine's. Stephanie would be waiting outside with her cell phone, to let Jinx, with his cell phone, know the moment the college van arrived. He would be stationed in the dorm stairwell, on the second floor, out of the blast zone. Kurt and Ford waited on the landing for the signal. I had Felicity in my room. The tricky part would be triggering the EM burst if we needed it, but not frightening or angering her before we needed it. Yet at the same time, we would need to build up the emotional outburst. There was also the problem of letting those kids who were linked to the dream box stay inside Divine's Emporium for too long. It was bad enough

Angela felt it necessary to let them in the door, inside the protective barriers that made Divine's such a magical place, and quite frankly kept a lot of weirdness under control. What if letting them inside the door, now that they were linked to the box, was like poking a balloon filled with explosive gas with a pin?

Kurt called down to me when Jinx yelled up that the van had arrived at Divine's. I told Felicity what had happened so far that day, the Reader's Digest condensed version, as we walked from my room to the stairwell landing. She had looked at the broken bench and the box when she came upstairs, and even said something felt wrong, but hadn't pushed me when I refused to fill her in on the details. Just knowing that Felicity could feel something was off, odd, was encouraging, and yet a little frightening. How strong was the invasion power or energy, that she could feel it?

Maybe what bothered me more: how come I couldn't feel what Kurt and Felicity were sensing? Not that I wanted to. Who wants to be the equivalent of a smoke detector?

By the time we reached the landing area, little blue sparks were curling up on the ends of Felicity's hair. She was primed, which was good. Or not. Depending on how much shock and creepiness she could take before an explosion. Her eyes got big when she saw the firecracker string of chemicals and other substances in their protective glass vials. This was the first time I had seen what Kurt and Ford had put together, and it gave me second thoughts about what exactly those two did when they played in Ford's workshop. I had an image of lightning filling the sky and big, scary shadows dancing against the wall, and mad scientists cackling, interrupted by blasts of thunder.

"They're all inside," Jinx called up to us. "Stephanie is going. She says something is reacting."

"Go," Ford said.

He didn't have to. Kurt nodded to me as he picked up the leading end of the string and shoved it into the slot. I picked up the middle, prepared to give a good hard shove with my telekinesis if something inside the box decided it didn't want whatever we were force-feeding it. Ford had the end, a good three feet away, where the battery pack attached to it.

Chapter Twelve

We didn't have to worry. Maybe the box liked the taste of the glass and wires and the lower current battery charge, or it could taste the chemicals and metals through the glass. There was a subliminal slurping sound. The string of vials raced through my hands, sucked down into the box so fast the wires cut my fingers. The slot widened and the edges warped, and I had the mental image of a mouth opening up. Big enough to suck us all in?

Ford flipped the switch as the battery leaped from his hands.

Kurt grabbed me around the waist and lunged at the railing with his other hand. Ford did the same with Felicity. I envisioned something trying to suck us down.

Felicity shrieked fury. Lights flared from behind us, so our silhouettes were almost burned into the wall of the stairwell. Like those images from nuclear explosions in science fiction movies from the 50s and 60s.

We kind of hung on the railing, all of us with a white-knuckle grip, and for a few seconds there was silence. I was positive the explosion behind us had been so loud we were all deaf. Any second now, kids were going to come bursting through the fire doors on either side of the floor, and we were going to have a lot of explaining to do.

Then I heard footsteps coming up the stairs. Okay, not deaf. So maybe there was no audible explosion, just the lights? Looking down, I saw Jinx come into view, holding his cell phone up to his ear, his eyes wide. He sagged against the wall and grinned at us.

"They're all fine," he said, and nodded to whatever Stephanie was saying.

"That's a matter of opinion." Ford let out a raspy kind of chuckle. "Kids?"

"We're good," Kurt said. "I think."

He let go of me, and I almost whined about it. There was something really comforting about all of us clutching at each other and the railing. However, now that the scare was past, it was kind of uncomfortable. I stood up and felt like I had gone a couple dozen rounds with that stupid electronic bull a very short-lived steakhouse had in its waiting area. Five dollars to ride it, or anyone who ordered their twenty-four-ounce house special got to ride for free. The only drawback was that someone with a twenty-four-ounce steak in their stomach wasn't going to be very comfortable riding the bull, and people who rode before they ate weren't exactly hungry afterward. They kind of killed their business with their promotional gimmick.

Then we turned around to face our handiwork, and I forgot about all my aches and stiffness and the low-level throbbing at the back of my head.

The box had vanished. Curling wisps of multi-colored smoke rose up from a pile of ashes that sparkled and melted away as we watched. Soon there was nothing left but a sour smell in the air, like something had rotted and then was burned to ashes. That, and the debris of the broken bench and destroyed decorations.

"Hey, Dad?" Jinx came running up the steps, holding out his cell phone. "Better get to Divine's."

All our coats were in my room. Felicity and I ran down the hall to get them, while Kurt checked the debris, just in case, and Ford talked to Stephanie. When we got back with the coats, less than a minute later, Ford, Jinx and Kurt were already bombing down the stairs, which wasn't really safe, considering all the snowmelt incoming students tracked up and down. Yeah, I know, who cared about falling on wet tile after what we just did? Just showed how much strain we were all under, that such things leaped out to the front of my mind. Felicity and I caught up with them at the bottom of the stairs, where Alysyn waited.

It wasn't bad news, but it was a little frightening. There was no bad reaction in Divine's when the box blew up. The roof didn't crash in. Walls didn't burst into flame. No strange noises came from the attics, where I knew for a fact dangerous magical items were stored. Stephanie said the lights sort of dimmed for a moment, but there was no reaction from any of the students Mercedes had brought to the shop.

However — and this was the frightening part — Angela went a little pale, and Stephanie saw sweat break out at her temples.

Yeah. Bad.

Angela doesn't get sick. She doesn't faint. She doesn't sweat.

Whatever happened when we killed the dream box, when the energy linking it to the other kids on my floor got cut off or the lines snapped or whatever was going on, Angela felt it. Later, she admitted it felt something like when a rubber band, stretched to its limits, snapped. Not a lot of whiplash, but still somewhat startling since she wasn't ready for it.

Stephanie was in the main room of the shop when we got there, keeping watch on Angela, who certainly looked normal as she talked with her customers. Everything felt normal at Divine's, and I even saw one of the old-fashioned candy jars slide out of the shadows, full of penny candy, just before Angela reached for it. Rita Shipton exclaimed that she loved that candy and she hadn't seen it since she was like six years old.

Okay, maybe things weren't completely normal yet, because even though I expected it, even though I suspected it happened that way, I shouldn't have *seen* the candy jar come out of thin air, or through a dimensional slit. Even if I was a guardian, I shouldn't have seen and felt those things happen. Does that make any sense?

Stephanie handed over her watch duty to me and Felicity as soon as we came in and got our coats off. She headed upstairs, followed by Ford. Kurt signaled that he was going to walk around. I figured since he was attuned to energy and sensing whatever magical-alien stuff was going on, he might have a better idea if some damage had been done to Divine's. He headed upstairs with Jinx. When they came downstairs more than an hour later, after the kids from my dorm left, he had a box of spare parts from the bits and pieces room. He and Jinx were talking about an idea for remote controlled alarm systems. If Kurt could play with his gizmos, that was a clear sign everything was fine again.

Angela insisted she was fine, that it had been just a momentary weakness. Still, I had to wonder if maybe she was downplaying her reaction to the energy snapping when we killed the box. Stephanie took it the hardest of all of us, scared by the implied threat to Divine's, the town, and especially Angela's moment of weakness.

"Do me a favor?" she said, as we all dug into the feast she had prepared for us.

That was what she had been doing upstairs. One of Stephanie's tactics for dealing with stress and scares, and yes, good news and celebrations, was to cook up a storm. That was why she and Ben

Miller were so good for each other.

"I know I don't have any influence over it, and I know it's wrong to get in the way if she's chosen, but if there's any chance of her avoiding it..." She took a deep breath and looked around the table. "I don't want Bethany to be a guardian."

"Perfectly understandable." Angela rested her hand on Stephanie's. "If I had a daughter, I wouldn't want such a heavy responsibility to rest on her. At the same time..." Her usual hint of a superior smirk returned, and the sparkle touched her eyes again. "You really should have considered that before you asked me to be her godmother."

Stephanie groaned, but the sound turned into a chuckle. We agreed: until the girls displayed any unusual gifts, even if just sensitivity to magical energies and events, or being able to see what other people couldn't, we wouldn't mention guardians or our duties to Bethany and Athena. As Ford's granddaughter, Athena had just as much potential to be a guardian. It had skipped a generation with his three children, but it might show up in Athena, or any children Jinx or Lenore might produce someday.

~~~~~

With all the hustle and bustle and fuss of wrapping up the semester and term papers and studying for final exams, we missed seeing or feeling most of the side effects of destroying the dream box. Professor Winghast got sick. Serious enough to spend a couple days in the hospital. We heard later that he hallucinated about Mafia types, or at least people dressed all in black, interrogating him for hours on end. What they wanted, no one who heard him raving in his delirium could figure out. Just plain incoherent.

Later, both professors were heard to comment multiple times about how the first half of the school year felt like a dream. The experiment officially ended with Christmas break. There were even some attempts to rearrange the dormitories, to sort of shuffle around the roommate assignments.

Some judicious, careful snooping and asking questions and following connections revealed a few interesting details. Each freshman dorm floor had something like the dream box, which the students were asked to focus on. None had the explosive results like the third floor of Wickslow Hall.

Need I point out that was a good thing?
~~~~~

However, some after-effects of the dream box and its destruction took a long time to become visible. Some of that resulted from the reshuffling that took place. There was always some attrition between first and second semester of the freshman year. Some kids didn't adjust to the on-campus living situation, or just academic life in general. Some decided to change their intended majors, or wanted to be closer to home, or farther away from home. A few transferred out, and some transferred in. The ratio was about one inward transfer to every five or six outward transfers. Willis-Brooks College was in Neighborlee, remember. We had the "go away, we don't like you" vibe.

Whether news of the experiment with the freshmen had gone around despite efforts to keep it quiet, or some bad vibrations lingered from the destruction of the box, second and third floors lost a lot of kids. Maybe once the field Kurt sensed dissipated, people subconsciously sensed something weird going on, and they wanted out. That hinted at some sort of attempted mind-control field. It also supported the theory that something was feeding on the power of belief generated by the creative types on our floor. The thing is, how much energy did the enemy expend on influencing or even controlling the two professors, to set up the whole experiment in the first place? If all they wanted was energy, they failed colossally. By this time, the three of us knew better than to assume anything when it came to the other-dimensional creeps trying to influence, hurt, or invade Earth through Neighborlee.

Most of the drama, dance, and art students left if they weren't hardcore geeks and SF and fantasy buffs. The Time Lords stayed. When the bench in the stairwell was replaced, they could usually be seen sitting there, talking at all hours.

Who were the Time Lords? That was what Rodney and Rita, Colby and Yuri called themselves. From the name, I expected them to be uber-hyper Dr. Who fans, but they were the exact opposite. They were snobs about time travel. They loved pointing out all the logic and physics errors present in every book or short story or TV show or movie dealing with time travel, or the control of the time stream. Excuse me? If it was impossible to travel through time other than the old-fashioned way of moving forward, one second at a time, like God intended, then how could they appoint themselves as the experts on how *real* time travel should be handled?

Things were quiet, all things considered, for the first few months of second semester, our freshman year. Almost comatose, considering what had happened first semester. That was good, because the teachers stepped up the academic pressure. Maybe they let us ease into the whole college routine during first semester, and now that the wimps and dilettantes had been weeded out, the real academic life was about to begin. Kurt, Felicity and I did our regular flyovers of the dorms every few nights. Kurt was relieved to report that he didn't sense the energy building up. Of course, then he had to ruin that sense of "whew!" we were feeling, and qualify it by putting an emphasis on "building up." He did feel energy of some kind. Whether alien powers or magical, the levels were too low for him to determine. Like any of us had enough experience to know the difference, or even pinpoint the source and the location? We paid attention, and Kurt said the impression he got was of something sleeping. Wherever the energy or power or whatever it was had come to rest, it wasn't strong enough to do anything.

Of course, the six of us, the guardians of Neighborlee, had regular discussions at Divine's Emporium, because, duh, we had been given plenty of warning that an enemy was at work. We spent a lot of time trying to analyze what had happened and keep tabs on those who had been marked by the threads of energy coming from the dream box. None of those freshmen showed any tendencies to do magical things or start growing extra limbs or eyes or whatever. Angela even said she would have been more worried if no one had been changed by the exposure to whatever the box was doing, or what its creators were trying to do through it. So we kept watch. And when our every-other-night flyovers revealed nothing but that sleeping impression, we changed to every-third-night, then every-fourth-night, until we did it once a week.

We should have realized the sleeping sensation was because the people being affected, the people who had changed were, duh, sleeping. Just like we should have been.

In retrospect, we should have done walk-throughs of campus during the day. Then when Kurt sensed the energy at work, we could have followed the trail to the source and seen the perpetrators at work. Yeah, retrospect is always a lot clearer. It's easier to weed out detours and distractions.

The first clue that something new was wonky on our floor? The Time Lords stopped spending every waking moment together. I had all four of them in my world history class, and they usually sat right in front of me in the lecture hall. I could look down on the next row of the stair-step seating and see them writing notes to each other more than they took notes on what the professor was saying. Granted, the guy thought he was a comedian, but he did drop interesting bits in among the boring details we already knew. They should have been paying better attention.

About two weeks after spring break, the row below me in the lecture hall was completely empty. I didn't think anything of it until I saw the twins meeting up after class and comparing notes, without Colby and Yuri trotting along in their wake. That was odd, but not enough to notice, until Yuri walked into the dorm lounge when the *Tomorrow is Yesterday* episode of Star Trek was playing. As I mentioned earlier, the Time Lords were utter nitpickers when it came to time travel. They were always harping about how every book and TV show and movie violated laws of physics and were utterly impossible. The writers and directors were telling lies and confusing people. Well duh, that's why they call it *fiction*, y'know?

So Yuri walked in and saw the episode, and he exploded.

Usually when the Time Lords got into a snit, we could either walk away from them, or keep repeating, "It's just a story," until they calmed down. Some of us learned the best way to shut them up was to challenge them to explain how "real" time travel was done. Yuri stomped over in front of the TV, spread his legs and, according to those who were trying to watch the episode, started his wettest tirade ever. He spat a lot when he got emotional. No one could get a word in edgewise.

Someone got fed up enough to yell until they drowned him out. That didn't stop him. Alysyn finally came out of her apartment to see what the problem was. Yuri kept shouting. Rodney came into the dorm then, returning from class. He looked into the lounge long enough for a few people to see him. Yuri paused for the first time. Rodney glared at him and walked away. Yuri started stammering. Then someone tackled him and finally shut him up.

It was the talk of the dorm: the Time Lords weren't defending each other. Yuri and Rodney didn't fight, either out on campus or when they were in their room. As far as anyone could tell, they didn't even talk. Rodney and Rita met up, as far as anyone could tell, but Yuri and Colby just glared at each other every time they had to be in the same room.

They were also regularly late for classes or missing them altogether. Their academic advisors came to Alysyn to talk to them, and she got Mercedes into the act. I know this because I had a front row seat to what happened next, caught between the bathroom and my room.

About 7 on Sunday night, Rodney came stomping into the girls' side of the floor with Yuri on his heels, right after Mercedes finished talking to them. He banged on his sister's door, and shouted about Rita turning him in. He only got a few words in, when the door opened. Alysyn stepped out into the hall and Rodney shut up so fast I heard his jaw clack shut.

I was no dummy. I held perfectly still, there in the little alcove by the phone booth. Alysyn looked back and forth between Yuri and Rodney. She looked over her shoulder at Rita and Colby.

"Nobody turned anybody in. Talk to each other. Get your heads straightened out. Get a watch. I don't know what your problem is, but none of you can afford to miss another class." She looked each of them in the eye, sighed, then stalked down the hall.

"Rod," Rita began.

"I don't want to hear it," he growled at his twin.

I was in the perfect position to see what happened next.

Rodney whipped out a pocket watch. It was silver, with a green enamel design on the back that turned out to be a dragon. Yes, I saw the watch close up later.

"You're not!" Colby yelped, and jumped out from behind Rita, reaching for the watch.

Yuri stuck his tongue out at her. Real mature. Not! He grabbed onto Rodney's arm as Rodney twisted the knob on the top of the watch. Rita let out a screech and dove forward, through the place where Rodney and Yuri had been.

Had been. Past tense.

Because they both had vanished.

"I can't believe what a child he is!" Rita snarled, and stomped back into her room. Colby followed her and they slammed the door.

Chances were good nobody saw me. I just stood there. Not a sound, not a movement. There were no other witnesses to that little blip of SF-turned-real, because nobody freaked. Honestly, if someone vanished in front of me, I would have freaked. At least, if I wasn't used to various levels of weirdness my whole life, I would have freaked. If Rita and Colby, who didn't grow up in Neighborlee, didn't freak out when Rodney and Yuri vanished, that told me they were used to the watch doing that. If they were ticked at the two guys vanishing, maybe they were used to it happening a lot.

I stood there for a little longer, thinking hard. Not just because I was a guardian and I was pretty sure this was something I was supposed to keep an eye on. I kind of had one of those copyright-infringement moments. What were these newcomers doing, indulging in weirdness when they weren't residents of Neighborlee? Okay, they were temporary residents, but there was something like an unspoken agreement between town and college, a tolerance factor. We put up with the college students and didn't blow their minds too much, and in return they didn't infringe on our weirdness territory.

We didn't have a security system like on the *Enterprise*, where we could track energy emissions, or follow where the transporter took someone, or detect when someone transported in or out. However, we had Kurt. I called him. Then I had to figure out how we were going to cover his presence in the dorm if we had to hunt around and track down where Rodney and Yuri had gone. What if they had slid through the floor, and they were on another floor of the dorm? Especially on the girls' side of the dorm. We were used to the two of them violating the visitation-non-visitation time rules on our floor, and we had a lot fewer people this semester. The other floors, however, just weren't used to Rodney and Yuri popping in out of thin air. At least, I hoped they weren't used to them.

Then it hit me, as I was waiting for Kurt. If Rodney and his cohorts had access to a gizmo that could help them walk through walls or turn invisible or manipulate the space-time continuum in some way, how come they were in so much trouble this semester? How come they were always *late*, or missing classes altogether?

"They're still here," Kurt said when we got up to the floor.

I had met him in the lobby and told him what I had been thinking. I had been keeping him updated all along on the Time Lords, because we were monitoring everyone who had been marked or tagged by the dream box. That saved us a lot of time when the crisis hit.

"What do you mean? They're not. I walked right through the place where they were." I gasped, and usually I never gasped. "They're not walking around, looking at all the girls taking showers, dressing for bed, are they?"

"They're still in front of the door, right where you said they were. Here, right?" Kurt stopped about two feet away from where Rodney and Yuri were when they pressed the pocket watch knob.

"Yeah. What do you feel? Can you hear anything? Can you see anything?"

"There's this swirling of energy, shaped like two guys, but..." He chuckled. "You said they've been late for everything lately, and now they're in trouble, right?" He looked around and found the bench tucked into the niche by the phone booth. It served as a lost-and-found for the floor, such as when we found someone's shower soap or towels or dried laundry.

"Yeah."

"You guys call them the Time Lords for a reason, right?" He sat down and leaned back, visibly getting comfortable. "Can't wait to get my hands on that watch."

I gasped again. Record. I had probably used up my gasps for the next couple years.

"They figured out how to control time."

"Nope, they didn't." He gestured at the place where Rodney and Yuri had vanished, and where, if I understood him correctly, they still were. "Remember the movie, *My Science Project*? The first time they played with the gizmo they stole out of the old lab, it jumped them forward in time a few hours, and they missed a class or something. The trick with time travel is freezing a moment of time, so you can go somewhere else. What these geniuses are doing is freezing themselves, instead of freezing time. When the timer runs out, they're in the future, and they lost time."

Rodney and Yuri lost nearly two hours. Kurt and I kept watch. We talked around various possible problems. Like if the guys phased back into the present moment while someone was walking down the hall through that exact spot. Just like one of the laws of physics said something couldn't be in two places at the same time, two different items couldn't be in the same spot at the same time. It would get kind of messy. I remember a couple science fiction stories that used that law of physics to kill someone.

We ended up knocking on Rita and Colby's door and confronting them with our theory, just to get more information on what was happening, so we could avoid that mess.

"The watch is kind of obvious," Kurt said, as the two girls, wide-eyed, let us into their dorm room and closed the door so we could talk in privacy. As much privacy as there could be in a dorm, with cinderblock walls and about a half-inch gap under each door.

"We've had the watch for about ten years. Ever since some morons at a convention tried to convince people that *The Girl, The Gold Watch and Everything*, was on the same level as *The Time Machine*, and *Time After Time*, and—" Rita ended with a shriek and dropped on her bed. Then she sort of froze. "How did you figure out what happened? Can you fix the watch?"

"It's what we do." Kurt stayed standing, with his back against the door. He had his left hand pressed flat against the door, probably sensing the energy field out in the hall, to track Rodney and Yuri's journey through time, but not through space. "As for fixing it, I have to figure out what you guys did."

"We don't know. Rodney brought the watch with him, and he started carrying it all the time when Mercedes was playing her weird mind games with the box and all that. Did you hear that some shrinks were playing games with us?"

"Yeah," I said. "Professor Tudderman and Professor Winghast put us in the dorms in specific rooms and floors to study us, see how we'd react."

"That's ancient history," Kurt said. "It's the box again. When we killed it, all that energy had to go somewhere. It was probably keyed to Rodney."

"So they programmed the watch, but since they didn't know they were doing it..." I wanted to laugh, but Rita was starting to look both scared and relieved. Relieved that someone seemed to know what was going on, and scared because yeah, someone else knew what was going on.

Kurt spent the next half hour asking questions and theorizing and getting a better idea of what the four of them had been doing. What was interesting, and probably complicated the whole situation, was that Rodney had been tinkering with the watch ever since he bought the movie prop at the convention. He had added things like colored crystals to store energy and generate a time distortion field when the watch was activated. All in his imagination, of course. He had no real hope of making it work.

Too bad the incident with Curtis and Ricky's prop gun coming to life hadn't discouraged them, or at least made them all think. The Time Lords had been playing with the watch, dreaming over it, for months. They believed hard enough, dreamed hard enough, so that when the energy burst out of the dream box last winter, something settled into the watch and made it come to life. Probably because the watch had been so much on Rodney's mind.

The funny, ironic, and scary thing was that the Time Lords, for all their theorizing and refining and mocking of others' time travel theories, still didn't know what they were doing.

"We can't figure out how it started working," Rita said, cutting Kurt off before he could ease into explaining what they were doing wrong. "Yeah, my twin exchanged all the plastic gears for metal, and it's like the Velveteen Rabbit, but it still shouldn't work."

Kurt and I slid into one of those moments where we didn't exactly share thoughts, but we knew what the other was thinking. That came of spending nearly our whole lives working together.

"Do all of you believe, completely, with everything you've got, that the watch really does work and help you travel through time?" I asked, after Kurt tipped his head to me. Essentially, he was giving me the job of easing them into the truth of Neighborlee. I had the awful feeling we were going to need a trip to Divine's and some shock therapy before this mess was fixed.

"I want to," Rita whispered. Colby just kind of froze there.

"Want to bet the guys do?" Kurt said.

"That's what you guys have been fighting about for the last couple weeks, isn't it? Let me guess. Rodney made it work, completely by accident, just pushed the knob one day, playing around, but wishing. He vanished, and when he reappeared—" I exchanged a glance with Kurt, then tipped my head toward the hall, where the energy cloud was waiting to release Rodney and Yuri. "—he hadn't experienced any time at all."

"Yeah, but it got kind of blurry for him. That's all that happens for us," Colby said. "He grabbed onto us and yanked us forward with him. Everything blurs, like everybody is racing around us, and lights flicker, and one time we got completely drenched."

"It rained while we were inside the time bubble," Rita said. "What use is a time machine if it doesn't protect you from what's going on around you while you're traveling through time?"

"Earth is a time machine," I offered, echoing something Pop had said once. He and the other guys in Pastor Rocky's retro band had got into a really funky, fun, philosophical discussion one night after rehearsal at our house. "We're not protected from what happens." I waved my hands to cut them off when both Rita and Colby opened their mouths to argue. "The thing is, Rodney and Yuri probably believe utterly that the watch works, but you two have your doubts."

"I believed at first. Completely. I mean, look what it did." She sighed and slumped and shared a glance with Colby. "Then all our experiments just flopped. We couldn't make ourselves believe when we had evidence it wasn't working."

"Yeah," Colby said. "We've been fighting like crazy. The guys keep trying. They keep grabbing onto us and making us late for class. What's really irritating is that sometimes we're not just late ten or twenty minutes, but we miss class, maybe the whole day. You know how many tests I've had to make up? The guys were weird enough before this started, but now they are serious freaks."

"What's really bad is that Yuri and Rodney are fighting now," Rita offered. "They aren't even working together to figure out how to make the thing work. They're constantly fighting over who took the watch, who used up all the energy, how long they have to wait for it to build up again."

"And it doesn't do them any good to try to run away from the other one." Kurt's voice got thick, meaning he was fighting not to laugh. "Because they're still in the same place when they come out of the time bubble." He gestured out into the hall. "Just like those guys are going to be in the same place pretty soon."

"Is it changing?" I asked.

"Something is kind of winding down." He rubbed his fingers together, meaning the energy vibrations were changing. "I think we need to get the Time Lords to Divine's and have a long talk with Angela right away." He gestured for all of us to get out into the hall.

Chapter Thirteen

I called Angela to find out if it was all right to come over, since Divine's wasn't ordinarily open on Sunday. Kurt set us up for the confrontation. I had already described to him where the guys were, the positions they were in when they vanished, and Kurt had a good idea of where the watch would be. Rita's job was to distract her twin. Colby, who seemed to have some hurt feelings to work out, got the task of leaping in and tackling Yuri, separating him from Rodney. Kurt would grab Rodney's arm, and my job was to mentally yank the watch out of his hand, so he couldn't activate it again. Although, after Rita's comment about the watch running out of energy, chances were good the guys wouldn't be able to use it right away.

Kurt started a countdown, just after we were all in place and Angela had given permission. An underwater effect filled the air in a rippling bubble. The guys appeared, looking a little green, and they were frozen in place for a few seconds. Another strike against the malfunctioning time traveling abilities of the watch: when the travelers emerged, they were vulnerable. Later, it occurred to me that having people walk through me while I was frozen in time, out of phase with the rest of the universe, could get really disturbing. How many times would I have to feel like a ghost before something went wonky inside my head?

We didn't even need Rita to distract her twin. Rodney and Yuri's knees partly folded. They still looked green even after the underwater rippling ended. Kurt caught Rodney's wrist and squeezed. His hand opened and I mind-yanked the watch away, and then took a half-dozen unnecessary steps down the hall. Just in case one of them was crazy enough to try to chase me and get it back. I'm pretty sure Colby was disappointed she couldn't tackle Yuri and work out some of her frustration.

Nobody argued when Kurt announced with a stern look that we were all going on a field trip. Of course, all four of the Time Lords were staring at me. Maybe seeing the watch zip through the air a good four feet and slap into my hand shocked them. They could believe in time travel, but a little display of telekinesis freaked them out?

Interestingly, all four seemed a little scared when Kurt announced our destination. I remembered them having a great time when we went to Divine's Emporium last fall. They all loved it, and they all talked about going back and spending more time there exploring. I followed along on automatic pilot as we grabbed our coats and headed downstairs and outside. My mind was too busy doing some backwards time travel of the safe variety. Well, maybe not that safe if I was so distracted.

"What?" Kurt demanded.

I must have made a sound that went with my spinning thoughts, pulling images and ideas together into a semi-coherent picture. Specifically, images of Rodney and Yuri going nuts in the bits and pieces room last fall. We were about two blocks away from campus by then. We had to walk, since the six of us sure couldn't fit into Kurt's truck.

"Rodney, did you get the new parts for your watch from Divine's?" I asked.

"Some of them." He kept his shoulders hunched and really wouldn't look at me.

"What do you mean, some of them? Which ones?" Kurt asked.

The inventory of replacement parts and talking through the process of rebuilding the watch took the rest of the walk across town to Divine's. All four Time Lords had been involved in the project. That put an interesting twist on the girls' previous attitude that the guys were a little too obsessed about getting the watch to work. Granted, they didn't do even a quarter of the work the guys invested in it, but they had helped. For a while. The girls stopped working on the watch after the dream box blew up.

That made sense, in a scary way. The box had been influencing them. Maybe trying to get a time traveling watch assembled for someone else's benefit?

Even more scary: the watch parts they didn't find at Divine's Emporium came from Professor Winghast. He walked by them in the Student Center and a couple other places, like the library, when they were researching watches and talking time travel, and making sketches of the pieces they needed to replace. He "just happened," in his words, to have a friend who rebuilt watches, and he offered to look for the pieces and parts they might need.

Even more interesting, Professor Winghast got a little insistent, almost nasty, when the guys told him they didn't need some of the gears and things he found for the watch project because they had already replaced them with parts from Divine's.

As a *piece de resistance*, when Ford Longfellow and my Pop did some investigating, Professor Winghast vehemently denied having a friend who rebuilt watches. He also had no memory of helping the guys find parts. Of course, that could be blamed on his hazy memories of the entire first semester.

So the question left from our investigation was what the enemy behind the freshman class experiment was trying to gain. Was the watch part planned, or just the first convenient outlet? Would the parts Professor Winghast gave the guys have been different, if someone else had been building a different magical gizmo?

We turned the corner to head down the street where Divine's Emporium perched on the hill looking down over the Metroparks. Kurt had the watch in his hand the entire walk, sometimes flipping it open to look at the face, then flipping the case open to look at the gears inside. He jerked to a stop. We all did.

"What?" I asked.

He told us the watch had vibrated for a moment. He held out his hand. "You guys see anything?"

They all shook their heads. Rodney looked like he wanted to see, wanting it to the point of being in pain. Colby looked like she most definitely did not want to see anything, with the same intensity. Rita and Yuri were somewhere in the middle. I saw a faint glow, more visible from the corner of my eye than straight on.

The glow didn't change as Kurt moved the watch in a circle, holding it closer to each of them in turn so they could get a better look. We were standing on the edge of a puddle of light from a streetlight, and the glow didn't change even as Kurt moved it in and out of the light. He nodded, with that grim look he wore when we were kids and something turned out just like he feared, not the result he wanted. Back when he was experimenting a lot with gizmos and learning about his talent for machines.

"So, is it happy to get to Divine's, or afraid?" I said. "Some of the parts are coming home, and other parts aren't."

Kurt bared his teeth at me and turned the watch over. He

flipped the back of the case open, revealing the gears and other pieces and parts. I couldn't make out the difference, but he could see and feel a difference in energy around each part, as he told me later. He dug in his pocket for the little tool kit he always carried, tiny screwdrivers and Allen wrenches and wire cutters, screws and nails and a couple widths of wire, all in a slim pouch like a large manicure kit. I opened it for him. He pulled out a skinny little screwdriver and used it to point out different parts as he asked the guys where each one came from.

I still couldn't see the difference, but I could *hear* a difference. Like when a TV is on but the volume is on mute. The sense of almost-sound wavered between sweet and sour whenever Kurt touched a part with the tip of the screwdriver. Sweet for the parts that came from Divine's, sour for the parts that Professor Winghast gave the guys. There were six or seven gears and such that the guys found at a craft shop in Medina, so they didn't glow or chime or do anything when Kurt touched them.

General consensus: those mundane, ordinary, un-magical pieces saved us. They held back the damage and power of the chaotic magical forces, as the friend and foe pieces and parts fought inside the watch case.

Kurt had me run ahead to warn Angela we were coming and tell her what was happening. The girls came with me. They showed the good sense to be freaked out. Maybe they couldn't see or hear, but after my demonstration of telekinesis, they had to believe.

The guys stuck with Kurt as he walked down the sidewalk, holding the open watch in one hand and his keyring flashlight in the other, focused on the pieces inside the watch. They stayed with him for pretty much the same reasons the girls wanted to get away: freaked out, and fascinated. The kind of fascination that kept people watching horror movies even when they crossed the line into sick gore.

Angela didn't need to be told. She felt the battle between the parts imbued with warring energy the moment we turned down the street. Kind of like an advance warning system, soaked into the pavement and the soil and the trees, maybe even the air in this part of town. She came outside with a round oil lantern that made me think of the Wishing Ball, except the glass was blue and green and gold streaked, and the three flames inside it were clearly visible.

She held out the lamp at arm's length, and had a peacock patterned shawl wrapped around herself. Her long hair wavered in the freshening breeze, and she was barefoot on the flagstone slabs of the walk leading up to her front door. She stood two flagstones away from the front step, and for a moment I had the strangest impression that she was afraid to go any farther away from the house. That made no sense. Angela wasn't afraid of anything.

Then I thought of that morning in the fall, when we went to look at that Darbyville house, and how pale she got. Yeah, there were some things that frightened her, or at least made her a little more cautious than usual.

"Well, I haven't seen you two for quite some time," Angela said, her expression warming back into her usual smirk that offered all sorts of wonderful surprises, if we were smart enough to trust her. "I should have guessed someone was causing you trouble, when you didn't come back."

"They're not guardians, are they?" I knew that was a stupid question as soon as the words left my mouth, but I couldn't take them back. They couldn't be guardians for the simple fact that they weren't orphans, Lost Kids, and had never been anywhere near Neighborlee until they came to town last spring on a senior class trip to explore different colleges.

"No, but the shop likes them. *Likes them,*" Angela repeated. "Most people, the shop either welcomes or ignores. Some, it rejects. It likes them, meaning they have..." Her smile deepened, and she gestured with a tip of her head for us to come through the gate. "Potential."

"Uh huh."

Colby and Rita and I stepped through the gate, and I had the momentary sensation of something sticky and cold and gritty falling off me. That was bizarre, because I hadn't been aware of that icky feeling until it left.

By this time, Kurt, Rodney and Yuri had caught up with us. Kurt stopped short, staring at the watch in his hand. More light came from it. Some golden, some a dirty olive shade touched with hints of sick red. It reminded me of the time I had an infected cut on my leg that mixed the blood and puss and other junk together, before the skin finally broke and let all that poison out.

"Angela, I'm scared to bring it inside." Kurt put his flashlight in his pocket. When he gestured for the guys to go through the gate ahead of him, they gave Angela the same scared looks they had been giving the watch. Which, in retrospect, was kind of smart.

The best we could figure, something nasty was trying to get its claws or tentacles through the protective energy of Neighborlee, maybe get at Angela, and get into Divine's.

"No, not inside, but closer," she said. "You are restraining it. Telling it not to do what it is meant to do."

"That's what I'm afraid of. Anybody else have a couple dozen movies in their heads right now, with bombs and terrorists and the good guy getting his hand blown off?" He held the watch out at arm's length as he spoke, so his hand almost touched the barrier created by the wrought iron fence.

The watch didn't seem to like that, because the colors flared and swirled together, the shades shifting, some of them to healthy greens and reds, and some of the swirls looking even more sick and diseased.

"Hey, Angela, is it just more of that silliness like whether Fae have wings, or is there some kind of power in cold iron and all that?" I said.

"Iron, forged metal of any kind, has power." She tipped her head slightly to the left and got that thoughtful little wrinkle between her eyes. "Like so many things, the power of belief has some influence over what iron does or doesn't do. Not that it matters, but most Fae I know avoid iron simply because they have an allergic reaction to it."

"Okay, so what is your fence doing to the watch?"

"Let's see, shall we?"

"I have an idea," Kurt said. "Lanie, you take over. Lift it..." He tipped his head back, eyeballing the distance to where the trees ringing the property leaned in. There was a clear area over the gate, going almost straight up. "Get it up at least fifty feet, straight up, and then inch it over the gate and into the yard."

As soon as I had my mind wrapped around the watch, Kurt hurried through the gate. He didn't augment my lifting, not that I needed his help with something so small, but it was important to get the watch entirely free of whatever influence he had over it.

The Time Lords just stood there, the guys with their mouths open, the girls with their arms wrapped around themselves and their eyes bigger than the guys' mouths. Well, maybe it was good they were getting a demonstration of what sort of things we dealt with in Neighborlee, especially if, as Angela said, the shop liked them. Maybe that was why the enemy working through the dream box and now the watch had chosen them: their potential. As Angela had told us earlier in our lives, potential was neither good nor evil, just like a hammer was neither good nor evil, just the use to which the tool was put.

I got the watch up around fifty feet overhead, which was stretching my limits for lifting things and holding them. Granted, pulling, especially when it came to heavy objects, was harder work, but the job was usually over quickly. Kind of on the order of sprints being a lot easier than marathons. Then I inched the watch toward us, standing on the front porch. It hovered above the gate. Kurt said nothing about the power fields having changed. I couldn't see any difference in the light. Another inch closer to us. No difference.

When the watch had moved about one-third of the way across the front yard, Kurt lifted a hand and I stopped moving the watch. I swear, he hadn't blinked since I lifted it out of his hand.

"Bring it down. Try to do it at the same distance you bring it closer," he said.

It took a few seconds for me to understand. All right, closer to us, closer to the ground, closer to whatever protective field was around us.

At nearly the halfway point, when I had brought the watch down about four feet, and forward about four feet, a ripple shot through the air toward me. A visible ripple, like in the water. Then in a split second, I had a vision of a shark arrowing up from the depths straight toward the fisherman holding the fishing pole, and the shark with fishing line in its mouth. The ripple turned into a flash of light, kind of on the order of a nova. Kurt yelled and flung up his hands, jumping to stand in front of me. Nice gesture, but what exactly could he do?

I pushed with enough force to give myself a killer sinus headache and a bloody nose. The watch shrieked and burst in a shower of sour-smelling, burned-smelling, poisonous green and yellow and black sparks.

We searched for days, but found no remnants of it. The power that burned it up devoured everything. Angela assured us there was nothing left.

That was good enough for us.

The problem with destroying the watch was that we had nothing to examine and learn from, and maybe backtrack to the enemy.

Kind of frustrating.

We tried to answer the Time Lords' questions without blowing their minds completely. After what they had gone through, first with the dream box and now the watch, they either had to adjust and accept the weirdness that was Neighborlee, or do what some people did as a self-defense maneuver. Essentially, convince themselves that what they had seen and done and experienced hadn't happened. They either dreamed it, or everything was exaggerated, blown out of proportion.

The four of them went to Divine's a couple times a week to talk with Angela. She was always ready to answer their questions and offer them help, even if it was just tea to help them sleep, or concentrate better as they prepared for final exams, or books to help them with research for their final term papers. Just like a priest or a counselor, she didn't tell us what she talked about with them.

When the semester and the school year ended, the Time Lords went home for the summer. Angela said it was time to wait, and whatever happened, not to worry.

Honestly, having her say not to worry made me worry. Kind of on the order of the ancient enchanter who told his apprentice whatever he did, not to think about pink elephants, or the spell would go wrong. Well, naturally being told not to think of them ensured he did think of them.

When summer ended and our sophomore year started, Rodney and Rita came back to Willis-Brooks, but Colby and Yuri didn't. They had lost touch with the twins over the summer, first taking a long time to answer emails and then not answering emails at all. The twins pretty much gave up.

Angela assured us that Colby and Yuri had made up their minds. It was better to leave them alone, to make it easier for them to forget all the odd incidents from their freshman year, as if they had never happened. The twins weren't in any of my classes our sophomore year, and since I didn't live on campus after that, we really didn't run into each other except when we visited Divine's at the same time. They went into a kind of training with Angela. It wasn't like they had any powers or talents or gifts or whatever, but they had been touched and changed by the struggle that would always take place around or under or within Neighborlee.

They'd had their eyes opened. It would be cruel not to train them to be alert to the weird and wonderful happening around them, if only so they could defend themselves. Kind of like refusing to teach someone how to use a sword, when there were weapons all over the place. The best way to avoid serious injury was to teach the people how to use the swords.

We called them the twins, after that. No more Time Lords.

~~~~~

The next couple of years were quiet. Maybe that was proof that the whole mess with the psycho-social experiment and the dream box and the watch were all attacks from the same enemy constantly trying to break through into Neighborlee and drain the magic. The battle had drained its energy. At least, that was our theory. We were glad of the quiet, glad of the illusion of having ordinary, normal lives. As normal as living in Neighborlee could be.

We heard from Jake and Emma Crowder just before I started my sophomore year. They were parents. Pete was born early spring that year. The summer between my junior and senior years, we met up with them in Toronto, following up on a few leads in their hunt for a treasure trove of documents relating to the dark days after the French Revolution.

The first time I saw Pete, he was in one of those carrier baskets with a handle, the kind that fold up to turn into a combination seat and bed, so the baby can sit on the dining room table to be fed and fall asleep while the parents are having dinner, and then lock into another contraption like a dock that stays in the back seat of the car. He was asleep, and I wasn't that much into babies, since I had had my fill of changing diapers and burping when I babysat Athena and Bethany. I got over my fascination with babies like dolls once the girls got on their feet and developed personalities. I found them a lot more fun than warm, cooing, sleeping, peeing baby dolls, which was the stage I thought Pete was in when I first saw him. I forgot he was more than two years old.

Pete was just tiny for his age. Small enough to make me think of changelings and faerie babies exchanged for Human babies.
~~~~~

Which I found out really didn't happen all that often. Angela told me bits and pieces through the years about the Fae. The general Fae didn't steal Human babies and put their own in their places. Most of the time they put their own babies in the cradle with the Human babies. Usually there was something going on, such as political warfare or intertribal feuding, and they needed to get innocent parties out of the way. So Fae babies were raised *with* Human siblings. When things calmed down back in the Fae enclaves, someone came to thank the Human foster-mother with gifts of gold or jewels or some magically enhanced tool and take the baby home.

The other explanation for the tales of Fae babies exchanged for Human was the result of Fae men marrying Human women and settling down to raise a passel of kids. When whatever drove them out of the enclaves cooled off and settled down, they faked their own deaths so they could toddle off home to their former lives. Changelings were half-bloods. Someone with strong enough Fae blood could go through the equivalent of gene therapy, to turn on the magical potential in their genetics and become Fae in truth.

Back to the subject of Pete. Once he woke up, he proved he was a lot more advanced than his two years warranted, meaning he was talking coherently, self-mobile, and quite frankly, jet-propelled. When he ran out of steam, he was dead weight. Hence the baby carrier, which his parents found very convenient for helping with shopping or stashing notes and sometimes even incriminating evidence, such as rolls of film or memory cards.

Pete woke up soon after we met up with his parents, and proved he had a great future as an escape artist. He undid the harness that kept him in the carrier and climbed over the side and managed to fall off the bench where the carrier sat before anyone realized what he was doing.

Fortunately, he was a curious little kid and wanted to know what was going on and who these strangers were, laughing with his parents. That curiosity held him in place long enough for Jake to get hold of him again and put him astride his hip.

Lunch was like a refueling mission in mid-air for Pete. He was off and running as soon as he got half his sandwich in his stomach and the other half smeared on his face and hands. I was relieved enough not to have a tiny nothing-to-do-but-hold-him baby around, I volunteered to keep an eye on him.

Yeah, my stupid. I had been spoiled by my experience with Bethany and Athena. Those two little girls liked being read to, playing dress-up and building forts with tables and cushions and chairs and blankets. Pete just liked to move. It didn't matter what was in his way, people or chairs or tables, he was going through.

I got a headache from mentally twitching things out of his path, or in the case of crowds of people, mentally tweaking Pete so he toddled at near-light speed around those forests of legs instead of through them. I had to do all that work with my telekinetic powers because despite my legs being longer than Pete was tall, I was always a good five or six feet behind him every step of the way. Exhausting. And I ran track! By the end of our afternoon with the Crowders, I was wiped out from running herd on a kid who would make the Flash give up and drop out of the race.

We spent two weeks with Emma, Jake and Pete, talking research and upcoming books our folks wanted to write, and discussing a collaboration in a year or two, when the current contracted project had gone to print. Then it was time to head home to Neighborlee. I had my senior year ahead of me, which meant student teaching.

I found out a few things had been changed, rearranged and shuffled around while I was out of town. Some paperwork didn't get filed, and people who were responsible for several small, important steps had personal crises or simply misplaced the paperwork. I didn't get to put in a year of student teaching at Neighborlee High like I'd planned, like I had been promised.

First semester, I had to drive to a school district an hour away. Not so bad when there was a good radio station and I had books on tape to listen to. Plus my Star Trek club had gotten into fanzine writing big-time. Some of my friends and I were collaborating on a humongous, multi-episode crossover story, where we included the heroes from more than a dozen SF TV shows, movies and books. There was a lot of picky detail work we had to straighten out, timelines that needed to be explained, conflicts, and inside jokes.

I spent my commutes dictating ideas into my microcassette recorder and brainstorming solutions. It was a lot of fun. Especially when people in the cars on either side of me would give me weird looks. I would have gotten even weirder looks if they had been able to see that my hands were busy steering, and I was running the recorder with my brain.

The commute was the only good part of my student teaching experience that first semester. I had a high school in the morning, the longest leg of my commute, and then I spent my lunch break driving half an hour toward home, for my afternoon assignment at a middle school. It was kind of like going through an airlock, or decompressing as I rose up from the depths of a really deep, murky dive. I won't name any names, but the high school was a major rival of the Neighborlee Pikes. We in Northeast Ohio take our sports very seriously. It's not just the professional sports. The high school and college rivalries are legendary. Just ask OSU and Michigan.

I was the sports stringer for the *Neighborlee Tattler*, and I recused myself from reporting when that high school played the Neighborlee Pikes. I figured that was the ethical thing to do, and Conrad at the *Tattler* agreed with me. However, people at the high school expected me to favor the "home" team. Well, they weren't my home team. When people investigated why and found out I was "a spy for the enemy," it got uncomfortable.

Well, the sports parents, members of the staff, and athletes among my students demanded I prove my loyalty to *their* school. Umm, excuse me? No temporary student teaching assignment could ever make me turn against the Pikes. As the rabid sports fans of Northeast Ohio were prone to do, people expressed their displeasure in many creative ways.

The first time my car was keyed, I went to Kurt for help. He developed a great car security system on the spot that dealt with vandals on several different levels. First, it sounded an alarm when someone came within five steps. That necessitated I park at the far edge of the parking lot, farthest from the door into the school. Fine. I needed exercise. If the alarm and the stern voice of warning didn't drive the attackers away, lights flashed. If they approached within two steps, more lights flashed and they were warned their pictures had been taken. If they persisted and got close enough for thermal sensors to kick in, they were warned and given a countdown of three seconds to flee the vicinity. If they touched my car or stayed in defiance of the warning (all recorded on video for later evidence), they were doused in a diluted solution of tempera paints, in the Neighborlee High School colors of green and gold.

The very first person caught on camera attacking my car stuck his tongue out at the verbal warning. Very mature—not. He counted down with the Star Trek computer voice, and then got a mouthful of that green and gold paint. Who? The head of the English department. My immediate supervisor.

The ignominy of him trudging back into the school, spitting out paint, worked in my favor. Quite a few teachers and office workers despised him. They couldn't have cared less about the school sports rivalry, but they had been cool to me for the sake of peace among the faculty and staff. After that morning, they were friendlier. Life got a little more comfortable after that day.

Kurt got several custom jobs designing security systems for cars and homes. The sports booster parents at this school took it very personally when their team didn't win, or didn't win by the huge margin they felt their team deserved. They took it out on the coaches and the sport staff, usually encouraging their kids in juvenile pranks such as TP'ing, soaping windows, stealing lawn furniture and firewood from back yards, vandalizing landscaping, turfing, and the ever-popular burning bags of dog poop on front steps. The coaches nearly wept when I gave them Kurt's contact information, so they could ask him to design a security system for their homes and cars. Some of those jobs turned into home remodeling and carpentry work. Kurt liked building things. Anything and everything.

The middle school assignment started out pleasantly enough. Then the staff decided they wanted me to commit to coming back as a teacher when I graduated. I let them know I was grateful, but I was already committed to teaching at Neighborlee High when I graduated. I had a scholarship and a signed contract. I was to transfer my student teaching to Neighborlee after Christmas break. The plan was written down in enough places that only a blind man would have missed that detail. The middle school staff insisted that no one had told them that.

I found out later that they were desperate to get rid of a woman who considered herself the queen of the town, a mover-and-shaker, and wife of a municipal judge. It wasn't that the middle school loved me, but they needed someone as a wedge to get rid of her. Part of me wanted to help them, because I knew the woman really was an arrogant twitch. I had encountered her when I was helping at the *Tattler*. When she brought in the engagement and wedding announcements for her four children, three-quarters of the wording discussed her husband's accomplishments and her social activities. Whenever someone reminded her the announcements were only for Neighborlee residents, which she and her husband were not, her response was always a Botox-stiffened smile and a cheery, "Well, do your best."

Translation: *Make an exception for me, I'm the most important person you will ever meet and you have a duty to make me happy.*

The middle school staff was not pleased when I told them I had a commitment to Neighborlee High. I was their last hope of winning the latest round of nasty politics. They denied receiving the documentation that spelled out my transfer, even though my advisor at WBC had the paperwork with all the school board signatures.

Desperation has a tendency to make some people really nasty. Some of the staff gave me the cold shoulder from Halloween onwards. Others tried to use our supposed friendship and guilt trip tactics to get me to break my contract. One of the ladies in the office gave me her psychotherapist's business card and told me she would make an appointment for me. Yeah, school politics were even more extreme and rabid than sports in Northeast Ohio.

What a relief to switch to Neighborlee High after Christmas break, and ease into my teaching and coaching responsibilities. It wasn't *like* coming home; it was *absolutely* coming home.

Chapter Fourteen

Felicity and I started house-hunting that spring, to share an apartment or a rental house. She was finishing up her freshman year at WBC, which meant in the coming school year she wouldn't be required to live on campus. However, plans fell apart, thanks to a transfer student in the veterinary program named Emilio Santori. Felicity transferred to the veterinary medical assisting program. She got an efficiency apartment close to campus to be close to Emilio. No need for me to be a third wheel in their budding romance. Their plan was that when he graduated he would set up his own veterinary practice and she would be his office manager. He adored her incredible talent for all animals, dogs in particular.

Felicity never did get around to telling him about her semi-pseudo-superhero talent, and that turned out to be a good thing. He went home to Greece for summer break at the same time we went to France to meet up with the Crowders for another five weeks of intensive research work. When Harry and I came home ahead of our folks, to get ready for the coming school year, Emilio hadn't returned to start his school year. All Felicity could find out was that he had been living and studying under a false identity, and he wasn't returning from Greece. There were hints that he wasn't really Greek.

She dropped out of college and went into telemarketing and dog-sitting work. She had a year's lease on her apartment, and liked the silence and solitude, so we gave up on sharing an apartment for the time being. I stayed at home and started my first year as an official high school teacher at Neighborlee High.

The situation with Felicity and Emilio-whatever-his-name-really-was got us thinking. If the time ever came that we found the love of our lives, what would or could or should we tell that person? If our significant others came from Neighborlee, the news of our semi-pseudo-superhero abilities and our duties as guardians might not even raise a blip on the radar. However, could we guarantee we would only fall in love with a Neighborlee resident, someone inoculated by the background weirdness?

Kurt speculated that it might be kind of programmed into us. Whatever magic guided our lives ensured we would only "click" with someone who would fit into our team without a moment's hesitation. Felicity wasn't so sure. She was still hurting from Emilio and hadn't given up on love. She believed what she felt was real. As for me? I wasn't sure what to believe. I was too busy for a dating life, for one thing. For another thing, as one of our youth group leaders had commented long ago, working with kids of any age sometimes served as effective birth control. All parental and romantic urges kind of died after enough exposure to the results of other people's romantic urges. Our hormones were effectively silenced after six to eight hours a day, five days a week, nine months out of the year locked into a classroom with twenty to thirty results of moonlight and roses.

We agreed: if the time ever came that we were ready to settle down with someone, full disclosure was mandatory. We gave each other permission to make the revelation in as embarrassing and mind-blowing a way as we could manage, if the revelation did not occur before an engagement ring appeared on someone's finger.

We brought Angela in on the discussion and our agreement. She just laughed at us and promised to help the ones responsible for making the revelation. I caught a wistful look in her eye at one point. I remembered some of the cryptic things she had said about having a sweetheart, or at least someone who meant something to her. Did she miss him? Did she remember him? Or was he still waiting somewhere in the misty future?

Was Angela ever lonely?

Weird thought. Maybe the question should be rephrased. Did Angela ever have a spare moment to feel lonely?

~~~~~

Between the school newspaper, yearbook, coaching basketball and track, my plate was full. There was talk of adding a creative writing and a journalism program once I had settled in as a teacher. The school board took things slowly, so I wasn't overwhelmed, which let me keep stringing the sports beat for the *Tattler*. I loved hearing my students point me out to their parents when we met up in town. I was Miss Lanie to everybody. Some kids had a hard time pronouncing Zephyr. Go figure.

All that exposure to the kids and their parents and being
~~~~~

involved in community activities helped me as guardian, keeping my finger on the pulse of the community. I lost track of how many rumors I overheard, hints of pending trouble, that let us short circuit trouble before it happened. I also developed an iffy ability to sense lies. It was unreliable because it required close proximity if not actual physical contact to catch images in the mind of the person speaking with me. How those images lined up with what they were saying revealed if they were lying or telling the truth. Sometimes I could tell if they were scared, and of what, or if they were trying to deny something awful or weird had happened to them. Sorting through the images and translating them took time and practice, and wasn't a very reliable talent. Whenever I did get images from someone's mind, I needed to pay attention. The talent only awoke in reaction to great stress and distress.

Felicity didn't go back to college. She took the occasional night class or online class, trying to figure out what she wanted to do. She turned her talent for dogs into a full-time job exercising pets in Neighborlee and three other communities, and hit her stride when she found a tiny apartment over the kennels of the Neighborlee Veterinary Hospital. She worked as assistant to Doc Huckman, but never did return to pursuing veterinary school. Probably still stinging from the whole Emilio situation.

The monster in the dark returned early in the summer I turned twenty-two. Felicity was nineteen, Kurt was twenty-five. Since Bethany Miller was affected (meaning so was Athena Longfellow), I should note that the girls were nine that year.

I volunteered at Eden that summer, coaching girls' track for eight-through-twelve-year-olds. Felicity and Mum, Stephanie Miller and Charlotte Longfellow helped me, because I wasn't foolish enough to believe I could handle fifteen little girls all by myself. We won our first tri-county tournament. No, let me clarify. We smeared the competition.

To celebrate, we packed up our girls for a day of canoeing at Mohican, about an hour or so south down I-71. We packed everyone into two city vans before sunrise, drove down and had a picnic breakfast beside the water, before spending a lazy couple hours paddling down the shallow river. Around lunchtime, we landed and had a picnic, and spent the next couple hours just playing in the water. We were miles away from Neighborlee, separated from the protective field that I could swear over the years made our town invisible to nasty outsiders.

Felicity and Stephanie and I felt a subliminal thrumming go through us when we crossed back into Neighborlee. Usually it was a good thrum when we returned home, kind of on the order of a puppy greeting us with happy barks. However, that afternoon, with storm clouds starting to scud across the sky from the north, there was something sour in the unheard vibration.

Later, we learned the attack on the protective field was long-term, with subtle consequences. It affected our sensitivity and our ability to bounce back from consequences of performing our duties. Specifically, better regenerative powers. We were blinded to that loss by the gradual, creeping, long-term subtlety of the attack.

That day, we got out of the vans in the parking lot of Eden and just looked at each other. No need to talk about it. We could see what each other was thinking, clear in our faces.

Kurt showed up while we were handing our girls over to their parents. He had felt the energy change the moment we crossed the border into town, kind of a reaction to us reacting to whatever was going on underneath Neighborlee. He let us know he was going to be on patrol for a while, then drove off. Charlotte knew that look, so we didn't even have to explain or ask. She volunteered to take Bethany home with her and Athena, while Stephanie, Felicity and I headed over to Divine's.

"I've been trying to come up with a way to describe what happened all day," Angela greeted us.

She was sitting on her swing in the backyard, looking out over the Metroparks. We could just see her there as we drove up, and didn't bother going inside.

"When did it start? Was there a definite starting point?" Stephanie settled down on the swing with Angela, while Felicity and I took a chance on the ground being dry and sat.

"The moment the three of you crossed over the boundary line and left our town." She waited for our response, and nodded, her mouth flattening a little, when that "oh, okay, ugh," comprehension slid through me.

"Kurt said he felt something when we came back into town," Felicity offered.

"So... What does that mean for the future?" Stephanie said. "We can't leave town?" She smiled as she said it, but there was almost a pleading look in her eyes.

"Hmm, I wouldn't say that, except maybe you can't *all* leave town at the same time." Angela caught hold of her hand. "I'm sorry, but there is something in Bethany, some energy… I had hoped that it came from her father, rather than you, but you need to be aware."

"What about Ben?" She frowned, so puzzled it was almost funny. Then her eyes got wide and she muffled a little gasp. "I know I've teased him about having pointed… No… Angela… It isn't possible." She swallowed. "Is it?"

"No matter how far down the line, blood holds true, and usually awakens at the most unpredictable time."

"Wait a minute," I said. "You're saying Mr. Miller has magic blood?"

"I would say the situation is something like Typhoid Mary. He will never be affected, but he is a carrier." She squeezed Stephanie's hands. "You have my promise that I will be here to guide and guard Bethany in whatever the future holds for her. After all, I am her godmother. All I am saying now is that there is more magical potential in Bethany than we anticipated, and our enemy may have felt that power leaving town today, along with the rest of you."

"It could go after her because she's young and untrained." Stephanie stood and took a few steps away, rubbing her arms like she was cold. "Affect her, impact her, while everything is unknown and misty and unpredictable."

"That will not happen as long as I live." Angela's voice didn't change, but all of us felt the reverberation in the ground and in the air, like a magic spell had been invoked. "You have my word."

"And mine," I said.

"I'm being silly, aren't I?" Stephanie tried to smile. "Panicking like that. What kind of guardian am I?"

"One who has yet to learn arrogance, despite the number of battles you have won," Angela said. "Now, we need to plan our next move. Kurt is walking all over town, trying to sense the central point of the attack."

"We'll fly patrol tonight," I said. "As close to the ground as we can get, and tight overlapping pattern. Maybe with the three of us together, all that energy concentrated in one spot, we can tempt it to try something before it's up to full power."

"We're gonna have weird dreams tonight," Felicity said with a groan. "I just know it." That got all of us to smile, if not laugh.

When we met up with Kurt that night, he was exhausted, and nearly snapped at me when I suggested that maybe he was too tired for us to fly patrol. He had followed the reverberations of unfriendly power all over town. Every time he thought he had located it, the pulses faded out and started up stronger somewhere else. Whenever the pulses got within two blocks of Divine's, he felt it split into smaller strands and swirl away. The only solid detail he could give us was that the energy was underground.

The lowering clouds kept threatening rain, but it never came. Unseasonably cold gusts made for a miserable night of patrol. The early darkness and heavy atmosphere let us fly closer to the ground than usual, which was the only benefit we had that night. Everybody got indoors and stayed indoors, anticipating a storm. We flew four complete passes over town, crisscrossing, and even landing every twenty minutes or so, to try to tempt the enemy to approach us.

Nothing. When we checked with Ford Longfellow, he hadn't sensed anything, either.

Only Felicity and I had dreams that night, and they were useless. The usual nebulous, misty fragments, impressions of snake-like things tunneling through the bedrock below town.

Stephanie, Ford, and Kurt were to take turns walking patrol the next day. Charlotte would take Bethany home with her and Athena at lunchtime, after team practice, freeing me and Felicity to join the effort. We would all meet up at Divine's in mid-afternoon to report what we had found, if anything.

The skies got darker and the winds blew colder and wetter, starting before 10 in the morning, so that by 10:30, all the teams had to retreat indoors. I talked with Gina, who had just been put in charge of Eden's recreation programs, about getting a school bus to take our kids home, rather than making a lot of them walk or ride their bikes. The impression we all had was of an approaching downpour that would be painful in its intensity and the size and weight of the raindrops.

Just as my girls were settling into one of the long back hallways, for relay races, the storm struck hard. We lost all power. A couple girls screamed just to be able to scream. Then the emergency lighting boxes clicked in, battery-operated rotating spotlights at each intersection. The delay in activation should have warned us something was off about this storm.

I got my girls sitting down with their backs against the walls. Good thing I chose an inside hallway. We didn't have any windows to see what was happening outside. We hunkered down and listened to the roar of the rain coming down and I shivered, thinking of Stephanie and Kurt out there in the sudden downpour. Did they have any warning at all? Or did it just drop on them like a chunk of cliff falling on the Coyote in those old Road Runner cartoons?

Later, I wished I hadn't called up that imagery.

The temperature plummeted, at least ten degrees in as many seconds. I swear, the floor heaved underneath us like something big undulated through the ground, turning the foundations to liquid for about three nauseating, seasick-inducing seconds. Since no one screamed or clutched at me, I was pretty sure that sensation was all in my head, not real and physical.

That off-key, sour thrumming rang through my bones, stealing my breath for another couple seconds.

Then it was over. That fast. No warning, no explanation.

The rain died away while the girls were still squealing and trying to get more comfortable. The regular lights came back on about ten minutes later. This time the emergency lights reacted like they were supposed to, fading away within seconds.

By the time I got to my feet and herded my girls down the hall to the lobby area, where all the other teams and coaches were gathering, the sky showed widening streaks of sunshine. Those thick black clouds that looked like they were made of dirty rubber cement instead of angry water vaper evaporated as we watched. The parking lot was covered in water, and little white specks that turned out to be hailstones, about the size of thumbtacks. By the time parents started showing up, the hail had all melted away. Some drying strips of parking lot emerged from the water, and the air warmed and even had streaks of steam in it. That drastic shift in temperature couldn't be good, could it?

Maybe I had a jaundiced view of the rapidly improving conditions because I was still cold. No, I felt frozen solid in my chest, and like I had rods of ice for marrow in my leg and arm bones. I stood outside to soak up that intense sunshine that seemed to be trying to make up for wimping out on us a short time ago.

I had two girls on my team whose parents worked Downtown Cleveland, and it was understood that in inclement weather, I would get them home. Charlotte got a call that a branch had broken through a window at home, and Ford was nowhere to be found. I told her I would take Bethany and Athena so she could go home and not have to worry about them. I loaded them and the other two girls in my Jeep, and we headed south and east, to drop off the other girls. Sad, but I can't remember their names. I went to Miller's Diner, intending to feed the girls and check with Stephanie.

Ben Miller was busy on the grill, tethered to the long black cord of the phone that was tucked between shoulder and ear. He waved at Bethany when she called to him, but I had the impression he really didn't see her. Peggy Caldecott had the counter and she beckoned me over after I sent the girls to the back corner booth that was reserved for family.

"Stephanie went walking more than an hour ago, on an errand she said, and she's not back yet." Peggy glanced over her shoulder at Ben, who seemed to be listening more than he was paying attention to the burgers on the grill. The diner was hopping, like everyone had been hiding indoors until the weather broke. "Something feels wrong."

I changed my plans right then. I asked her for malts for the girls and left a note for Ben that I was taking them to Divine's. Angela was the best person to look after the girls while I started looking for Stephanie.

We had just turned the corner to head down the dead-end street to Divine's when I heard the ambulance sirens. Athena and Bethany were both on the floor in the back seat, giggling and playing at being smugglers, needing to stay out of sight of the guards at the gate. How come I can remember those details, but not the names of the other girls on the team?

What matters most is that the girls didn't hear the sirens. I decided not to break into their fun. My instincts started screaming, and I prayed they were wrong. I prayed for Stephanie the rest of the way down the street, and as we walked up to the porch of Divine's. Angela opened the door before we got there, and she smiled and hugged the girls. She held onto Bethany longer than

Athena, and when she stood up and looked at me, I saw the tears making her blue eyes glisten with extra facets. Of course Angela knew. How could she not know?

The coroner theorized Stephanie had a heart attack, that the same electrical atmospheric imbalances that brought on the freak storm had unbalanced her body systems. She was found lying in an alley, drenched and peppered with hail from the storm, and not a mark on her. Other than being as pale as the ice in her hair, she looked like she had fallen asleep.

Our theory was that she had tracked down the weak spot the enemy had made in the fabric of reality. The storm was the snake starting to break through. Stephanie slapped her unique energy over the weak spot and gave everything she had to her duty as a guardian.

The battle had become personal for Stephanie. She wasn't just protecting the town, but Bethany. Who knows? Maybe the attack was focused on Bethany, because of the double whammy of her heritage. Because yes, after that little revelation, I paid more attention to Ben Miller.

He had pointed ears. Nothing like Spock, or the characters in Elfquest, but enough to be noticed and to make me wonder. Especially since I discovered Bethany had slightly pointed ears too. If anyone else ever noticed and wondered, they obviously didn't say. Maybe some magic interfered to keep them from noticing.

I remembered what Angela had told me all those years ago about the Fae, how she talked about them as if they still existed in the modern world, visiting from time to time, and how they didn't have wings anymore. She never said they didn't have pointed ears.

Between her guardian mother and her father's much-diluted Fae blood, and with Angela as her godmother... Oh, yeah, Bethany was destined for something, no matter what her mother's wishes for her might have been

For Stephanie, we agreed to give Bethany no clue about her heritage. We detoured her away from the weirdness whenever we sensed magical ripples and had hints of otherness poking at the borders of Neighborlee.

We should have kept a closer watch on Athena Longfellow, as it turned out. She was the granddaughter of a guardian, after all.

~~~~~
~~~~~

Spring of the year I turned twenty-four, we made some major adjustments in our lives and household. Harry was seventeen. Pete Crowder was six. We had visited him and his folks in England the fall before. Mum and Pop were out of town on a research trip and kind of hard to get hold of, shuttling back and forth between Australia, New Zealand, and Papua New Guinea.

That afternoon, I was outside on the track, working with my girls relay team. Harry could have gone home after school without me, but he was working on something that I suspected would factor into his project for Senior Prank Night. He was at the top of the grandstands, tossing all sorts of futuristic designs for balsawood planes off the top and racing them down to the track. Then again, maybe it wasn't for his prank, but just to be visible. A couple of my girls were paying more attention to my brother's antics than they were to the pacing during the baton transfer.

Yes, I said a couple of the girls. Not that Harry played the field or wanted to be known as his class's Casanova. My brother just happened to be gor-gee-ous, and he wasn't one to deprive the female population of a chance to admire God's handiwork.

Col. Hayward showed up about the time I was letting the rest of the team go and asking the relay team to stay an extra fifteen or twenty minutes. I felt something change in the air, but it wasn't the weather. The boys' track team had been dismissed already, so I couldn't blame them for any "disturbance in the Force." I didn't notice the Colonel at first because he wasn't in uniform.

Note for future reference: When Col. Hayward doesn't show up in uniform, that usually means the situation is ultra-serious, and security issues of some kind are involved.

Chapter Fifteen

Harry recognized the Colonel when he came down to retrieve his latest batch of test planes. He gathered up all the pieces and came over to sit on the bench behind me. I felt him watching me. That, combined with a growing sense of tension, prompted me to dismiss my girls early.

As soon as I turned around, Harry gestured to the right along the grandstand with a handful of balsa wood parts. Even out of uniform, I recognized the Colonel right away.

"You know our folks are out of the country?" I said. He stood up and walked down to meet us. Even with the intervening years, and my having grown some, he was still tall. "Is something wrong with them?"

"Emma and Jake Crowder were killed this morning. I can't go fetch the boy. For her sake, I have to stay as far away as possible."

Doggone it, that big tough military man had tears in his eyes, just for a moment.

"You're asking us to go get Pete. How is our getting him letting you stay away from him, since there's a connection between us?"

He snorted and managed one of those crooked grins that always gave me a shiver, because it threatened so much damage to anyone who got in his way. Even knowing that I was included in that threat in a protective, defensive way, I still shivered.

"It only makes sense for you to take care of the boy, since you're friends. He knows you. He doesn't know me. I've kept my connection with your family as distant and as invisible as possible."

"Did you do something to get them in trouble?" Harry demanded.

"I hope not. I pray God I didn't do anything, that it's just a coincidence, but..." He looked past me, and it was like he was looking across the ocean, to wherever little Pete Crowder was right that moment, probably scared and fighting the strangers who were taking care of him.

"Emma has been living under Witness Protection most of her life. Her father was—well, you don't need to know those details.

Suffice to say the people whom he managed to hurt very badly have long memories. The Taliban could take lessons from them. Emma's father and my late wife were distant cousins. I am now Pete's only relative. Your family are the only ones I can fully trust to look after him. I need him out of England as quickly as possible, and safe in a good home. Charlie and Rainbow came here to be safe, and I can only hope this town will do the same for the boy." He spread his hands, gesturing as if he handed something to us, and let out another deep breath. "Please."

"Well?" Harry stepped away to toss his plane parts in the trash barrel.

"Do you remember the combination for the fireproof box where Pop keeps our passports?" I tossed him my keys. He caught them and ran to get my car.

By the time I got to the end of the field, Col. Hayward had filled me in on all the details. Yes, it irritated me a little that he had already arranged for our flight out of Hopkins to LaGuardia, and from there to Heathrow. He also had passports and other identification for us, all sorts of paperwork, including credit cards and driver's license and even an overview of our new biographies. Yes, new biographies, because he had given us entirely new identities. So we didn't need our own passports. What was a little creepy was that everything looked worn, like it had been used, not freshly minted.

I had to wonder, as Harry and I hurried home to pack, if maybe we would ever need that kind of extreme protection and a way to escape from deep trouble. If Jake and Emma Crowder could get into trouble and killed on a historical treasure hunt, then what kind of trouble could my parents get into, to the point that we would need to vanish?

Harry and I discussed our new biographies on the short drive to Cleveland Hopkins Airport, just so we wouldn't make any mistakes that would attract attention. Col. Hayward's people were good, because they created biographies pretty close to our reality. We just had to remember our names. Elaine and Jerry Westland. Close enough that if people heard us call each other by name, their ears would essentially skip over the differences. Our cover story was the truth: the Crowders were friends of our family and the child welfare authorities in England had found our contact information in Jake and Emma's paperwork, so they had contacted us as the closest thing Pete had to family. We were taking a long weekend, flying out on Thursday night and hopefully returning early Monday morning. If all went well. If all Col. Hayward's arrangements worked out as planned.

In case something went wrong, and Jake and Emma had indeed been murdered, and their enemies latched onto us, we had contingency plans. Multiple plane tickets, assigned to several spare identities. We had options for switching flights, and even contacts who would provide us with new clothes, haircuts, dye our hair, other little details to help us disappear into thin air. The important thing was to keep the enemy from knowing that Pete Crowder was going to live in Neighborlee, Ohio, with the Zephyr family.

We spent our flight from Cleveland to New York studying the fragments of details the Colonel provided. Something was suspicious about the accident that killed Jake and Emma and their team. The treasure hunt relating to the French Revolution had led to an underground chamber full of mystical symbols carved into stone walls. The official report said the archeologists had hit a gas line that had intersected the chamber decades ago, triggering an explosion that killed everyone.

Really? No one knew the chamber was there when they ran the gas line through? I didn't believe that, even before we turned the page and found Col. Hayward's note. All records indicated the nearest gas line was several hundred yards to the west of the site. His people were investigating whether local officials were part of the coverup or had been duped. Once they knew that, they could investigate who on the team had been the real target. Until then, we had to assume Pete was in danger, in case he overheard something the team discussed.

By the time we landed in England, I was exhausted from thinking and worrying and praying. We left the airport and all the lovely bureaucracy of Customs just in time to find a car and get caught in the morning commute chaos. Then we had to deal with foreign currency. After that, foreign traffic laws, driving on the wrong side of the road, and finding the people on Col. Hayward's list, so we could get into the hotel and get Pete out of there. Nope, it didn't happen as quickly as it sounded. More's the pity.

The second we walked into the hotel room where Pete was

waiting, his blue eyes got big and filled up with tears. He spread his arms and jumped off the couch where the nanny hired by the child welfare people had put him for a nap. He called for Harry first, and then me even before he tripped coming off the couch. We ran to him and the three of us kind of clung together in a weepy ball for a few minutes. That went a long way to convincing the nanny. I never did learn her name, but she impressed me as a combination of Nanny McPhee and a prison matron. Tough and loving and quirky. We passed her inspection. Her approval went a long way toward greasing the wheels so we could gather up Pete and what he wanted to take with us on the trip back. Then there was the matter of throwing the rest of his parents' belongings into crates for shipping home to the States, before we could head home.

Of course, none of that went as easily as it sounded, either.

We untangled ourselves from our crying heap on the floor of the hotel room. The nanny gave us a grim smile of approval, murmured that we would do very nicely, then started firing off orders like a drill sergeant. She sent Harry into the bathroom for a wet washcloth for Pete, scooped Pete back onto the couch to put his socks and shoes on, and showed me where his luggage was waiting. Three little bags, mostly clothes, some books. I pulled the identification papers out of my backpack and she waved them away.

"Doesn't matter, does it, if you're approved or not? The little lad wants you and needs you, and that's what matters. He's what matters, yes he does." She switched into high gear, getting Pete's face washed and loading us up with his bags and filling my hands with all sorts of official paperwork.

She wrote down all the instructions she gave us, and didn't expect me to remember. People we needed to check with, various public officials to avoid at all costs if we wanted to be home before Christmas, and advice on alternate roads to take to get back to the airport the next morning. Then she told me five separate times to let the officials pack up all the Crowders' belongings to ship home. We shouldn't "fash" ourselves over the books and papers and clothes and such, but let someone else help us.

Being Charlie and Rainbow Zephyr's daughter, my knee-jerk reaction is to investigate anything that someone takes such care to tell me to ignore. Besides, what else could the three of us do for the rest of the day, once we got Pete to our hotel room in the next town? We had the rental car, we had the tourist books Harry picked up at the airport, and we had memories of our last visit to England. To top it off, Pete wanted some things that weren't included in his clothes and books. He told us people got angry when he wanted to go to the flat his parents had been renting, to get his art kit and his action figures. That just made both Harry and me determined to do what we thought was right, not what others told us.

Col. Hayward had given us names of people who could get around the official people who might get in our way. None of them were on the list of people the nanny told me to contact, to answer questions and deal with tasks. Such as packing up the shipping crates with the Crowders' possessions. Not naming any names, to protect our sources and keep them and us from getting into trouble if there are ever any repercussions. I contacted one of the Colonel's people, and we had a set of keys for the Crowders' flat waiting at the front desk when we left our hotel room to go in search of lunch.

We got lunch to go and stopped at a roadside picnic area near the village where the Crowders had lived. Pete said his parents took him there a lot. He showed us the path down to the edge of the stream where he and Jake made boats with bark and twigs, with leaves for sails. We found a boat, and Pete cried a little when he held it, sitting in the back seat as we drove on to the village.

The Crowders' flat wasn't that hard to find, since it sat right over the combination bookstore and tea room in the middle of the village. The lady who ran the shop came running out to hug Pete and exclaim over him and insisted on having us stay for tea with her and her family. She wanted to know all about us. Pete broke our cover entirely. Well, it wasn't his fault. We didn't tell him we were there under false identities. Besides, Mrs. Guilderoy was very good friends with Jake and Emma. They had told her about several chapters they had contributed to one of Mum and Pop's books. Mrs. Guilderoy had all their books, prominently displayed in a corner of the store, right next to a memoriam display for Jake and Emma. She had even seen pictures of us from visits with the Crowders, so eventually she would have recognized us.

In the long run, breaking our cover didn't really matter. Having Mrs. Guilderoy on our side did. She was a fountain of information without being a gossip. More important, she was one of the most trustworthy and knowledgeable people in town. She simply felt there was a great deal we needed to know, and very little time to tell us. Before we even said we wanted to go to the Crowders' flat, she warned us there had been "considerable traffic, at all hours, quite annoying, traipsing up and down those stairs with no respect for people trying to conduct their ordinary lives."

What kind of traffic? Most of them were police or people who looked very official, but she had caught and chased away several folk whose faces she didn't like. More important, they were faces she didn't recall ever seeing before, and that was a sign of danger to her. If she didn't recognize them, they had no business on the back stairs, going up to the flats she rented out over her shop. Her renters knew better than to have people over without telling her they were coming. Everyone knew the polite thing to do was to have them come through the shop and introduce themselves, even if only to say they were on their way up to visit.

"Maybe I should come with you," she said, after giving us that bit of information.

My instincts agreed.

Mrs. Guilderoy was more surprised and slightly puzzled than angry, when I produced the set of keys for the flat provided by Col. Hayward's contacts. According to her, only the police and two officials involved in the investigation should have had keys. She had made sure to take back the keys she had given Jake and Emma.

"The people who notified us of the accident gave us some contacts, people to help us get around roadblocks," I said. "We had no idea of who would be on our side or that you would be looking out after Jake and Emma and Pete. We certainly wouldn't have chosen to hurt your feelings."

"Oh, dearie, don't worry about it. I've got a sense for folk, and our Peter here certainly vouches for you." She ruffled up his hair and chuckled when Pete just rolled his eyes. He was holding my hand, and I was positive that was a big point in my favor.

The four of us went through the back of the shop and up the second, private set of stairs reserved only for Mrs. Guilderoy and her family. She chuckled and her voice dropped to a whisper as she explained that most of her tenants didn't even know the stairs were there. Family legend said they were used when the village was part of a smuggling network. There were reputed to be caves and tunnels running under the village, possibly from the days of the Celtic tribes, when they fought against the Roman invaders. That was an interesting piece of information, and I filed it away mentally to pass on to Mum and Pop. They would get all the cooperation in investigating they would ever want from Mrs. Guilderoy, their biggest fan in this part of England.

Those private stairs were incredibly sturdy and didn't creak in the slightest, being carpeted and braced. We came out on the third floor through a door in the back of the little laundry room. It looked like a door into a storage closet. Yes, we could believe quite easily those stairs were used for smuggling and other secretive activities.

Jake and Emma's flat was three doors down from the laundry room. The doors for the flats all opened out onto a shared porch, and their flat was the largest, the last one on the corner, facing down over the river and a little walking trail.

We were just passing the door of the flat next to the Crowders' when their door opened and a man dressed all in brown, with an odd green hat, kind of like a beret but with ragged edges, came out. He turned and looked at us. His eyes sort of flashed, visibly angry, when his gaze focused on Pete.

"Here, you, what do you think you're doing? You got no business in there, do you?" Mrs. Guilderoy shouted.

The man snarled something at her that sounded sort of Gaelic. Hard to tell, because everything happened so fast. He raced toward us, snarling under his breath, and shoved aside Mrs. Guilderoy, who was leading the way. He swung at me. I ducked to keep from getting his fist in my face.

He swooped down, snatched up Pete, and flung him over the third-floor railing, out over the river.

Mrs. Guilderoy screamed and fell back against the wall. Harry slammed into the railing, reaching for Pete. The man tripped over him, and he knocked me off balance as I jumped over the railing. I nearly missed him, but I grabbed hold of Pete by one kicking foot and pulled him tight against me. We flew over the river, about ten yards wide at that point, to land on the opposite bank. We landed in mud and skidded and got generally filthy. Even now, I shudder at the mental image of the cows on that side of the river, who gave a couple snorts and mumbling moos but really didn't react to us landing among them. If we stank of cow droppings, my mind has completely blanked it.

By the time the police showed up, Mrs. Guilderoy had sent two of her sons to come fetch us in a little motorboat. It had a strangely quiet engine that I could easily believe was used in modern smuggling. We crossed back to the dock that was part of her property and she bundled us into her living quarters to get washed up, and took care of laundering our clothes. Two more of her sons investigated the Crowders' flat and made sure it was securely locked up again. Harry saw the mess that man in brown had made, and he was more furious than afraid. Every crate that Mrs. Guilderoy and her sons had packed up and hammered shut, ready for shipping, had been pried open and the contents pulled out. If something had been taken, nobody had any idea. Pete certainly didn't know. The intruder hadn't torn anything apart, all he had done was empty out the crates. Maybe he found what he was looking for.

Thanks to Mrs. Guilderoy's influence, the police believed my story. Between adrenaline, the height, the wind blowing at my back, my being a track coach and lettering in the long jump and pole vault (okay, that last was a definite lie), and a heavy dose of the grace of God, we got across the river without being hurt. That was my story and I stuck to it. The mud we landed in did a lot to make the story credible, too. We got muddy from skidding when we landed, rather than needing it to cushion our fall, but I wasn't about to give them that information. There was no telling what the English police would do if they had even the slightest hint that I could kinda-sorta fly. We weren't in Neighborlee, after all, where the police were family friends and shrugged off the odd things that happened every day.

Pete, however, knew firsthand and close up that we *flew*. He was almost giddy with excitement, but he had the smarts not to tell anyone. Not even Mrs. Guilderoy, who I suspected was on the verge of offering to keep him in England and adopt him. What was one more boy when she had six of her own? Her sons ranged in age from fifteen to thirty, and Pete was something of a pet for them.

His excitement and the way he just kept watching me, his eyes big, his cheeks flushed and that trembling kind of disbelieving grin on his face could all be explained away as shock. I was his hero. I was amazing. I was all his comic books come to life. He couldn't wait to go flying again with me, and he was smart enough to know from reading those same comic books that if he told anyone, I could get in a lot of trouble.

Harry took charge of Pete and had a long, whispered conversation with him while I was talking with the police, supported by Mrs. Guilderoy and several neighbors. They were down at the river's edge for their afternoon naps or walks and saw the whole thing. Everybody embellished what they saw, translating what the man said variously into curses or magic spells. Several insisted I had leaped up on the railing and shoved off and performed some acrobatics. One of them swore he knew from experience the people who performed freefall stunts from airplanes, so he could vouch that I had spread myself out just right to catch the breeze and make my body into a glider to get across the river safely and land without getting hurt.

I almost didn't have to say anything. Between all the odd additions and details that contradicted each other, the police were probably so confused they didn't want to ask any more questions. Nobody protested when I told them that we had tickets to fly home the next morning, so I wouldn't be available to answer any more questions.

We spent the rest of the afternoon re-packing those crates and letting Pete take out anything he wanted to bring home with us on the plane. I didn't care what extra fees we had to pay, just as long as we could ensure that Pete would have it when we got home. After all, we had no guarantee that any of those crates would make it across the Atlantic, much less without someone ransacking them again. I called Col. Hayward's contact and explained the problem we ran into. He already knew about it, making me think he might even have been there, cleaning up the mess without anyone noticing. He took charge of the crates and assured me Mrs. Guilderoy would not interfere or be upset or suspicious in any way.

Then we went back to our hotel and had an overpriced room service meal. We answered all Pete's questions about our little flight, and I demonstrated my telekinesis for him until I got a headache. That distracted all of us from thinking about the actual danger he had been in. I woke up from at least one bad dream of Pete going over that railing and hitting the docks, or landing in the river with enough force to knock him out and drown, or at least break bones. He didn't have any bad dreams that I knew of, but that was no guarantee, just because he didn't wake up crying.

"We're gonna have to adopt him, aren't we?" Harry said, early the next morning.

We were busy packing up and I was checking the layers and layers of packing tape and the address labels on the three boxes of Pete's extra belongings that we were taking to the airport with us. He was still asleep. I couldn't sleep in, despite London being seven hours ahead of Ohio time. Harry got out of bed soon after I did, and got to work washing up and dressing for the day and packing.

"Like, you and me, adopting him?" I said.

He just groaned and shook his head. Then he grinned. "What do you want to bet Mum and Pop are already thinking about it? If the Colonel got hold of them with the news by now."

"You don't mind?" I flashed back to the awkward questions when we brought Harry home. Mum and Pop had worried I would be jealous or upset that they hadn't offered to adopt Kurt and Felicity.

"He's already passed the test of belonging in Neighborlee. He thinks you're cool. And I like him."

"Why do I feel like this is the same conversation you'd be having with Mum and Pop if you wanted to get a dog?"

We laughed about that. The good feeling stayed with us, helped energize me for getting to the airport, checking in and dealing with our extra boxes and bags and getting on the plane. I slept most of the way across the ocean, which was made a lot easier by having the boys sit together in the row in front of me. We had most of first class to ourselves. Whatever the boys talked about during the time I was asleep, they had already come to an agreement and understanding. Basically, my brothers were ganging up on me before Pete was officially our brother.

All our extra boxes and bags made it kind of awkward navigating out of the airport. I cheated a little and proved just how un-observant people in New York are, by using my telekinesis to move Pete's extra boxes. Nobody noticed. We got to the car rental hub and rented a van and drove to Erie. Col. Hayward's connections took over, switching us to another rental, this time a nice SUV, for the remainder of the trip home. If anybody followed us from the airport, we lost them on the highways and back roads, and then changing cars. It was a relief to get home and collapse and sleep around the clock.

I took Pete to Mrs. Silvestri at NCH and told her the truth (well, most of the truth) and asked her what we needed to do to process the adoption. She laughed and asked if I had told my parents yet about adopting Pete. Of course, I hadn't. And I didn't have time to do any more explaining, because I had to get to work. When I got back to the orphanage after school, Mrs. Silvestri had taken care of most of the work, including tracking down my folks in the middle of their hopscotch travel pattern between Australia, New Zealand, and Papua, New Guinea. She said my folks were very proud of us and approved wholeheartedly, and half the paperwork was being processed already.

That was just how things were done in Neighborlee. We took care of our own.

Harry was right, of course. Pete had already passed the tests for fitting into our town. Angela was waiting when we took him to Divine's after school, and greeted Pete like she had known him all his life.

~~~~~

We lived on alert status through the summer, waiting for some indication that someone had followed Pete's trail to find him in Neighborlee. His folks' crates with all their research and notes made it to us without any signs of tampering, or any delays. No one showed up to make trouble, and just before school started in the fall, Col. Hayward confirmed that Pete was safe. If anyone was hunting him to find something his parents knew, they had lost the trail, or had given up.

We got a new resident that summer. John Stanzer was a private investigator. At first, learning what he did for a living, he set off a few of our personal alarms. However, one of the first things he did, even before signing the lease on his office, was go visit Divine's Emporium. Angela approved of him without reservation.

Almost before the paint was dry on the plate glass window of his office, he had settled in and made friends. He joined Neighborlee Gospel Church, got involved as a stagehand with the summer theater program at WBC, and offered to sponsor a sports team at Eden, when we had more kids and teams than we had sponsors. The peewee soccer kids loved him, especially when he
~~~~~

provided slushy-pops after every game.

The next few years were quiet. Or rather, quiet for Neighborlee. We were grateful, because some of us had had more adventures and problems and puzzles to solve than we liked or wanted. Kurt's reputation as the Handyman grew, and he took on more custom-designed projects for people with security systems and special grownup toys. Projects like his Senior Prank train and snow blades for motorcycles and bikes. Felicity meandered from one job to another, and from one casual boyfriend to another. She picked up lots of dogs, and sometimes I teased her about being the resident dog lady, like other towns had cat ladies. She laughed at me, which was good, because getting her riled always managed to blow some small electronic device.

I actually dated from time to time, which was amazing considering how busy my life was, with school and sports reporting and tutoring at NCH and of course, patrolling the skies of Neighborlee every few nights. Not that I was looking for a steady boyfriend, much less my soulmate, and certainly not a husband. After a close encounter with disaster, I tended to shy away from even a suggestion that I look for a romantic encounter. Not to go into a lot of details, but a friend at the newspaper had a reputation for matchmaking. When she asked me to go on a date with this guy who was new in town, I was stupid enough to trust her and go.

At first he was a lot of fun, a good sense of humor. I have to admit, the glorious feeling of "He likes me!" overrode common sense. For a little while. After the fourth date, I took a step back to really look at him, and ask some questions. When I applied the tests that we had been taught since middle school Sunday school, he failed them, one after another.

Chapter Sixteen

Strike one: He wouldn't go to church with me, but he did want to volunteer at our Sunday school. On our second date, he volunteered to help me tutor at Neighborlee Children's Home. He was more upset than I thought reasonable that he had to pass a background check before he could spend any time on the grounds with the children. He provided his information, grudgingly. He was out of my life before I realized he failed the check.

Strike two: He didn't freak out when he met my folks. I love my parents, but they aren't your typical aging parents of a high school teacher. He didn't react at all. It was like he was prepared.

Strike three: He wanted to be buddy-buddy with eight-year-old Pete, but ignored Harry, who was closer to his age. Pete said he gave him the creeps. He kept trying to put his arm around my little brother.

Strike four: I didn't need the final test by this time, but I made him come with me to Divine's Emporium. My intended Romeo stopped at the wrought iron gate and said he just remembered important errands, then claimed he was sick as he ran for his car. He did look a little too pale, as he drove away, leaving me stranded.

I didn't have to talk to Angela to know he wasn't the one for me. My matchmaking friend at the newspaper couldn't understand why I said no more dates, when he called me at work the next day. He stormed into the newspaper office an hour later and threw a very public fit. He probably was trying to embarrass me into going out with him. Why was the guy working so hard?

Neighborlee's protective field was working overtime that day, because Gordon was in the office, witnessed the temper tantrum, and decided to investigate.

Two weeks of investigating revealed my ex-Romeo had records in a dozen cities across the country, under a dozen identities. He had romanced a dozen women, all teachers and youth workers, to access the children in their care, to hunt for his next victims.

Gordon was a true guardian of Neighborlee that time around.

Between my job, sports reporting, volunteering at NCH and being a guardian, and then the brush with near-disaster, it got easier every year to say "no thanks" to the possibility of a romantic relationship.

Name me some superheroes who had steady, consistent love lives. I can't think of any. By the time I crossed age twenty-five, I had pretty much convinced myself that I didn't need that kind of a relationship, although Kurt and Felicity were still looking.

Fact: No good deed goes unpunished. My life is living proof.

Just ask any superhero. Does Spider-Man get to swing off into the sunset with a happy ending? Hardly! And what about Superman? I don't have *that* much in common with Superman, other than the fact I now work at a newspaper. He's a guy; I'm not. He wears glasses; I don't. He has a cape; I don't. A cape would tangle in my wheels.

Yes, I'm getting ahead of myself.

My point? The happily-ever-after factor is conspicuously missing from most superheroes' lives. Kind of like in soap operas, when you think about it.

This next phase in my life proves I'm right.

It was June. Specifically, the first Wednesday night in June. Senior Prank Night.

Just because most of the high school teachers and a good number of volunteers, including off-duty policemen and firemen and city officials were on patrol on Senior Prank Night, that didn't mean Kurt, Felicity and I could slack off. We were guardians. We had been protecting the residents of Neighborlee from Senior Prank Night since before any of us were seniors. The Great One, Stan Lee, put into words what we had grown up knowing: *With great power comes great responsibility.*

Mum and Pop were getting ready for a long research trip for their next book. This time, with two of the three of us kids relatively independent, they were heading out on a globe-trotting trip that would take them away for at least two years, visiting places like Stonehenge, again, and the pyramids of Egypt and South America. They were looking for similarities and differences in mechanics, building materials, cultures and cultural legends, and then would see where those launching points took them. They were still trying to find someone to rent our family home while they were away, and only two weeks away from launch date. Harry was going to Cleveland State to study business and had a loft in a warehouse downtown that he was helping to renovate. Pete would live with me while our folks were gone, in the house I had just bought. Felicity had just broken up with a guy who came pretty close to needing to hear the "Superheroes are real and I'm one" speech. With the addition of two more dogs to her household, she needed new living arrangements. We planned to renovate the two-car detached garage at my new house into an apartment for her.

Between our track team going on to state finals and filling in for two stringers at the *Neighborlee Tattler*, I was a little more overwhelmed than usual that June. I was getting ready for graduation, grading final exams, and trying to figure out which contractor to bring in to renovate my garage. Felicity's five dogs were the main reason she wasn't going to move into the house with me. Plus the occasional EM burst she still couldn't quite control.

I was crazy-busy that day, with our thank-God-it's-over party in Yearbook and other activities, but I still noticed when Athena Longfellow didn't make it to school. I even imagined her, just for a few seconds, lying in a ditch somewhere. Her uncle, Jinx, regularly drove his motorcycle fifteen miles over the speed limit, and he usually brought her to school on it. Only something dire would have made her miss the party in Yearbook. I got to the office to ask if they knew what happened, but they hadn't heard. I meant to ask Bethany, because the girls were inseparable. I never did, because she was bubbling over with news about a new acting job she had landed in another commercial. She was turning into quite a little actress. Stephanie would be proud of her. Certainly if something was wrong with Athena, Bethany would know, and she wouldn't be so happy. They had a connection of their very own.

I kept kicking myself over not following up on Athena's absence, but there was always something distracting me. So when Kurt stepped into the door of my classroom that afternoon and said, "Senior Prank Night," with that big, eager, can't-wait-to-make-mischief look on his face, my first reaction was to mentally lob all four chalk-filled erasers at him.

Kurt knew me well enough to be prepared for something like that. He ducked out of the way and only got one rectangular yellow mark square in his chest. It would have been hard to explain a cloud of chalk dust slowly settling around him, turning his wheat-blond hair yellow and making his gray eyes water, when Principal Wellington showed up in my classroom a few minutes later.

"Come on, Lanie." Kurt lounged into my classroom, looking around for other convenient missiles he might need to dodge. "It's our big heroic night of the year."

"This year's seniors aren't as stupid as usual." I bit my tongue to keep from adding, *Now that there aren't any more Grandstones in school.*

I would have changed my mind about being a teacher at Neighborlee High if there had been any new Grandstones slithering their way up through the grades. So far, Reggie, Freddie, and Sylvia, the only Grandstones in our generation, had yet to reproduce.

Proof that God is merciful.

"Yeah," Kurt said, grinning as if he could read my mind. We still had no proof that there *wasn't* some nebulous mental connection between the three of us. "But Toby Malone is a senior, his dad has keys to the city garage, and I heard rumors about borrowing the cherrypicker to steal the bell from the Taco Bell by the highway."

Yes, our Taco Bell was still the old design that had an actual bell hanging in the Alamo-style building. So sue us for being nostalgic or retro or whatever.

"Toby aced his driver's ed class. He won't wreck the city's truck." I busied myself sliding papers into my files and basically neatening up my desk so the cleaning crew wouldn't disturb anything when they came in. "What are you doing here, anyway?"

"Delivery. I fixed that coffee machine in the teacher's lounge."

"Coffee instead of sludge. The caffeine addicts will bow down in adoration."

Actually, I was kind of relieved, because I wouldn't be hearing any more complaints or witnessing any more panic attacks when various members of the faculty couldn't make it through the afternoon without a dose of coffee. I had recommended they go to Kurt so many times I lost count. Obviously someone had listened to me, at long last.

"Ah, my hero!" Principal Wellington crowed, striding into the classroom. He gave the yellow rectangle on Kurt's chest a little frown, then slapped him on the back. With the hand not holding an enormous, steaming mug. "You have my undying thanks."

Did I mention Principal Wellington made the rest of the caffeine addicts in the school appear almost comatose in comparison?

"Lanie, I found a note that you asked about Athena Longfellow. Charlotte did call this morning." He waved the pink phone message slip and handed it to me. "There's been a little excitement over at their house. It seems a cousin showed up suddenly this morning, so Athena didn't make it in to school."

"Is she all right?"

"Fine. Playing big sister, from what her grandmother said. The girl's name is London. From what I gather, her parents are dead. Poor little thing came by taxi, all by herself. Nine years old." He shook his head as he turned to walk out, message delivered, and paused to take a big slurp of that fresh coffee. It must have jolted some memories to the front of his brain, because he turned around again, nearly slopping coffee over the side of his mug. "I almost forgot. It's alumni night at the Old Bean."

My face must have showed some of the horror that washed over me, because he laughed and wagged a finger in my face. Fortunately for him, it wasn't close enough for me to bite.

"You promised if we moved alumni night from the Copper Pot Bar to the Old Bean, you'd attend."

"I know." After a long day of closing-down-the-school-year activities, my brain wasn't exactly in gear for coming up with excuses. I couldn't use the excuse of Senior Prank Night and needing to go on patrol because he was part of the regular group on patrol. If I claimed I couldn't participate in the alumni talent show, he would just counter that we would be out in plenty of time to short-circuit whatever this year's self-destructive attempts might be. And he would invite me to patrol with him.

How could I say no without revealing that Kurt, Felicity and I had our own…ahem…methods of patrolling? Nope, I couldn't use that as my trump card. Especially not with Kurt standing right behind Principal Wellington, making faces at me, almost daring me to spill the beans.

I really wanted to lob a couple dozen dirty erasers at him with a mental heave-ho, but that would break our premier rule, to never reveal the existence of semi-pseudo-superheroes in our town.

"What's at the Old Bean?" Kurt wanted to know. "Alumni night?"

"Willis-Brooks alumni," Principal Wellington said, heading back to the door again. "Talent night. It's been a tradition ever since there was an alumni group."

"Cool." He winked at me. "So, what kind of talent do you have?"

"Come with Lanie and find out." He raised his mug. "You have a marvelous talent yourself, Handyman. Don't be late, Lanie. We lost boys have to stick together." Then he vanished down the hall.

"So what's with the lost boys?" Kurt had to know. He settled down on a desk while I slid a last few papers into my filing cabinet. "Or hasn't your principal figured out you're a girl yet?"

"Why should he, since you haven't?" I grabbed my backpack—I had never gotten into the habit of a purse—slung it over my shoulder, and gestured at the door. "Not that it would matter," I had to add, "since you are so not my type."

"That's my line." Kurt jammed his hands into his back pockets and sauntered down the hall with me. A quick mental yank had my classroom door closed securely behind us. "I don't go for religious chicks."

Faith: one of the few areas where I differed from Kurt and Felicity. Admittedly, the existence of our superpowers and some of the strange, magical things we've witnessed have created a big hurdle to overcome. I've always believed our powers proved God existed and had a nasty sense of humor. Those same powers made my friends doubt. I've never been able to imagine a universe *without* God, no matter what kind of weirdness existed alongside Him.

He waggled his eyebrows at me. "We gotta get our minds back on track for tonight."

"One thing at a time, okay?"

By this time, we'd reached the side door that led out to the teachers' parking lot. Principal Wellington was ahead of us, somehow balancing four ten-ream copy paper boxes as he tottered across the parking lot to his car. We had to hurry over to help, of course, before he dropped something and the nearly empty lot was carpeted with papers or whatever was in those boxes.

"What's with the lost boys?" Kurt had to ask, as we stood there with our arms full and waited for the trunk to open. "You're not talking about Peter Pan, are you?"

"Precisely." Principal Wellington grunted satisfaction and jammed his key into the trunk lock. "I was referring to Lanie and me being abandoned children. There are quite a few of us in town, actually. Neighborlee seems to have this remarkable attraction for having abandoned, lost children ..." He gave Kurt an assessing look. "Thanks very much." He slid the boxes from our arms into the trunk. Then he stepped back and frowned. "I don't get to as many service nights at the children's home as I'd like, but it occurs to me I've seen you there every time. Are you a graduate?" He looked back and forth between us, visibly connecting dots.

"Yeah, he's a lost boy too," I said.

He chuckled. "I'm curious. Hanson. Is that your family name, or the name the authorities gave you when they found you? Or did you choose your name when you were emancipated?"

"Gave and found." Kurt gave me his 'what's he up to?' look. I could only shrug. I hadn't faced that inquisition when Wellington found out I was a Lost Kid, but that could be because my folks adopted me. "So Wellington wasn't your...orphanage name?"

"Hardly. I was on a British military history kick and Wellington was my hero. Maybe a little foolish, but it does help break the ice at meetings." He winked at us and stepped over to unlock his car door. "See you at the Old Bean."

"Yeah, yeah," I muttered, nodding and smiling like I actually looked forward to it. When his engine started up with a roar, and I had put a good fifty feet between me and his car, I relaxed. "I really do need to be a superhero to do the alumni night at the coffee house and then handle Senior Prank Night."

"Don't worry." Kurt slung an arm around my shoulders, shaking me for a moment. "The monsters don't come out until midnight. That's when the shifts change for the police, and that's the best time to pull pranks, when one shift is half-asleep and the other is still getting out there on the road."

~~~~~

"I always wanted to be a superhero." I struck the classic George Reeves Superman pose, fists jammed into my hips, legs slightly spread. That got almost as much laughter from the alumni jammed into the Old Bean coffee house on the campus of Willis-Brooks
~~~~~

College as the words I said. "Specifically, I wanted to be one of the X-Men. Not that I would be caught dead in yellow spandex, but there's just something about Wolverine..." I sighed loudly, earning more laughter.

In the second row, just outside the glare of the single spotlight someone had rigged for the talent show, Felicity gave me her "you are so dead" look. A rainbow-shaded flicker like a halo made me think she was going to change her hair color while sitting there — in public — to punish me. Kurt closed his eyes and shook his head. I mentally stuck my tongue out at them and continued.

"No, seriously. Can you imagine how cool it would be to have superpowers? Nobody could accuse me of cheating, but I'd be able to read all the answers in the teacher's desk — because honey, I'm a teacher, and I *know* those desks aren't made out of lead. Cardboard coated in aluminum paint is more like it." That got some chuckles from fellow teachers.

I went on for another five or six minutes, talking about how cool it would be to have superpowers, followed by the downside of having to wear one of those stupid form-fitting outfits. Just like the problem with the costumes-slash-uniforms in *Star Trek: The Next Generation*, said superhero would have to always be aware of his or her figure and diet/exercise routine. Every indulgence would show up in the waistline or the buttocks.

"You're paying me back, aren't you?" Kurt muttered, when I finished spouting my inspired lunacy and sat down at the wobbly little pedestal table, one of many that filled the coffee shop.

Was there some law of physics that said tables that small were never allowed to sit square?

"Nope. Why would you say that?" I fluttered my eyelashes at him and sipped at my iced chai, which had melted sufficiently so the spices and sweetness weren't overpowering.

He tried to glare, but his lips kept twitching. Felicity just giggled at both of us. The next act came on stage and we gave up trying to communicate over the banging and clanging of a one-man band. He was pretty talented for a geezer of ninety-five. I hoped I would be in that great physical condition when I was that age.

The alumni talent night closed down just before eleven, giving us plenty of time to drive to my place, where we had stashed our night maneuvers gear, change, and head back out. We didn't usually need our official gear for flying in the summer, other than long-sleeve black t-shirts and black jeans, to help us blend into the night sky. Tonight, though, we needed the waterproof jackets and hoods to keep us warm and dry in the pouring rain that started during the talent show.

For early June, it was a viciously cold rain, slashing down hard enough it felt like it had ice at the core of every drop. Since none of us had super night vision, we had the goggles Kurt had created that let us see in the dark and didn't fog up even in the coldest weather. One less excuse to sit out Senior Prank Night.

We piled into Kurt's pickup and turned on the police band receiver. There was a lot of chatter, a good portion of it in code, and it took us ten minutes of the twenty-minute drive to the target Taco Bell for us to decipher the hubbub centered around two vehicles missing from the city lot.

"The monsters don't come out until midnight, huh?" I said.

What had happened to the supposed plan to just take the cherrypicker? Why two trucks?

Kurt growled under his breath. No more conversation until we pulled up to the Taco Bell. It was still open, and there was no sign of a cherrypicker or any other big truck anywhere in the area, waiting for the lights to go off so the pranksters could attack.

"What would you do with big pieces of equipment, knowing the police are probably looking all over town for you?" Kurt said.

"Not stay in town?" Felicity offered.

"What's the use of pulling a big, flashy prank like that if nobody in town knows what happened?"

"The quarries." I felt a little dizzy. Maybe it was foresight, or maybe it was just exhaust fumes from the junker car, painted in four different colors of primer, belching blue-gray smoke directly in front of us.

"Makes sense," Kurt said with a sigh, and put his truck back into gear. He pulled around the kid ahead of us and headed for the driveway. I rolled down the window to let cold, fresh air gush in.

On the drive back across town, we discussed all the possible places for Toby and his friends to park their stolen equipment. We knew the quarries well, from our days of going there to explore or to test our developing powers. Or try to contact the aliens who might have dropped us on Earth when we were toddlers. The quarries on the west side of town had been mined for decades for gravel and sandstone slabs for the construction industry. Several small streams ran through them, and a few of the deeper pits were perpetually full of water, summer and winter.

Decades ago, the state turned the southern part of the quarries into part of the Metroparks, and diverted some of those streams into a river that ran through it, as well as filling some of the shallower pits and turning them into fishing and swimming areas. The more inhospitable parts in the northern section were left as ragged cliffs and deep pits. The park service had chains across the access roads and patrols by the local police and park rangers to keep intruders out. And more important, to protect the lives of idiots and daredevil kids who just hopped the chains and fences or got in through the park roads.

The quarries were a good location for idiots to show off their accomplishments, such as stealing city vehicles and equipment, or dare each other into pulling stupid stunts, like riding their bikes down steep access roads to the edges of sheer drops. It wasn't too far from town, and patrolled regularly enough that someone would see the trucks before dawn. Word would get around town fast enough that the perpetrators of the prank could bask in some glory. Best of all, it wouldn't be that hard for the city to get their equipment back. An important element of Senior Prank Night was avoiding expense and trouble and possible police charges.

The only problem that I could think of as we drove through all that rain was that there were no lights up at the quarries. If I was having trouble seeing the road in front of us in the headlights, what kind of trouble navigating were Toby and his friends having?

I had learned a long time ago to listen to that prickly feeling up my back that warned of impending disaster. Common sense said to make sure we had backup if my prickly feeling of trouble turned out to be something more than sunburn from washing my Jeep and mowing the lawn the afternoon before. I pulled out my cell phone and called Gordon.

"You expecting trouble?" Kurt said, after I got off the phone with Gordon, telling him the truth: we had heard Toby was going to steal a truck and steal the bell. Since the missing trucks weren't there at Taco Bell, our next guess was the quarries.

"I hope it's just my imagination, but I can see Toby and his pals trying to park the trucks on the highest cliffs, and not being able to see where to park, thanks to all this rain." I glanced at Felicity, who sat between us on the bench seat. She gave me a big-eyed look, and we held hands for the rest of the drive.

The last time we had a weird storm like this in the summer was when something tried to come through from another dimension, and Stephanie died patching the weak spot. I did a lot of praying I was wrong.

"I've been thinking about what your boss said," Kurt said, after we had turned down the back road that led from behind the municipal complex to the quarries. It was the most direct route, and had no streetlights or stoplights.

I was about to ask what he was talking about, because Principal Wellington hadn't spoken at all during the talent show. He juggled and danced a jig. Before I could ask a dumb question, Kurt went on to tell Felicity about the comment about being another lost boy.

"Did you ever wonder how many Lost Kids there have been through the years? The ones who developed powers, and the ones who didn't?"

"The ones like Mr. Longfellow, who became guardians?" Felicity offered. "I've thought about them, but I was kind of scared to ask."

"You mean the other guardians who died?" I said. "We could ask Angela, but … I figure she would have told us by now, after all we've gone through together."

"Maybe there just aren't as many of us as we thought," Kurt said, and frowned at the blurry road ahead of us.

"Then we hallucinated the kids who vanished without any explanation?" I could get snarky because Felicity sat between us, and Kurt would have to go through her to either dig me with his elbow or push me out the door.

Kurt's talent for controlling machines sometimes extended to car doors opening for no reason at all, or activating windshield wipers to distract nasty drivers ahead or behind him. Or lights turning on or off at the most inopportune moment. I wouldn't put it past him to shove me out the door into the rain without touching the door. But Felicity sat between us, like always. Just like we didn't get Felicity riled up when we couldn't afford an electro-magnetic burst, I didn't hack off Kurt when we were in his truck unless someone sat between us. My mama didn't raise no dummy.

"There have to be others with powers. Maybe some who are older than us and have figured out some answers," Kurt said, barely sparing me a curled-lip sneer and a sideways glance.

"The trick is finding the others," Felicity said.

"I thought about that." He leaned a little closer to the windshield as we reached the outer boundaries of the quarries. Just like I expected/feared, the triple chains across the road were down. "We need to get into the orphanage records for a starting point."

"Mrs. Sylvestri guards those records like the Library of Alexandria," I offered. "Just how are you going to get into them without telling her the truth?"

"Forget about lying to her about anything," Felicity added with a crooked grin. "For all we know, she has superpowers too. She's a better lie detector than even Lanie."

"Okay, suppose we get that information, somehow," I said. "What do we do when we find those other Lost Kids? Just ring the doorbell and ask each one if they're aliens with superpowers?"

"What if the kids who have vanished were taken away by people who want to take over the world, like evil mutants in the movies?" Felicity said. "What if there's a whole army of evil super kids out there and they're getting ready to invade Neighborlee?"

"If they outnumber us, why haven't they?" Kurt said. He grinned at us. I had to say what I knew they were both thinking.

"Who'd be stupid enough to come up against Angela, and all the fury of Divine's?"

Kurt's smile faded and he brought his truck to a stop and turned on his brights. "Well, we know they're definitely here."

There, clear in front of us for less than a dozen feet, were deep tire tracks, gouged through the mud and gravel and clay, filling up with water as we watched.

Chapter Seventeen

"You guys up for flying tonight?" I asked, and prayed they would say no.

"In this rain?" Kurt looked at the torrents slashing through his bright beams. As if he hadn't been gauging the ferocity of the storm all this time? "Nope. We'll have a hard enough time seeing where we're going without having to battle the winds. You do lookout duty if you can, and call us. We'll see what we can do on foot."

"I was afraid you were going to say that," Felicity mumbled.

What was she grumbling about? She would be down on the ground, while I would be up in the air, battling that wind, trying not to run into trees and cliffs in the dark.

I'm sure there's some law of physics that says the longer and farther something falls, the harder the impact, because when I got about one hundred feet up in the air, the rain didn't feel as hard or as cold as it did down on the ground. I was grateful for those goggles of Kurt's, because of course, I didn't have super-vision to see in the dark and in adverse conditions.

I spotted both trucks. Tom Malone was going to be so fired if anything happened to those trucks, because his son had stolen his keys. Naturally, the trucks weren't together. Toby and his friends were splitting them up. I wondered where they had their car hidden, to help them make a fast getaway. Of course, it wasn't beyond believing that they hadn't thought that far ahead, and they had a long, cold, dark walk back to town waiting for them.

I went back to the ground to relay to Kurt and Felicity the directions the trucks were going. And to get a break from the rain and wind in my face. We knew the quarries pretty well, so it was easy to guess where the stopping places might be. I took the garbage truck to follow, leaving Kurt and Felicity to follow the second truck in his pickup. I went aloft again, silently grumbling about my lack of a force field to keep me dry.

I said it before and I would say it again, and until my dying day: the half-baked state of our superpowers was simply more proof God had a nasty sense of humor. He didn't even give us half the required superhero package. We weren't invulnerable to bruises and broken bones and diseases. I didn't want to find out we weren't invulnerable to bullets, thanks very much. It was some comfort to know Spider-Man got beat up and Superman had kryptonite to worry about. Maybe we were better off that our weaknesses were simply normal human weaknesses, rather than something freaky that could give away our secret identities at the worst possible times. Not that we had secret identities.

I followed the garbage truck off to an arm of the quarry that extended south, toward the Metroparks. After about two minutes, its taillights brightened and stayed bright, meaning the driver was riding the brakes. Meaning he was trying to stop and failing. I glided closer, and decided the truck was still moving just as fast as before. Definitely there was some trouble stopping.

A buzz whispered through the air. I could have sworn an odd bluish light flickered over the truck. Just once. My stomach twisted with an awful suspicion I didn't want to even consider.

I lowered my altitude more, and realized the truck had gone down a side access road that was usually blocked with chains and a board barricade. It was easy to envision that truck smashing through the barricade and the driver being totally oblivious to it until it was too late to stop. That road sloped down at a pretty nasty angle that made the descent hard to control in good weather. The same access road where some kids were stupid enough to ride their bikes in the summer.

This particular road wound around some sheer rock faces as it dropped down, and the bumps in the road often led to bikes smashing into those rock faces before the careening path took them over the cliff at the end. The smart kids jumped off the first time their brakes locked up and their bikes kept going, and they weren't hurt too badly. If any of the kids who purposely went down that access road could be labeled "smart." The dumb or just plain scared stiff ones stayed on until the last minute, and usually ended up breaking bones or getting cut up pretty bad, but at least nobody had gone over the cliff with their bikes. So far, anyway.

"Call for help," I said, as soon as Kurt answered his cell phone. I relayed where the garbage truck was. When the driver finally jumped out, he was going to need paramedics, at the very least.

Just as I shoved my phone back into my pocket, the door

opened, and in the cab light, I saw Toby Malone. I groaned, wishing it had been one of his stupid friends. Toby was a good kid, and pretty smart. Until tonight. I swooped down, ready to help him when he landed.

That buzz zinged through the air again. That flicker of bluish light/non-light wrapped around the door of the truck.

Toby didn't jump. I wiped the water off my goggles and moved in as close as I dared. I figured, I could be close enough to touch him, and Toby wouldn't see me. I got close enough to see the door had closed on his coat and left him hanging, dangling, kicking and unable to twist around to get the door open.

That drop over the cliff was getting closer by the second.

I landed hard, hitting the garbage truck. It had those old-fashioned running boards, giving me something to stand on. I grabbed the side bar the mirror hung off and scrambled to get secure footing before I fought with the jammed door. Toby gaped at me for a second, then grabbed onto me like a drowning man. That made it hard to pull on the door handle to free his coat. I wasn't worried about him falling as soon as he was free.

That was kind of the plan, actually.

A prickle of warning went up my spine, hot and sharp. That flicker of light pushed against the opposite side of the truck. I turned around as I yanked on the door handle, to see a dark wall come swinging at me out of the rain.

Had that light … *pushed* the truck closer to the rock wall?

We were closer to the cliff than I thought. Toby wasn't able to adjust the way he hung from the truck, and the increasing momentum was going to smash him face-first into that rock. I flung myself against him, trying to press him flatter against the side of the truck and maybe tear his coat loose.

I swear, I heard the crunch of that rock wall against my back before I felt anything. Then it was all fire and jagged knives stabbing at me and the sensation that I could only compare to ripping about a half-inch layer of flesh off my back. I hoped that tearing sound was my jacket and sweater, and not flesh. A rattling sound reverberated up from my back to my head. I nearly looked to see if chunks of my spine had stuck to the wall as we passed.

I couldn't breathe, but that was okay because the rain was slapping me straight in the face and I would have drowned. Toby was screaming my name and that got me moving again. Nothing like, "Miss Zephyr, Miss Zephyr, help me! I don't wanna die!" to make me feel old.

What kind of semi-pseudo-superhero was I, letting a little thing like getting slapped with about two tons of rock stop me?

After all, what was terrifying about the awful suspicion that the dimensional invader was breaking through and using a semi-innocent but stupid kid to attack me?

I got the door open somehow. Toby fell free and I went with him, just as the truck hit a pothole and swerved. Right into us, like it wanted to follow us. Or *something* wanted it to follow us. The impact threw us over the front of the truck. Toby grabbed onto me, screaming like a girl. I still couldn't seem to breathe, so at least I had some dignity. That zing wrapped around us and a blue flash of light filled my eyes. We fell and a big, hard, round battering ram slammed into my back. Forensic investigation later revealed it was the old-fashioned iron bumper of the garbage truck.

This time the crunching in my back and rattling up into my head was more like gravel thundering down a chute at the supply yards. I landed hard, knocking what little air I had in my lungs right out of me. I landed mostly on my back, but it didn't hurt. The rain kind of felt good on my face, until I realized I was starting to pass out. I had to get my lungs working, even if I stood a good chance of drowning in the rain.

I must have passed out anyway, because I opened my eyes and found Chief Tanner kneeling next to my shoulders, leaning over me, keeping most of the rain off my face. I heard lots of sirens and voices shouting and a sound like something hissing and sizzling in the rain. Later I learned that was the garbage truck that had exploded when it hit the rocks at the base of the drop and was still on fire. All that gas and oil kept burning, despite the flood spilling off the cliff edge on top of it.

"Hey there, Lanie." Chief Tanner reached down and wiped hair and mud off my face. I appreciated that. Everything felt kind of limp and empty. "Don't you worry. I'm staying with you right until the doctors throw me out. Your folks are on their way."

Okay, that answered my question. I had been out for a while, not just a few minutes. Not a good sign.

"You're something else, girl, you know that?" He blinked

rapidly, and I really hoped that was just rainwater streaming off his saggy old hound dog face, and not tears.

"Is Toby okay?" I managed to ask, when I finally got my breath back.

"A little bruised, a lot shocky." He shook his head and tried to smile. I really hated to see a man's lips tremble like that. "Don't you think about anything but holding yourself together, you hear me, girl? I've got your hand and I ain't letting go until I hand you over to the doctors. It'll take the Jaws of Life to separate us." He lifted up his hand, to show me he was holding mine.

I lost my breath again. Even though he held on tight enough for a white-knuckle grip, I couldn't feel it. I couldn't feel anything other than the wet and mud on my face and the pebbles under the back of my head.

~~~~~

They tell me I stopped breathing twice on the way to the hospital. I guess it was good I couldn't feel anything from the shoulders down, because I've seen people who've gone through resuscitation, and they were pretty bruised and achy afterward from all those compressions and big, burly paramedics pounding on them.

At least the guy working on me was cute. I knew Doug from high school and the youth group at church. His parents were Aunt Jane and Uncle Dan when we were little, so Doug always claimed that was why he couldn't ask me out. You didn't kiss your cousin. When I opened my eyes and found him leaning over me, and felt his fingers on my neck, I had a pretty good idea of what he had been doing. He had taught a first aid class that concentrated on CPR at school just a couple weeks before, in preparation for the usual summer hijinks and stupidity. I hated the way his face was all shiny with sweat and effort and wrinkled with worry. He was putting down the mask that connected to the resuscitation bag gizmo, so no mouth-to-mouth in the EMT truck. That struck me as kind of unfair, after the rough night I had had.

"Still can't get you to kiss me, huh?" I said.

It came out a raspy whisper. Not a good sign. Doug burst out laughing, sputtering and crying at the same time. Any other time, he might have threatened to strangle me. But since he had been fighting so hard to resuscitate me just a few minutes before, that
~~~~~

wouldn't have been a smart thing to do.

"So help me, Lanie, how can you make jokes at a time like this?" he said, when he finally got himself under control again. He grabbed my wrist—the hand that Chief Tanner wasn't holding, and that I still couldn't feel—and checked my pulse.

"Only way to stay sane at a time like this," Chief Tanner said.

"Yeah," I said. My voice sounded a little stronger. "Otherwise I'd be scared to death, and even though I'm ready to go, I don't really want to, not yet."

"Don't you dare. We're not ready to let you go just yet, girl. God's got a lot of other things for you to do."

We pulled into the hospital emergency entrance right then, and everything turned into a rushed blur for me. Doctors surrounded me, and I could hear Mum and Pop calling me from somewhere, letting me know they were there. I saw a nurse stick a syringe into one of those bags on the end of a tube, and when I followed the tube down with my eyes, I saw it went into my arm.

It must have had something to knock me out, because I blinked and opened my eyes, and found myself in a hospital room with Angela standing next to my bed. There were all sorts of contraptions and monitors, and wires and tubes attached all over me. All I cared about was that the pillow under my head was soft and my hair was dry. So was my mouth, and everything smelled like antiseptic.

A faint echo of something snarling frustration whispered through the back of my mind, then faded. My mouth tasted even worse. That was probably the taste of fear.

"Slowly," Angela said, bringing a cup with a straw over before I could clear the cobwebs out of my head enough to ask for something to drink.

When she leaned over me to hold the straw to my lips, I was startled to see streaks of drying tears on her face. That scared me more than realizing I still couldn't feel anything below my shoulders. Angela simply never cried. She was always serene, with a slight hint of a Vulcan smirk of superiority. It felt good that she was concerned enough about me to cry. But it scared me, too. How bad was I, to make her cry?

I drank slowly, because nobody with any sense disobeyed Angela.

"You're not going anywhere, Lanie. You and I are guardians. We're needed. I'm not letting you go." She cupped my cheek for a moment. Her hand was warm and soft and soothing. "It's the most amazing thing to see. Our whole church is outside, filling the hospital and on the steps and the park, praying for you."

It was kind of funny, and put a twisty feeling in my stomach (which was odd, since I couldn't feel anything else, so maybe it wasn't really my stomach reacting?) to hear Angela talking about prayer. She's always been part of the *otherness*, the weirdness at the heart of Neighborlee. But it was comforting, too, because it confirmed a theory that I'd had all along: *God has a place in His plan for weirdness, too, and Angela is on the good guys' side.*

"There's no way in the world you'll be allowed to leave, even if you wanted to." She blinked, and another tear ran down her cheek. I could almost hear her thinking of how we had lost Stephanie.

"The snake," I whispered.

Angela went very still, and icy-alert pale.

"It was there. At the quarries. Trying to get through."

"I know. I felt it in the storm." She closed her eyes, and two more tears escaped her lids. "Lanie, I failed you."

"It's back where it belongs, isn't it?"

"Because it squandered all its power attacking you."

"Then it's stupid. But we won, right?"

"But at what cost?" She opened her eyes and cupped my cheek again. "And I couldn't stop them removing you from Neighborlee. The defensive field …" She shook her head.

"When I go back, it'll help, you think?"

Angela didn't answer right away. She offered me more water. I waited. She sighed.

"It didn't help you. Just like it didn't help Stephanie." She took a deep breath. It shattered slightly.

Then I heard a sharp intake of breath, my first clue that someone else was in the room. Angela stepped away as Mum and Pop came up to my bed. I realized they had been sleeping somewhere out of sight in the room. I was pretty sure she had something to do with them waking up right that moment, to stop that line of conversation.

~~~~~
~~~~~

Do I need to say that I didn't make it to the hearing to deal with the theft of the city trucks and the accident that left me in the hospital? Toby and his two buddies, Steve Muldoon and Jay Parker, didn't make it to their graduation. They were still sitting in jail, because a lot of people, including the defense attorneys, were in no hurry to get them out onto the streets again. There was talk for a while of denying them their diplomas and making them go through the senior year all over again. The judge in charge of their sentencing gave them a choice: military enlistment or spending the next five years dividing their time between drudge jobs for the city and community service. They chose military enlistment.

I had some hard times, that first week or so. Pastor Rocky walked in on me when I was indulging in a pity party. If I could have lifted my arms, I probably would have been throwing things around the room. Then again, if I could have moved my arms, I wouldn't have been feeling so sorry for myself. As it was, I was drippy and gasping for breath and tears were in my ears and I was just on the point of one of those screaming prayers when you're demanding answers from God and ready to start hurling some pretty nasty names. Not a smart idea for someone who was helpless and only alive by God's grace. But still, that was the mood I was in.

I was finally alert enough to consider what my shattered back—think jigsaw puzzle—meant for my life. No more track and basketball. No more hiking from the Rapid station to Progressive Field to watch the Indians from the nosebleed section. I had a vague idea of how long rehabilitation would take, and I certainly wasn't heading back to teach school and coach in the fall. I couldn't imagine teaching, period, confined to a wheelchair, depending on someone to help me with all my bodily functions, eat, drink, comb my hair… Everything just piled up on me, and I was clear-headed enough to be angry enough to rage at God. I mean, if you're going to complain, start at the top, right?

So when Pastor Rocky walked in, I had that snarl ready to burst out of my throat. I swallowed and choked on it when I turned my head and saw him standing there, looking like he wanted to laugh and cry at the same time.

"Why?" was all I could manage to say without screaming.

He stood there for a moment, his head tipped to one side, just looking at me until I finally took a breath. Then another. Then the pounding slowed down in my head.

"Why not?" Pastor Rocky yanked a chair over next to my bed, turned it around, and sat down, straddling it backwards.

"What do you mean, why not?" If my mouth hadn't been so dry, I would have spat.

"You're acting like someone broke a promise to you. When did God ever promise that you'd go sailing through life unharmed? When did He promise that if you bounced off a garbage truck speeding down a muddy slope, that you wouldn't get hurt? When did He promise that if you risked your life to save somebody, you wouldn't get hurt?"

He had a point. I was starting to calm down enough to listen. That was the thing about Pastor Rocky. He looked like a slightly overweight former rock'n'roll star, and he had an amazing gift for projecting calmness and getting everybody to listen, even a speed freak holding a gun on him. Been there. Saw it. Awesomely scary experience.

"It isn't fair." I knew the moment I said it, that was probably the stupidest thing to come out of my mouth, even counting the times I had been doped to the gills on pain medication. Although, as far as I knew, I didn't have gills…

"Hmm, maybe not." He patted my hand, then reached up and squeezed my shoulder, where I still had some feeling, although it was mostly tingles and numbness, like the nerves couldn't decide if they were alive or dead. "But you have to consider that with all the damage you took, you shouldn't be alive at all. I think some thanks are in order. And I think it's proof that God has more work for you to do."

"Work? From here? Sorry, but I am not an inspirational speaker, and I couldn't do art when I had both my hands, and Joni's already done that gig. What am I supposed to do?"

"Wait on the Lord. If He has work for you to do—and I'm firmly convinced of it—He will provide the means and the people who will work alongside you."

"What if this is a punishment?" slipped out of that tangled knot that seemed to fill my stomach all the time lately.

"For what?"

"For not doing what God wanted me to do before this." I took a deep breath. "Pastor, I used to be able to fly. But I used it for goofing around. You know those great aerial shots of Stonehenge? I took those photos. Without a plane or a kite or anything. Just me."

"Uh huh." He looked me in the eye and just sat there for a few seconds.

"I'm not on drugs, and I'm not delusional. I used to be like…well, not a superhero, obviously. But I could do things. And now I can't. God took it away. Like He took away my legs. Maybe I was supposed to do something with my freak talents, and I didn't and now I'm being punished? You think?" I desperately wanted to wipe my nose and get up and pace. Any minute now, Pastor Rocky was going to call the nurse and tell her I needed to have my meds checked.

"I think if you don't have your gifts anymore, you had them for a certain time, and that time has ended. The purpose they were intended for has been accomplished." He smiled, and it wasn't that humor-the-crazy-girl smile I expected. He had tears in his eyes. "I wondered how in the world you got on that truck to save Toby's life. Flying makes perfect sense."

"You believe me?" My voice cracked and screeched like nails on a chalkboard for a moment.

"Lanie, when you've lived in Neighborlee as long as I have, you…accept the fact that what other people consider natural laws don't quite apply here. Things that belong only in the movies or in comic books might just be real here. And what we would consider magic — the province of angels and demons — might not be within the boundaries the rest of the world gives them." He sat back and gave me that thin little smile of his, like he was inviting me to join mischief. "What else could you do?"

He just listened and nodded and didn't show a bit of doubt when I stumbled through my fragmented abilities. I told him how we first made ourselves protectors of the town and the seniors, and some of the stupid pranks we either short-circuited or turned harmless. He laughed when I grumbled about invulnerability not being part of the package.

"I think God made you vulnerable so you wouldn't get arrogant or take stupid risks."

"Like that night at the quarry?"

"No. That was not a stupid risk. That was a necessary risk. I truly believe you made our Father very proud that night, Lanie.

You put the welfare of another soul ahead of your own. If you had died that night, do you know where you would have awakened in eternity?"

"Yeah. Definitely," I whispered. By this time, I had learned the behind-the-scenes events of that night, including the fact that I had died a couple of times, momentarily. Had God sent me back for another job, or had it been the power of Chief Tanner's prayers and Doug's CPR skills?

"Do you know where Toby Malone would have gone?" Pastor's smile widened and went a little crooked when I just shook my head.

"My back versus Toby's life. I've been pretty selfish, huh?"

"Not in the least. You're entitled to be angry, to be afraid." He sighed. "I certainly would have liked to have seen you perform some telekinesis, though. Are you sure you lost all your powers?"

Three days before, I had tried to lift my plastic cup of water from my bedside table, so I wouldn't have to use the tongue control on the headset they had given me, to call the nurse. I had given myself a nova-sized headache that put purple and black spots in front of my eyes. After all that Pastor Rocky had done, giving me something new to think about, listening and caring and helping me get some bad stuff off my chest, I was willing to risk the headache again. So I turned my head enough to see the cup of water and I wrapped my thoughts around it like I always did when I wanted to lift something.

I didn't lift the cup. But I did lift the straw. I got it six inches above the cup before I realized I wasn't breathing. I lost control of it when I started hyperventilating. Pastor Rocky picked it up off the bedside table and put it back in the cup, and his hand shook a little. Even though he didn't *dis*believe what I said about my powers, obviously he didn't quite believe me, either. Until that moment.

I tried again, this time moving the cup enough to tip it over and spill about half a cup of lukewarm water across my chest. I didn't care. Even if I could have felt the wet, I wouldn't have cared. I burst into tears.

Pastor Rocky poured a fresh cup of cold water and held it for me so I could drink through the straw. Then he wiped my eyes and helped me blow my nose, and kissed me on the forehead before he turned to go.

"I think that's a sign that God isn't finished with you yet, Lanie

Zephyr. Your life is going to be a lot easier with telekinesis. But I'd caution you not to use it too much outside of town. In Neighborlee, you can get away with using it in broad daylight, and nobody would look twice. However, we're not in Neighborlee right now, are we?" His smile went a little sad when I shook my head. "Be careful. Hurry up and get well and come home, and we'll see what God wants you to do with the rest of your life."

~~~~~

From that afternoon, things got better. I had no idea if it was my freak genetics or a true miracle, coming from all the prayers from everybody in my church, surrounding me day and night. I didn't heal all the way, but I did heal, when the doctors said I shouldn't have even been able to breathe on my own.

I thought about what Angela said, about the protective field around Neighborlee not helping me. Like it should have? Like she expected it to?

Like maybe our enemy had been winning all along, in tiny ways, diluting the protection that we had grown so used to, we just expected it to be there? Maybe Stephanie shouldn't have died, that day of the storm. Maybe I should have been able to bounce back from having my back shattered. Or maybe I should have been protected from having my back shattered. Maybe if I had stayed in Neighborlee, instead of being taken to a hospital outside the protective barrier, and the delayed or diluted protection or magic or whatever had been given a chance to work ... who knows?

So what if they were winning? Whoever they were, the snake, or maybe the people from outside who had been stealing Lost Kids, they weren't going to win in the long run. Lanie Zephyr was down, but not for the count. With my whole church praying for me, and the protection that came from being a guardian, and with whatever God still had waiting for me to do, I was not giving up. I was going to come back. That snake or whoever our enemy was, they were in for a big surprise. Eventually.

First, I got feeling back in my arms. I thought I was imagining it, like ghost pain, until the prickling sensation got downright irritating. Then my fingers twitched. Involuntary muscle spasms, the doctors said. I didn't say anything about it, but I worked myself into headaches constantly, trying to concentrate and force feeling and muscle control back into my limbs. A nurse walked in on me
~~~~~

the day I picked up the cup from the table by myself, and she nearly fainted when she saw it.

Then came the day when the doctors gathered around my bed with puzzled looks instead of grave ones. It turned out the latest x-ray of my jigsaw puzzle back showed fewer pieces than the last time. Of course, everybody was blaming everyone else for bad imaging and faulty equipment and misdiagnoses. I didn't care. I knew what was going on.

The doctors thought I'd be numb and limp from the shoulders down, but every time they looked, there was less gravel and more spine. They finally agreed that it was just a "temporary paralysis."

By the end of the summer, I was out of therapy and tooling around town in a wheelchair. Not an electric wheelchair, either. My own arm power. I didn't need a ventilator or braces or a corset to help me sit up. What the city's insurance policy and my insurance through the school district didn't cover, was handled in other ways. Anonymous gifts showed up at the hospital. The town took up a collection to pay my bills, and adapt my house and car for my use. I could stand for short periods of time if I leaned against something, but I had regular spasms and flashes of numbness in my legs that meant walking was completely out. I would essentially be confined to my wheelchair for the rest of my life.

There were times I'd get upset, because why was God doing a halfway job on me again? Halfway-decent superpowers, now a halfway healing job. But I made myself remember that conversation with Pastor Rocky in my hospital room, and I told myself to be grateful. Maybe God had a job for me to do that could only be done from a wheelchair. I mean, I grew up in Neighborlee, so anything was possible.

I had no right to complain. I was alive when I should have been dead. I was self-sufficient, when I should have been depending on everybody to do everything for me, and maybe tied to a ventilator, too. But I could drive and wash and dress and feed myself.

Felicity moved into the garage apartment and became my official aide. My folks didn't go on the research trip for their book until a year later. I moved to full-time work covering sports and doing copy editing work at the *Neighborlee Tattler*, and gave up on teaching, even though I probably could have gone back to work the next school year.

Somebody tattled on me, and word got around that when I went in for therapy, I told jokes and entertained some of the other patients. By the time the holidays rolled around, I was invited to do some comedy material for small Christmas parties. Suddenly, I had a comedy career. People wanted to pay me to make them laugh. Cosmic concept, huh?

Nothing could persuade me that my life had been spared and I regained my arms and most of my legs just so I could do a sit-down comedy routine from the comfort of my wheelchair. Although having a doorknob-level view of life did make for some pretty wry, twisted humor. The comedy career that sort of fell on me out of nowhere was just to distract me so I wouldn't go nuts while I waited for my marching orders.

Or in my case, rolling orders.

Is it any wonder that when I let my friends and fans talk me into self-producing a comedy CD, the title was *Living Proof that the Good Times Roll*? I was living proof of something. I just couldn't figure out *what*, yet.

END

Afterword

Homage, kudos and apologies must be made here, to the source of much of Lanie's snarky sense of humor and doorknob-level view of life.

My hero is my brother, Dean. Probably 95 percent of Lanie's comedy performance material in future books comes from Dean, in his own words, "the world's greatest sit-down comic." Because he, too, is in a wheelchair. I'm still not sure why God chose or allowed Dean to get CP in infancy. Maybe he was put here to slow the rest of us down, to make us think, or something. Since the day he learned how to talk, Dean has been playing with people's brains until they bounce off the ceiling. His humor has helped us through many trying situations and broken the ice and won people over who were ready to let his wheelchair put up a wall between them and him. (Because, you know, a physical problem means there's something wrong with his brain, too, and maybe, like, you know, it's a contagious disease!)

For instance, at a wedding, the bride's father walked up to our table and said, "We're here to enjoy ourselves. Get up. Have fun. You're not tied to your chairs." He was standing right behind Dean, even resting his hands on the push-handles of the wheelchair. Dean tipped his head back and looked upside down at the bride's father, who he had never met before, and said, "Really? That's news to me!" We all laughed, the bride's father tried to sink through the floor, and the newlyweds had a fond memory of the day.

Or the time some volunteer roadies were picking up his chair to put him on the stage at a comedy venue where the stage (such as it was) was about two feet high and there was no ramp. They DROPPED his chair. In Dean's own words, the collective gasp from the audience sucked all the air out of the comedy club. Once he was back in his chair, he looked around at all of them and with his typical Pac-Man grin said, "I hope you all appreciate the fact I do my own stunts." (Confession: he stole that from Kermit the Frog, from the Muppet Movie, but the fact he thought of that and found the perfect situation to use it ... well, that's Dean.) They were putty in his hands from that moment.

So that's what I grew up with, and that's partly (maybe greatly) to blame for my own slightly wacked viewpoint of things. Maybe becoming a writer and diving into made-up worlds was an act of self-defense. Who knows?

Here's to Dean H. Levigne, my brother, my buddy, my parking pass, my living shopping cart, my hero.

Neighborlee, Ohio

(Title, Original Title, Release Date)

Confessions of a Lost Kid (Growing Up Neighborlee) 05/20
Semi-Pseudo-Superheroes (Dorm Rats) 07/20
Virtually London (London Holiday) 09/20
Living Proof (that no good deed goes unpunished) (Living Proof) 11/20
Night of the Living Proof, 01/21
Quitting the Hero Biz (Hero Blues) 03/21
Bride of the Living Proof, 05/21
Shrunk: The Exile of Maurice (Divine's Emporium) 07/21
Return of the Living Proof, 09/21
Allergic to Mistletoe (Have Yourself a Faerie Little Christmas) 11/21
Dawn of the Living Proof, 01/22
Angela's Knight (Divine Knight) 03/22
The Living Proof Gets the Blues, 05/22

ABOUT THE AUTHOR

On the road to publication, Michelle fell into fandom in college and has 40+ stories in various SF and fantasy universes. She has a bunch of useless degrees in theater, English, film/communication, and writing. Even worse, she has over 100 books and novellas with multiple small presses, in science fiction and fantasy, YA, suspense, women's fiction, and sub-genres of romance.

Her official launch into publishing came with winning first place in the Writers of the Future contest in 1990. She was a finalist in the EPIC Awards competition multiple times, winning with *Lorien* in 2006 and *The Meruk Episodes, I-V,* in 2010, and was a finalist in the Realm Award competition, in conjunction with the Realm Makers convention.

Her training includes the Institute for Children's Literature; proofreading at an advertising agency; and working at a community newspaper. She is a tea snob and freelance edits for a living (MichelleLevigne@gmail.com for info/rates), but only enough to give her time to write. Her newest crime against the literary world is to be co-managing editor at Mt. Zion Ridge Press and launching the publishing co-op, Ye Olde Dragon Books. Be afraid … be very afraid.

www.Mlevigne.com
www.MichelleLevigne.blogspot.com
@MichelleLevigne

Also by Michelle L. Levigne

Guardians of the Time Stream: 4-book Steampunk series
The Match Girls: Humorous inspirational romance series starting with **A Match (Not) Made in Heaven**
Sarai's Journey: A 2-book biblical fiction series

Tabor Heights: 20-book inspirational small town romance series.
Quarry Hall: 11-book women's fiction/suspense series
For Sale: Wedding Dress. Never Used: inspirational romance
Crooked Creek: Fun Fables About Critters and Kids: Children's short stories.
Do Yourself a Favor: Tips and Quips on the Writing Life. A book of writing advice.
Killing His Alter-Ego: contemporary romance/suspense, taking place in fandom.
The Commonwealth Universe: SF series, 25 books and growing
The Hunt: 5-book YA fantasy series
Faxinor: Fantasy series, 4 books and growing
Wildvine: Fantasy series, 14 books when all released
Neighborlee: Humorous fantasy series
Zygradon: 5-book Arthurian fantasy series